DESPERATE CROSSING

DESPERATE CROSSING

The Jenny Sanders Pryor Story

BARBARA RIEFE

A Tom Doherty Associates Book / New York

DESPERATE CROSSING: THE JENNY SANDERS
PRYOR STORY

This book is printed on acid-free paper.

A Forge Book
Published by Tom Doherty Associates, Inc.
175 Fifth Avenue
New York, NY 10010

Forge® is a registered trademark of Tom Doherty Associates,
Inc.

Library of Congress Cataloging-in-Publication Data

Riefe, Barbara
    Desperate crossing: the Jenny Sanders Pryor story /
Barbara Riefe. —1st ed.
        p.   cm.
    "A Tom Doherty Associates book."
    ISBN 0-312-86071-4 (acid-free paper)
    I. Title.
    PS3568.I3633D47   1997
    813' .54—dc21   97-24762
                                                          CIP

First Edition: December 1997

Printed in the United States of America

0 9 8 7 6 5 4 3 2 1

This book is respectfully dedicated to
Helen Luchsinger

This book is respectfully dedicated to
Helen Luchsinger

O you daughters of the West!
O you young and elder daughters! O you mothers and you
wives!
Never must you be divided, in our ranks you move united,
Pioneers! O pioneers!

—Walt Whitman
"Pioneers! O pioneers!," 1865

1865

Three days of almost continuous rain had reduced this stretch of the Oregon Trail to a slough. So deep was the mire, wagon wheels sank to well above their felloes, making it impossible for the oxen to move forward. One by one, the eighteen wagons in the train had to be muscled free of the quagmire and moved laboriously up the long grade to the top.

Earlier that day, the train had left Scott's Bluff to cross over from Nebraska to Wyoming. Jenny Pryor's husband John, the wagonmaster, worked with other men shouldering the Pryors' wagon, leading the train up the roughly fifty-yard stretch toward the summit. With Mary, her seven-year-old adopted daughter, Jenny walked off to a stand of trees to escape the broiling sun of late June and to pick wildflowers. They quickly found blue and purple lupines and delicate wild pinks.

Mary stooped and clutched a fistful of lupines.

"Pick one at a time, sweetheart," advised Jenny. "That way you won't crush them."

"What do we do with them, Jenny?"

"Steal a little water to keep them from wilting right away. Enjoy them while they last. Just don't feed them to the oxen, lupines are poisonous to cattle."

Jenny spied a patch of wild pinks and ran to them, hitching her skirt up with one hand. She stopped suddenly; directly ahead stood Mr. and Mrs. Foley from the wagon train. He was a farmer from Indiana. Over the six hundred miles the emigrants had traveled from their jumping-off place in Independence, Missouri, Jenny had yet to see a smile soften Foley's stubbled glower. Mrs. Foley—Amelia—was shy, somewhat withdrawn, as were most wives suffering from husbandly intimidation. But she had a pleasant smile and was pretty; blessed with a lovely complexion which she diligently protected under the poke of her slat bonnet. The couple had not seen Jenny; she edged behind a tree.

"Cut it, woman."

Jenny saw something in Amelia's hand catch sunlight; it was a pocketknife with the blade extended. Without a word, she turned and cut a switch from a nearby thicket. When she turned back to her husband she returned the knife which he snapped shut and pocketed. He gestured, she handed him the switch. He tested its pliancy and slapped his side with it. Amelia started. Jenny caught her breath. She watched as Amelia turned to one side and bend slightly. He began to beat her. His grim look darkened, he was suddenly the instrument of righteous vengeance. Amelia's face tautened; she had closed her eyes and color flushed her pale cheeks. With every blow she flinched, biting her lower lip to hold back a scream.

"Stop! You contemptible bully! Stop, I say!"

His switch high, Foley froze. And gaped. He had set a hand on Amelia's back. He slowly lifted it then caught himself, restored his hand and readied to resume. Jenny shouted, lowered her head and rushed forward, butting him in the ribs. Down he fell; out shot her hand, snatching away the switch. She moved to thrash him, paused the switch in mid-air, and instead snapped it in two, flinging away the pieces. Foley slowly got to his feet.

"How dare you!" she shrilled.

Attracted by her shouting, others in the train came running. Everyone stared as Jenny stood seething and glaring at the man.

"How dare *you?*" he snarled. "You'll regret poking your nose in, Missus. . . ."

He growled unintelligibly and swept past her, striding toward the trail. Jenny went to Amelia, who had straightened and now appeared dazed. And she was trembling. Jenny placed an arm around her, but almost at once the woman recovered and shook her off resentfully. Without a word, she, too, brushed by Jenny. She headed after her husband, hurrying to catch up.

Jenny felt foolish; she could feel her cheeks glow. She debated whether or not to explain to the others. Disregarding their stares, she decided against it. It was over, walk away from it, get away from their eyes.

"What's going on?" her husband asked, pushing to the forefront of the gathering.

"Nothing, John, I'll tell you later."

Mary, who had come up behind Jenny, spoke. "Mr. Foley was beating Mrs. Foley with that switch." She indicated the pieces. "Jenny made him stop . . ."

"Please," murmured Jenny, "can we just forget the whole thing?" Her hand went to her chest, covering the heart-shaped locket with Mary's silhouette in it.

A blood-red sun was dripping behind the jagged ridge of the Laramie Range when the last wagon reached the top of the grade. Camp was made for the night, the supper fires lit, the oxen fed, watered and unyoked. Jenny leaned against the tailgate of her wagon, holding a tin-plated hand mirror and running a comb through her long, bright red hair—so bright her husband swore that on a clear day he could see it half a mile away. Jenny was nineteen and the two had been married only seven months. Unlike most of the wives in the train, she eagerly looked forward to arriving in Oregon where John planned to start a new life as a carpenter. His first wife had died of pneu-

monia two winters before, less than four months after the couple adopted Mary.

John Pryor had fallen in love with Jenny Sanders at first sight
and did not hesitate to so inform anybody who was curious as
to how they met. John was approaching his thirtieth year, of
medium height, raw-boned and the possessor of a classic Irish
temper. He had been to Oregon before he married his first
wife. He had scouted the area near the wooded south bank of
the Columbia River almost in the shadow of the Hudson's Bay
Company. At the time, settlements were sparse throughout the
Willamette Valley and north as far as Astoria. A job as a brick-
layer with his father-in-law's construction firm and his first
wife's rejection of anywhere except Cincinnati had delayed
John's return to the Northwest; but now, four years after his first
visit, he was well on his way with Jenny and Mary by his side.

Jenny had just finished explaining what had happened with
the Foleys in the woods, with Mary adding her own observa-
tions.

"What I can't fathom," sighed Jenny, "is why Amelia
couldn't have shown at least a smidgen of gratitude."

"She's a strange one," said John.

"He ordered her to cut that switch and she couldn't do his
bidding fast enough. It was disgusting, it turned my stomach to
see it. I know there are men who beat their wives, but why
should he beat *her*? She never crosses him, not two words. And
yet you should have seen his face, he was livid . . ."

Amelia was coming toward them; John saw her before Jenny
did. "Shhh, here she comes."

"Jenny Pryor," snapped Amelia, her expression pure disgust. "In the future, kindly mind your own business!"

"See here . . ."

"Stay out of this, John," said Jenny. "Amelia . . ."

"You heard me. Don't you dare interfere again. Jeremiah
has told me to tell you that if you ever butt in again there'll be

h-e-l-l to pay." She leaned close, tight-lipped and glaring; her words came out like darts. "And he means it!"

She spun around and walked off, leaving Jenny with her mouth open, her pretty green eyes testing their sockets.

"Well of all the . . ."

"Shhhh, keep it down, dear heart."

Mary had come up clutching Jenny's favorite doll, which Jenny had entrusted to Mary's care on the trail. The doll was apple-cheeked with a mohair wig, go-to-sleep eyes and a pink organdy dress and bonnet.

"Go play with the Wilcox girls, sweetheart," said her father.

"Daddy and I are talking," added Jenny.

"About the Foleys."

"Go . . ." John shooed her off with both hands.

"Do you believe Amelia?" Jenny asked. She was rapidly getting angry—breathing hard, nostrils flaring. She set down her mirror on the tailgate so hard she nearly cracked it. "I saved her life . . ."

"Saved her a good deal of pain, for sure," he cut in. "Maybe we're missing something here. Neither of us really knows them, what their relationship is."

"What's that got to do with anything?"

"Jenny, please keep it down, why put on a show for the whole train?"

"He was beating her! The way he was going at it she wouldn't have been able to sit for a week!"

"I know, I know."

"You don't, you weren't anywhere near there. It would have made your blood boil; it did mine. What does he think she is, one of his oxen? He's the one should be beaten, thrashed black and blue. I don't understand you men, I should think you'd take him aside and read him the riot act. If I were a man . . ."

"If I were you, she'd be the one I'd be upset with. You come to her rescue and she bawls you out."

"Weren't you listening? She was following orders."

"I should think women like that would make you sick."

"*He* does, not her. Don't you understand? She's helpless. It's so frustrating, let's just drop it. The fire's burned down, I have to get supper. Go find Mary while I get the food and the skillet out, would you? Men! Disgusting! How I wish I had a horse-whip, I'd beat the seat off his britches!"

John managed a weak grin, gestured helplessly and walked off.

TWO

Jenny lay in John's arms in a tent pitched against one of the wagon's rear wheels, while Mary slept in the wagon.

"Tell me about Oregon."

John hugged her and grinned. "You ask me that practically every night."

"I like to hear it, it *is* where we'll be spending the rest of our lives. Tell me about our house."

"No stone, no brick; homes in the woods up there are all logs. At least no sod houses."

"We must have a wood floor."

"We will, I promised."

"To keep out bugs, especially spiders. I hate spiders."

"It won't all happen overnight, Jenny. I can't just wave a magic wand. First we have to find a prime piece of land, make legal claim to it and file the claim with the nearest recorder. Then we start building. By the time we get there it'll be October and the start of the rainy season. That's one thing about the Northwest, it can rain for twenty days straight. And by then the oxen'll be so tired they won't be of much use. By then, too, you'll be sick of the sight of the wagon, but until we get walls up and a roof over our heads we'll have to live in it."

"Food won't be a problem; you promised I could go hunting with you."

"Next spring, not in the fall. The weather's too poor for hunting. Besides, we can't spare the time away from building the house."

"We'll have to buy so much when we get there."

"If we're lucky, and if there's any type of store within a hundred miles."

"But John, we'll all need clothes desperately—at least cloth so I can make them."

"Oh, we'll find a store somewhere. There wasn't one last time I was there—not within hiking distance—but one's been built since."

Jenny grinned. "One good thing: I'm sure not going to be homesick. I couldn't wait to leave Cincinnati; that gloomy old house on Rice Street gave me nightmares. And all that soot and smoke in the neighborhood. And you had to walk eight whole blocks to get out where the grass was green and the air fresh and you could see Deer Creek."

"We were only three blocks from the Ohio River."

"It was always too crowded down by the docks, and all you could see were dirty boats and dirtier barges. At least out here everything's clean, the air especially. And in Oregon it'll be even better, won't it?"

"It will, honeybee, Oregon is God's country." He hugged her so tightly she squealed. "You'll love it: The Cascade Range to the east and the coastal mountains to the west wall you into prairie and timberland so beautiful they'll bring a lump to your throat. And Oregon soil grows anything. There's plenty of water, great rivers, and hundreds of streams; the springs, which are all over, are as sweet and pure as any water in Christendom.

"There's all sorts of game—millions of deer. You can step outside your front door and pot supper as easy as picking berries. There's grouse and quail, there's salmon, trout, and sturgeon in the rivers and streams.

"It never gets too hot in the summers, nothing like here or back home. Never too cold in the winter. Oh, the rivers freeze and there's light snow in January and February, but it melts quickly."

"Maybe by next summer, when we're all settled in, we should think about having a baby," murmured Jenny.

"That's up to you, honeybee."

"I say yes. I want you to have at least six sons and four daughters for us."

"Oh my, we'll have more redheads than any family west of the Mississippi. Come here."

He kissed her playfully and too loudly.

"Be tender, John Pryor, kisses aren't supposed to wake up the oxen."

She kissed him soulfully. He responded; minutes later they were making love. He was a tender lover, exploring her gently, igniting her passion, bringing both of them up to a stage of wild abandon.

Later, after he'd fallen asleep with—she noted—a smile on his face, she lay awake speculating on what lay ahead of them. Unlike some of the women in the train, she harbored no fears of the future. She did not lie awake worrying about the evils and dangers of the trail. Indians roamed the area they were passing through, and from here to Fort Laramie. Why shouldn't they? These were their hunting grounds. The hunting grounds of some other tribes stretched from Fort Laramie to beyond Fort Hall, though she didn't know one tribe from another.

But army units were scattered all over the territories. At Fort Kearny, where they'd stopped to rest and resupply, about ten days out of Independence, they were told that they would encounter roving hunting parties but they could expect no trouble with any hostile warriors. Long-time enemies were too busy skirmishing with each other to be bothered with passing emigrants.

Also, like every wagon train, theirs was heavily armed. A story made the rounds shortly after the train left Fort Kearny. It was claimed that fourteen wagons following the Oregon Trail along the Platte River the summer before had successfully fought off 150 Pawnees, killing nearly half.

Jenny went to sleep with her mind at ease, focused on Oregon and their arrival there less than five months hence. Her one wish was that there would be a school for Mary not too far from where they settled. For Mary, for all eleven of their children.

Poor Mary, she'd be the only one whose hair wasn't red.

THREE

The next morning—after a breakfast of Mormon Johnnycake, bacon, and coffee, with milk for Mary from the Armbruster's cow—Sarah Larimer came up to the Pryor wagon with her eight-year-old son Willis, a shy, tow-headed boy who displayed a galaxy of freckles on his slender face. Sarah, a widow Jenny had made friends with before leaving Independence, was a vivacious blond who laughed as easily as she breathed and was good for everyone's morale—especially the more morose pessimists among the women in the train, like Amelia Foley. Sarah picked up everyone's spirits; John had liked her from the moment Jenny introduced her to him.

Sarah planned to leave the train at Fort Boise, in Idaho, and set up shop in the area, to earn a living taking pictures of miners and soldiers. She showed up at the Pryors' wagon carrying her heavy, square, bellows studio camera, solid oak pillar–stand and all. Willis trailed her, his hands deep in his pockets, scuffing the sides of his shoes as he shuffled along and yawning every third step.

"I want you, John, and Mary for my sample book," announced Sarah.

"Again?" asked John.

"Shhhh," said Jenny, pretending exasperation. "But, Sarah, you do have scads of pictures of us already."

"Only none are as good as I know they can be. I want at least one absolutely perfect group shot."

She positioned her three subjects, pausing impatiently while Mary got out Jenny's doll—"the perfect touch," Sarah insisted. She then turned to working the rack-work to raise her camera and made other necessary adjustments. Declaring the sunlight to be insufficient, she got out her flash light powder holder. She poured a quantity of powder on it full width, inserted a parlor match, stuck her finger through the trigger string ring, took hold of the pneumatic release with her other hand, and cleared her throat.

"Ready, everyone. Not so stiff, John. That's better. When I say smile. Here we go. One, two, three, smile!"

The Pryors obligingly smiled, the flash light powder detonated with a muffled *poof*, Sarah squeezed her bulb and the family portrait was slowly exposed and fixed on the plate. While everybody waited for the process to be completed, Sarah began raving about her certain success.

"It'll be beautiful! Everybody can relax; you, too, John. Jenny, I'll go straight back and develop and print it. I can't wait to see this one. It went off like clockwork, it's bound to be my best work ever!"

Willis helped his mother carry her equipment back to their wagon.

*   *   *

The family portrait would have been perfect had not Mary moved slightly. Sarah very much wanted to keep trying until perfection was achieved.

The wagon train had moved eighteen miles closer to the protection of Fort Laramie when, around four in the afternoon, John called a halt. Everyone's supply of firewood was either badly depleted or exhausted; off to the left of the trail at a distance of less than 125 yards was a thick stand of trees. John led the men off with their axes while the women took advantage of the respite from the continual jouncing of the wagons to repair bonnets and tend to other chores.

Sarah brought the photograph back to show Jenny.

"Mary's the only blur, everything else is as sharp and distinct as can be. You can even see the little lines on either side of John's mouth."

"Don't tell him, maybe he won't notice."

"Oh, why even show it to him? I'll take another when we get to Fort Laramie. When I can take the time to set up properly. How far is it from here, Jenny?"

"I heard John telling Walter Armbruster and a couple others a little more than twenty miles."

Jenny shifted her eyes to the north and the foot of the mountain slopes. Dust rose in a fat yellow cloud.

"What's that, do you think?"

Sarah had turned to look. "A sandstorm?"

Carried on the breeze came the muffled sound of galloping hooves, and even as the two of them reacted in fear, the shrilling war whoops began.

"Oh my God," murmured Jenny. "Mary, Mary, out of the wagon! Come, hurry!"

Sarah ran off to find Willis. Mary came over the tailboard and Jenny clutched her with one arm and stared at the charging horde.

FOUR

In full warpaint the Indians came thundering in brandishing rifles and lances, shooting arrows, whooping wildly. Wagons were toppled, their contents ripping canvas covers; water casks were upended, shattering, spilling; oxen, many still in their yokes, lowed and milled about in confusion. Women and children ran in all directions, screaming and shouting. The few men left to guard the train fumbled with their carbines while their families crawled under the wagons for want of better cover.

The woodcutters rushed back to the edge of the woods paralleling the trail. Warriors sighted them and opened up a withering barrage of arrows, sending them scrambling behind trees. Down on his belly, John Pryor stared across the sun-browned June grass at the carnage before him. He saw neither Jenny nor Mary, but did catch sight of Amelia Foley staggering about with a lance thrust cleanly through her. John heard bellowing off to his left and saw Foley start forward only to be jerked back down by the others as his wife fell and lay motionless. A gaudily painted warrior, stripped to the waist, ran his pony over her. Again Foley shouted, rose full height, and moved forward. An arrow found his chest, killing him.

Bullets whined over the woodcutters' heads, gouging trees and ricocheting off them. Arrows came whizzing, one vibrating to rest barely inches above John's head. Walter Armbruster, still clutching his axe, his rifle nowhere in evidence, his cheeks ashen, bellied up alongside John.

"They mean to massacre every last one of us . . ."

"No," said John. "Us they'll just keep pinned down back here, keep us out of it. They know we wouldn't dare try to make it across that open stretch."

"Millicent's dead, I just know it. I feels it! They's just no place to hide out there!"

"Maybe she got under a pile of blankets in the wagon."

As the words came out two canvas tops flared up simultaneously. Black smoke billowed skyward and the sound of crackling flames came at John and the others through the steady whine of bullets and whirring arrows.

"Crazy bastards," growled another man on Armbruster's other side. "They didn't even bother to loot before setting fire to 'em."

As if hearing this, the savages turned to looting in earnest. John sounded a small sigh of relief. Was the killing over? Were the emigrants' goods a more tempting prize than their lives and scalps?

Two women, each carrying a small child, crawled forward beyond the lead wagon, got to their feet and ran. John and Armbruster watched in horror as both women took arrows between their shoulderblades, dropped their burdens, and fell dead in the dust.

Burning with frustration, completely helpless, the woodcutters watched the massacre and the plundering until roughly a third of the wagons were totally destroyed and bodies littered the scene. Most of the wagons still upright and those lying on their sides didn't appear damaged.

The oxen, most of them freed from their yokes and wandering about, were in no danger; it was almost as if the savages did not even notice them. Were they horses or mules they would steal them along with the emigrants' goods, but oxen were of no value to any Indian, and too slow to keep up with the attackers' horses when they rode away.

The massacre lasted just under seven minutes by John's watch. The savages assembled quickly, all partially dressed in pieces of clothing they'd stolen, and with all the loot they could carry rode off to the northeast, toward South Dakota.

On John's order, the woodcutters waited a few minutes before venturing forth. Reaching open ground, they raced forward. With Walter Armbruster, John wandered about. At almost the same instant both men found their wagons. Armbruster's lay on its side but at first glance looked to be intact, with even the wheels undamaged. To his joy, out of the wagon crawled his wife; she was angry and shaken but John could see no injuries.

He searched his own wagon, still upright and also undamaged, although everything he and Jenny owned was scattered around it. But there was no sign of either Jenny or Mary. Fear set its cold hand on his shoulder, accelerating his heartbeat into a thunderous pounding. He wandered about shouting for them, until the Armbrusters came up.

"John . . . ," began Walter, stopping suddenly, lowering his eyes.

His wife looked deeply troubled. "They took both."

"No!" he shouted, drawing everyone's eyes.

Millicent nodded. "They took Sarah Larimer and Willis, too."

"Oh my God . . ."

He turned to where the attackers had ridden away. By this time their dust had settled; the terrain was uneven but there were no trees that might obscure his vision. For as far as he could see there was no movement.

"I need a horse," he rasped. "They've got my wife and daughter, I need a horse. . . ."

There had been four horses with the train; the Indians had taken all of them. Again he searched the landscape to the northeast and could see no sign of them.

"No," he murmured. "No, no, no . . ."

He sank to his knees, seizing his head with both hands and shaking it slowly.

When the attack came Jenny lifted Mary over the tailgate, practically throwing her inside the wagon.

"Hide in the big chest; pull the red and brown blanket over you and don't move an inch."

"But how will I breathe?"

"Just do it! Once inside with the top down set your mouth against where the top rests. Take small breaths, there'll be enough air; just whatever you do, *don't raise the top and give yourself away.*"

"What about you?"

"I'll find a place."

Jenny climbed in the wagon after her, stumbling forward until she reached the driver's seat. A tightly rolled comforter was thrust under the seat. Wrapping herself in the comforter, Jenny tried pushing under the seat, found that she could not fit, and settled for underneath the tall dresser, squeezing laboriously until she was completely under it and facing the side of the wagon. She wondered if anyone looking in would be fooled.

It was so close and hot that she was in place only a few seconds before she began worrying that she would suffocate by the time the Indians did find her. So muffled were the sounds of the attack around her it sounded as if it were taking place miles distant.

What had happened to John? God forbid that he and the others would try to make it back. They'd be cut down like ripe wheat. And what if the savages decided to set fire to the wagons?

"God!"

That hadn't even occurred to her. Both the cover and the wood were bone dry; the mere touch of a torch and they'd go up in seconds. She strained to listen. She thrust her head partially out of the roll, filling her lungs with air. The whooping and shooting was much louder. Was Mary doing as she was told, not lifting the chest top even a fraction of an inch? For a seven year old she had good sense; she wasn't spoiled, she minded. Jenny crossed her fingers and drew back her head.

The wagon began shaking; two or three Indians were climbing in. Once more she pushed her head forward. They were looting, jabbering loudly. One had come up to the chest under which she was hiding and was pulling out the drawers. She could hear the soft sound of the contents being dumped: bed linens and winter clothing. Now the chest itself was pulled over. They grabbed the free end of the comforter; suddenly she was spinning, being rolled out of it. She thudded to the floor.

A grimy hand seized her hair; she saw the tomahawk upraised; Mary was screaming; a brave clapped his hand over her mouth as she struggled. A brawny arm stopped the forearm to the hand gripping the tomahawk.

Pulled to her feet, Jenny was pushed toward the tailgate. Ahead of her Mary was being lifted out, still screaming. Jenny fell over a stool. The same Indian who had lifted Mary out pulled her over the tailgate. In the next moment she had fallen and lay in the dust. The attack raged around them. Jenny's knee felt as if it had been struck with a club. Nearby she heard protesting screams; her three captors, Mary, and she all turned to watch Indians smashing Sarah Larimer's camera and other pieces of equipment. As Jenny watched, Sarah flew at one, yelling shrilly and pounding his bare chest. He flung her aside and one of the others picked her up by the waist—kicking and screaming as she was—and sat her on a wild-eyed mustang. Another Indian brought up a horse with Willis astride it.

"Maw! Maw!" he bawled.

The sound of her son's voice stopped Sarah's screaming; she stiffened and in that instant full realization of what was happening swept over her.

Down from the horse she jumped, attacking the brave who was menacing Willis. He pulled his knife and would have killed her on the spot had not Jenny wrenched free of the brave gripping her and pushed between Sarah and her antagonist. The knife-wielder turned on her angrily.

Just then, an older warrior came hurrying up. A chief, Jenny decided, from his ornate attire. His deeply-fissured face was nut brown and unpainted; his gray-white hair, parted in the center, was very long with a single white feather. On either side of his chin braids began, each one tightly wrapped in red cloth.

One eye was milky, either partially or completely blind. He wore a plain vest over a white cotton shirt buttoned at the neck. It was open, revealing a quill bib. A string of blue and red beads circled his neck and descended the front of the bib. Around his neck was a blue ribbon, depending from it a liberty head silver dollar. He also wore antelope skin trousers and moccasins. On both hands a total of four fingers were missing.

He blurted something to the brave menacing Sarah. Slowly, the man lowered his knife, reluctantly backing off.

"Better get back up on the horse," murmured Jenny to Sarah. She did so.

"You are brave to risk Red Horse's knife to save your friend," said the chief. "What is your name?" She told him. "Jen-ny, *hou.* I am Ottowa, *Iyuptala* and chief of the Oglalas."

"Iyup . . . ?"

"*Iyuptala.* That is our war society. The society of our bravest warriors. Bravest of the brave, Oglala Sioux. You, your friend, and your children will come with us."

"No."

He had been staring at her hair. He reached forth to touch it and she shrank back.

"Yes!" he snapped.

"I want Annie!" bawled Mary.

"Her doll," Jenny explained.

Ottowa nodded. Mary was permitted to retrieve the doll from among the goods scattered about outside the wagon. Ottowa, his men, and their prisoners assembled. The order was given, off they galloped.

FIVE

The emigrants wandered about the attack site mumbling and dazed, picking up the pieces. Nine women and all five of the men left to protect the train in the absence of the woodchopping detail met their deaths. The Oglalas had been selective in their killing; none of the survivors could understand why. John Pryor chalked it up to whim. Fourteen dead; four prisoners.

Walter and Millicent Armbruster commiserated with John over his loss.

"What'll you do now?" Walter asked him.

"Get them back or die trying!"

Armbruster scratched his two-day-old beard, his pale blue eyes brimming with sympathy. "You daren't go running off half-cocked. You got to think practical."

"I am. Our oxen weren't harmed; I'll hitch up and go on to Fort Laramie with the rest of you. Leave my rig and then head on out and try to pick up their trail."

Millicent gasped. "Surely not all by yourself . . ."

"The Army'll help ya," said Walter. "That's what they're here for. Talk to what's-his-name in charge there."

John nodded. "Colonel Thomas Moonlight. The trouble is, with the war back East just ended and everything up in the air, the army hasn't sent out any reinforcements yet. All these posts have been getting by with a handful of men. I'll wager there's not one, from Fort Dodge up to Fort Assinnibone on Canada's doorstep, able to muster more than half a troop. And that's how it'll be until fall at least. No, Walter, if Jenny and Mary are to be rescued, I'll have to do it alone. I wouldn't want it any other way . . ."

"You'll get yourself scalped," muttered Millicent. "One man 'gainst hundreds, all armed to the teeth? What good'll your death do Jenny and Mary?"

Millicent's face darkened suddenly.

"I can guess what you're thinking," murmured John. "That I'll be wasting my time chasing after them. By the time I catch up they'll both be . . ."

"Don't say it," said Walter. "Don't even think it."

John called out, assembling the survivors. "Everybody finish picking up what's worth salvaging, then check your wagons and beasts; make sure they're in condition to travel. Those who've lost their wagons will have to double up with their neighbors for the time being. Fort Laramie's only about twenty miles up the line. When we get there you can decide whether or not to replace your wagons and keep going or quit."

Soon after captors and captives were on their way, Jenny turned full attention on the three braves riding closest to her. From the Oglalas' indifference to their prisoners and their eagerness to talk among themselves, she decided that none understood English. While they jabbered, she called over to Mary and was relieved to see that not one of the braves looked her way. All three wore pieces of clothing stolen from the emigrants, and one wore a skillet hanging from his neck by a strip of rawhide.

"Sweetheart . . . ," said Jenny.

"What?"

Mary's eyes were tear-stained. She persisted in knuckling them, streaking the whole upper part of her face with dirt.

"You're going to get away," continued Jenny.

"How?"

"Shhhh, just talk normally. In fact, don't speak, just listen. And mind. I want you to rip open Annie's stomach with your fingernail."

"What for?"

"I said don't speak. Just do it, keep her out of their sight. Then pull out pieces of stuffing and drop a few at a time. But you mustn't let them see you. It's starting to get dark, the sky's clear, there'll be a moon tonight . . ."

"Leave a trail that you'll be able to follow back to the wagon train," explained Sarah. "Just like hare and hounds."

Mary pouted. "That'd be a hideous thing to do to poor Annie . . ."

"Just *do* as I tell you," said Jenny.

"What about you and Mrs. Larimer and Willis?"

"We'll be fine," said Jenny. "This is your chance to get away, maybe your only chance. Get back to Daddy. Go ahead, rip open her tummy. And mind none of them see you dropping the stuffing. Let's see how good you are at hiding it."

"I can do it, I just hate hurting poor Annie. And I hate leaving you three. I just know Daddy and I'll come back and you'll all be dead."

"Do as I tell you, sweetheart. Get busy."

══ SIX ══

Darkness came swiftly over the southeastern corner of Wyoming; over the tall needlegrass and bluestem, over the buffalo grass. The moon emerged as flat as the liberty head silver dollar bouncing at the end of its ribbon on Chief Ottowa's breastbone. Stars swarmed, pulsing powerfully, and Jenny, riding close to Mary, the length of her horse ahead of Sarah and Willis, speculated on their plight.

Her first and most fervent hope was that John would not act rashly. Still, if he'd followed them away from the train he would have caught up long before now.

What *was* he up to about now? With the others on their way to the fort? Had they already arrived? How many soldiers could the colonel spare for a rescue mission? Would he even bother?

Of course he'd *want* to, it was his duty. But how many able-bodied men did he have under him? John had mentioned that thousands of Sioux roamed the territories as far down as southern Kansas. What could a handful of cavalry do against the ones around here?

And yet the army in the West had a history of bargaining with the tribes for the freedom of white captives. Out here it was normal procedure, with the Indians demanding guns, powder, whiskey.

This raised another question: What were Fort Laramie's commander's personal feelings toward the tribes? Most officers posted in the West hated all Indians, even the most peaceful ones, and would no more bargain with them than they would with a pack of wild dogs. What did whomever was in command at Fort Laramie think of them? As vermin to be exterminated? Suddenly she found herself holding little hope for deliverance.

On the other hand, was she shortchanging her own and Mary's value? Furthermore, John wouldn't let the two of them sit on their hands in this danger. She glanced toward Mary, who caught her eye and showed her Annie just long enough so Jenny could see that she was nearly empty of her stuffing.

"Give her to me, sweetheart."

"But . . ."

"Please."

Mary glanced furtively about and jammed what was left of the doll against Jenny, who sneaked it under her shawl.

"Listen closely," Jenny whispered. "Start drifting clear. Move away from me a little at a time."

"They'll see me, they'll kill me!"

"She's right," murmured Sarah. "The horses are tiring, they'll be stopping for the night soon. Why not wait till everybody's bedded down?"

Jenny considered, then nodded. A few minutes later, Ottowa raised his arm and shouted, calling a halt. Dismounting and collecting in small groups, the Oglalas carried on, celebrating their triumph. A few fires were lit; Sarah sidled up to Jenny.

"Forget the horse," she said, "let her just sneak off."

"It'll take her all night to get back walking. And get back to what? What's left of the wagon train'll be long gone."

"I can follow the trail to the fort easy," said Mary. "I'm not afraid of the dark and I'm not helpless."

"You sure aren't," said Sarah.

Jenny grinned grimly. "So I'm outvoted. All right, when they've all fallen asleep you just sneak away. I'll stay awake, wake you when the time's right, and off you go."

Chief Ottowa came up.

"You will be given food, Jen-ny. Then you must sleep. No harm will come to you, you will be treated well, unless you try to escape. I warn you all, do not try."

"Where are we heading?" Jenny asked.

"You will know when you get there. It is a long way: three sleeps counting tonight. Again, do not be foolish and try to escape. You will be caught and . . ."

He paused and slit his throat with his finger. Then he walked off. The Oglalas hobbled their horses and let them graze. They themselves ate dry buffalo meat, drank muddy water from a nearby stream that looked on the verge of drying up completely, then curled up in their ratty-looking blankets. The captives were fed and given blankets by a brave proudly wearing an apron stolen from the train. He looked about twelve and so bowlegged Jenny had to force back a grin when he stood before them sternly ordering them to wrap up and sleep. His English was comically broken. Willis laughed. The brave glared and menaced him with his knife. Sarah thrust herself between the two.

"Everybody calm down," said Jenny. "Let's just do as he says, go to sleep."

The brave grumbled something in Oglala, spat at Willis, and trudged off. Willis laughed quietly.

"Don't be surprised when you wake up and see the two of us have left," said Sarah to Jenny.

"I wouldn't try it if I were you," said Jenny. "You heard Ottowa."

"Mary's going . . ."

"I know, and I'm beginning to have second thoughts."

"You mean you won't let me go?" burst Mary. "After I killed poor Annie and everything?"

"Shhhh, you can go. You must run as fast as you can for as far as you can. Get well clear of here."

"She'll be fine," said Sarah. "They won't even miss her; what do they want with a seven year old?"

"I suppose," murmured Jenny.

Sarah smiled reassuringly. "Good night."

Rolling over, she fell asleep almost immediately.

Willis grinned. "My maw can fall asleep on a picket fence."

Jenny had no such luck. Ottowa was deadly serious; attempting escape was a risky business. But any riskier than remaining in captivity?

"Oh, John, wherever you are, do something. Get us out of this."

SEVEN

In the sixteen years since the U.S. government had purchased Fort Laramie, building had been almost continuous. By June of 1865 it had become an elaborate rambling complex of more than 150 buildings extending beyond the original walls. More than three quarters of the buildings were not in use, however. Since the beginning of the Civil War, Laramie—like every other fort west of the Mississippi—had been operating with a skeleton force.

Invited to confer with Colonel Thomas Moonlight, John Pryor found him to be pleasant, agreeable, dedicated to the job, but deeply frustrated. This last was understandable; upwards of an estimated three thousand mostly hostile Indians roamed the territory. Moonlight and his men lived in constant fear of attack. The colonel took the time to explain his situation before his visitor could get a word out beyond introducing himself.

The office was small, gloomy, and dusty. Moonlight was obviously not a chair-borne commander. Sitting opposite him, John got the impression that he wanted almost desperately to free himself from his chair. Unfortunately, the size of the enemy forces surrounding him precluded any semblance of armed action on his part. He was reduced to watching the calendar and counting the days until Departmental Headquarters in Omaha brought his command up to its full complement of fifteen hundred officers and men.

"That'll never happen, Mr. Pryor; not in my lifetime."

Both men puffed on cigars. John Pryor couldn't stand cigars, couldn't stand this one in particular, despite the praise heaped upon the brand by his host. To John it smelled like fresh buffalo droppings to which a torch had been applied. The longer both men smoked the thicker the smoke became, clouding the ceiling. And the stronger the stench.

"I'd settle for four hundred bodies, eight of those new Gatling guns, and two twelve-pound howitzers." He chuckled. "No regulation against dreaming, eh?"

Moonlight was a bull-chested man with the posture of a wooden soldier. He made up for the total absence of hair on his gleaming scalp with sideburns, mustache, and full beard.

"Getting volunteers is like pulling teeth. Army service has no attraction for a young fellow now that the rebels have been licked. A half-wit can earn a lot more shoveling horseshit than the sixteen dollars a month they pay privates. With no risk of an arrow parting his hair. But you're not here to hear about my troubles. Tell me what happened—everything."

John did so, including in his recounting a detailed description of the attackers.

"Oglalas," murmured Moonlight. "Ten years ago Thomas Twiss, the Indian agent back then, assembled all our tribal leaders, including the Dakota chiefs."

"The what?"

"The seven tribes of the Sioux. Dakotas are what they call themselves. Twiss ordered them to pack up and move south of the Platte. The irony is, the Oglalas were one bunch that complied. Twiss got together four hundred lodges of Dakotas alone near here. In fact the only clans that stayed out were the Brulés and the Miniconjous."

"I'm sorry, past history doesn't interest me. Where exactly do the Oglalas camp?"

"You want to go there and recover your wife and daughter . . ."

"Where?"

John stumped his cigar out in Moonlight's ashtray, a gesture intended to inform the colonel that time for socializing was over. He took the hint.

"Anywhere from down by the North Platte to up to the Black Hills."

"South Dakota."

"They're like most of the tribes, they're nomads."

"That's a big help."

"Now don't you go getting discouraged on me. Not this soon." He grinned.

"Colonel, there's nothing funny about this; not to me. My wife is nineteen, my daughter only seven. As we sit here stinking up your office those red bastards could be putting them through the tortures of the damned. I'm sure they can't wait to get their filthy hands on Jenny's red hair. A prize scalp if ever there was one."

"Please." The colonel held up one nicotine-yellowed finger. "If you think I'm treating this frivolously, you're mistaken. What seems like lightheartedness to you is merely a vent for my frustration." He leaned forward, his expression suddenly deeply troubled. "It's had me by the throat ever since I got here." He gestured helplessness. "I just don't see how I can help you."

"Somebody's got to do *something*."

"They will, just make sure *you* don't go off half-cocked."

"Small chance of that, how would I find them? The Oglalas rode off north a little to the east."

"That's helpful; their main camp is probably up in the Black Hills."

"What about the forts up there? Don't they have dealings with the Oglalas?"

"I'm afraid there aren't any forts in or near the Black Hills. The nearest is Fort Sully, just north of the Missouri River, about thirty miles from where it intersects with the Cheyenne River. Here." He had gotten up and indicated the area on his wall map. "That area's the Department of the Dakota; we're . . ."

"In the Department of the Platte, I know. Are you trying to tell me red tape is going to block any attempt at rescue?"

"I didn't say that . . ."

"All right, what can you do?"

"Better: What can Heffernan do?"

"Who?"

"The Indian agent around here." Moonlight puffed out a ring and watched it ascend to join the smoke snugging the ceiling. "I expect he can get in touch with his counterpart up in Wind Cave. Whoever *he* is must have dealings with the Oglalas."

"We'll have to pay a ransom. Money, goods . . ."

"It's customary. And good for your loved ones, if you think about it. The Oglalas usually take good care of people who have

a value for them. Your wife and daughter are worth guns and powder, whiskey, whatever. Out here the government isn't too choosy
about what they bargain with; whatever works they'll trade."

"With lives at stake they've no choice."

"Exactly. So cheer up, I predict you'll get them both back."

"When?"

"I wish I could predict that. How about another cigar?"

Jenny's heart moved up into her throat as she sent Mary running off, but the child got cleanly away. Jenny stayed awake just
to be certain no one in another part of the camp had caught sight
of her leaving and was riding out in pursuit.

She looked over at Sarah and Willis fast asleep before rolling
over and falling back to sleep herself.

When she was awakened it was still dark out, but in the east
the horizon was sending up a soft pink light. She smelled Ottowa before she got her eyes open and saw him. It was he who
had shaken her awake.

"Get up. Where are they?"

Jenny rubbed the sleep from her eyes and looked about.
Sarah's and Willis' blankets were empty. She gasped.

"Where is your child?"

"They escaped," she murmured. "And took her with them.
Isn't it obvious?"

"Why take her and not you?"

"That, you'll have to ask Sarah."

"She is gone; are you blind? They are dead!"

He walked off. Jenny's heart rose; so Sarah had gotten away.
Would that she'd awakened her so that she might join them.
Had Sarah stolen a horse? Too risky.

How far was it to where the wagon train parked to wait for
the woodcutters: fifteen, twenty miles? She turned to look
south; the sky was a metallic gray, the color of Amelia Foley's

hair. As she stared, it slowly grew lighter and in the east the sun
pushed through the horizon. About twenty yards from her Ottowa was engaged in what appeared serious conversation with
four braves. They then mounted their horses and rode off.

Her heart sank. How far had Sarah and Willis gotten? And
had they caught up with Mary? Bigger, stronger, they must
have by now. And they, too, would be following the bits of stuffing Mary had pulled out of Annie. Jenny had hidden the doll
under a corner of her blanket. First chance she got she'd have
to get rid of it, or Ottowa would rightly conclude that she was
behind the escape attempt.

Attempt. That's what it was, and now four braves were riding out after them. Sarah Larimer was no fool. She had spleen,
she had brains; she'd know better than to stick to the trail back,
knowing they'd be followed. As soon as she and Willis caught
up with Mary, Sarah would find a hiding place and hole up all
day. If she was brilliant she'd stay put all night as well, knowing
that when they failed to catch up the Indians would go off in
another direction.

Yes, by all means stay put all day, all night and part of the
next day before getting back on the trail. Wouldn't it be even
better to travel parallel to the trail, using trees and ledges and
boulders for cover?

They would make it safely to the fort—they would with
Sarah in charge. She found herself wistfully wishing she'd gone
with them.

EIGHT

Up the eastern end of Wyoming between the Front Range and
the Nebraska border traveled the Oglalas with their single captive. Jenny's pessimism, discouragement, and fear of her plight

were to some extent eased by her confidence that Sarah and the children had gotten away.

The sun was standing high over the Great Plains when they forded the North Platte, moving steadily closer to the southwest corner of South Dakota and Cheyenne River country, with the Black Hills just beyond. Jenny kept a sharp eye out for landmarks but the semi-arid alkaline plains presented few.

Ottowa had taken to riding beside her with two young braves who were among the homeliest men Jenny had ever seen. One, who called himself Pawnee Killer, displayed a nose that appeared entirely deprived of its septum and resembled a mushroom cap set in the center of his face. One cheek and his jaw were deeply scarred; one eye socket hung a half-inch lower than the other, and the skin of his face was so loose it looked as if he'd borrowed it from someone with a much larger head.

His companion barely came up to either his or Ottowa's shoulder and the bones in the sack of his skin looked badly out of arrangement. His face was unscarred but he was comically homely; his pouch cheeks hung down on either side of a mouth that even when open was half the size of a normal adult mouth. His eyes were as dull as an ox's and he dribbled saliva when he spoke. It occurred to Jenny that both Pawnee Killer and Ottowa indulged him rather than treating him as equal or friend. She decided that he'd probably suffered a blow to the head as a boy or young man, which had at least partially addled his brain. Ottowa called him Four Hawks.

"We go home to the *Papa saka*—the Hills Black,*"—said the chief. "A place our people hold sacred."

"What do you intend doing with me? What do you want with me? What good am I to you?"

"I like your hair, it is fiery like a summer sunset. Like a torch."

*The Dakota language places adjectives after nouns.

"You abducted me because you *like my hair?*"

"Ab . . ."

"Kidnapped me, took me."

"No. I took you because I like you."

"Please, you're old enough to be my grandfather."

The sarcasm sailed past him. "I like your bite."

"My what?"

"You are like the *sentayo*, the cat that lives in mountains; you have her strong heart, you have no fear." He chuckled. "And a temper . . ."

Reaching into his saddlebag, he brought out a battered pipe. The stem was long and intricately carved; the bowl was fashioned of some type of stone.

"For you."

She studied it, then his face. He was very old, at least seventy-five. His single good eye stared. He suddenly looked frightfully savage, despite his smile.

"I liked the way you pushed between Red Horse and your friend to stop him from killing her."

"Sarah." Jenny smiled. "She got away."

"Did she?"

"You know it."

He grinned and gestured behind them and off to their left. A cloud of white dust was bearing down on them. She swallowed as four riders emerged; the four braves Ottowa had sent after Sarah and the children. Ottowa reined up and waved both arms at the incoming riders. As one they veered toward him and seconds later came pounding up, reining sharply. Their horses were skinned with sweat and blowing hard. Ottowa addressed them. One unfolded an antelope skin. Another reached into it and held up a scalp.

Black. Sarah Larimer's.

"Oh my God . . ."

They produced a tow-headed scalp and then a smaller one: hair with bits of bloodied flesh still clinging to it.

"No!" She turned on Ottowa. "Murderer! Child killer!" She flung the pipe at him; it flew harmlessly past, striking a rock, cracking loudly.

He glared and barked an order to the two braves riding with them. By now the entire war party had stopped; everyone was watching them. The braves dismounted and pulled Jenny down from her horse. She struggled in their grip as they pushed her up close to Ottowa. His eyes slitted evilly.

"You helped them escape. *You* are their murderer. I close my eyes to that. But now you desecrate my gift of the sacred ceremonial pipe. Given to show I have opened my heart to you, and invited you to enter it. You throw it away, break it."

The pipe was brought to him. A long crack ran down the stem almost to the bowl. His expression grew even fiercer. He snapped a command. A hand seized the top of the back of her dress, ripping it down to the waist. Pawnee Killer and Four Hawks held her at arm's length on either side while a third man got out his quirt and began beating her.

The pain was like a torch slowly drawn across her back: firing deep, excruciating. She screamed. Again he struck, and a third time. Ottowa and the others began to swim before her eyes. She was passing out; she prayed she would. Again and again the braided leather struck, biting into her flesh.

Now the pain exploded. Everything in sight was gradually darkening until she could no longer distinguish faces. Still she screamed, sinking into unconsciousness. But the sound grew fainter as it drew further and further away. Then she dimly saw Ottowa's arm go up.

The beating stopped. She fell to her knees, reaching her right hand behind her, hesitating as she was about to touch the raw, bleeding flesh. Ottowa had gotten down from his horse. His knees cracked loudly as he crouched beside her. His stink assailed her nostrils. Gripping her hair, he lifted her head until their eyes met.

"Now you die."

NINE

Ottowa's voice was low and laced with menace.

"You will be tied to an unbroken horse. My braves will shoot arrows at you until our anger is appeased. You will not live long enough to know when it is."

Pawnee Killer spoke; Ottowa looked up and responded.

"He wants your fire scalp; I told him it is mine; because *you* are mine and it was my sacred pipe that you destroyed. Get up."

Pawnee Killer and Four Hawks pulled her to her feet. She retrieved her shawl to cover her exposed back. The wool fibers intensified the pain of her raw wounds.

"Bring the horse," commanded Ottowa.

"Wait..." Jenny filled her lungs, steadied herself, and struggled to drive the fear out of her voice and lower it to normal tone. "Listen to me, great Chief. Breaking your sacred pipe *was* sacrilege; but I did it in anger at your men killing my child. I thought that the Oglalas were brave warriors who killed their enemies in fair combat; not murderers of helpless women and children.

"I lost my temper, I threw away your gracious gift; for that I know I must pay."

From the pocket of her skirt she got out her leather bag, holding it for all to see. The braves pressed closer. Slowly, she opened the bag and got out a roll of bills. Dropping the bag, she peeled off ten dollars and handed it to Ottowa.

"Ten dollars. Enough to buy you a whole keg of whiskey; so

big, so heavy you will not be able to lift it by yourself. Or you can buy a rifle and enough ammunition to fight two battles."

Blank-faced, he held the bill and studied it. He knew its worth, she could tell. She began distributing the rest of the roll among the braves closest to her. Others pushed forward jabbering, hands outstretched. After giving out her twos and fives she had twenty-seven dollars in ones left. These she passed out while keeping up a running commentary on how lucky they were, what they should buy from white traders. She gave away 120 dollars, all she had. When she was done she showed her empty hands and picked up the bag, holding it upside down to show that it, too, was empty.

"There, Chief Ottowa. I committed sacrilege and I have paid for it."

Ottowa and those who had received money looked at her through new eyes; admiring eyes, their faces showing how impressed they were. Then they crowded around asking what the numbers in the corners meant. Again she explained the differences in value. The recipients of the ones looked enviously at those who'd received twos and fives.

Ottowa was most impressed that she had had the good sense to give him ten ones in one piece of paper.

She sighed, taking pains to not show it. So she'd bought her life back. For how long, remained to be seen. Ottowa ordered his men back on their horses; Pawnee Killer, who'd been given five dollars, helped Jenny up on her horse and the journey was resumed.

The beating, Ottowa's death threat—all of it—had happened so fast she'd had time only to react to the deaths of Mary and the Larimers. Now the cruel reality sank in and it was all she could do to keep from trembling. It drove the pain of her wounds out of mind; she felt as if someone had gripped her shoulders and was slowly pulling her in two.

Mary dead. And she was to blame. Sending her off to follow the bits of doll stuffing was the stupidest idea she'd ever conceived. How could she think for one minute that a seven year old on foot would stand the remotest chance of escape from these animals?

She recalled Mary's objection: *They'll see me, they'll kill me!*

She would hear that voice, those six fatal words, until the day she died.

TEN

Jenny had been walking by the river, had climbed up Mount Adams to Eden Park and was resting on a bench when a man walked by with his little girl. The child was beautiful, with long brown hair and twinkling mischievous eyes. She had been bouncing a ball and had missed: Off it rolled, coming to rest at Jenny's feet. She picked it up as father and daughter came over.

"That's mine," said the child, reaching for the ball.

"Is it?"

Jenny examined it. A black-capped goldfinch landed on the back of her bench, flicked its tail, sounded its bright *per*-chick-*o-ree* and watched them.

"I don't see any name on it," said Jenny.

"Give it here, please."

"Well since you say 'please,' here . . ."

"What's your name?" the child asked.

"Jenny Sanders, what's yours?"

"Mary Elizabeth Pryor."

"John Arthur Pryor," added her father, grinning.

"I don't have a middle name," said Jenny, feigning soberness.

"Your hair is beautiful," said Mary. "How old are you?"

"Mary!"

"It's all right," said Jenny. "I just turned nineteen."

"I'm six; my father is twenty-nine." Jenny laughed. "You're pretty. Isn't she, Daddy?"

Jenny invited them to sit. They talked animatedly for nearly two hours at which point John got up and reached for Mary's hand.

"We have to go, Jenny. *We* have to study our ABCs. *We* have a test tomorrow."

"I'll pass it easy. Do we *have* to go?"

They said good-bye. Jenny waited all week for Sunday, to return to the same bench. She got there a full hour earlier than the previous Sunday. She was late; John and Mary were waiting. Mary had passed Monday's test in a breeze. They spent the whole afternoon together and Jenny invited them home for supper.

A hand gently placed against her arm snapped her out of her daydream. Ottowa, Pawnee Killer, and Four Hawks had moved on ahead. The newcomer was handsome, his features clean-cut and well-proportioned, in contrast to Ottowa, Pawnee Killer, and Four Hawks.

"Are you in pain?" he asked in flawless English.

"I'll live." She scowled at Ottowa's back a few yards ahead. "You can't imagine how powerful my motivation is."

"Do not even think about that. I am Jumping Bear. I am a Christian. I have wanted to talk to you since we left."

Suspicion wormed through her thoughts. "Why?"

"To practice my English."

"It's fine, as good as mine. Where did you learn it?"

"I was brought up at the Jesuit Mission near Lacklund. Father Drummond taught me; I was an orphan." He sobered. "I am sorry for all of this. You should not be here, but Chief Ottowa took a liking for you."

"*This* is 'liking'? What would he do if he hated me?"

"Throwing away the sacred ceremonial pipe was not wise. It was very valuable, worth many buffalo robes. I have seen one traded for *two* horses."

"I didn't ask for his stupid pipe. Besides, I was furious. When they came back with the scalps if I had a knife within reach I'd have cut his heart out!"

Jumping Bear grinned. "I think you would have. But he *does* like you."

"Sure, for what he can get for me in trade; if he doesn't beat me to death first."

"If you want to stay alive, be careful." Edging his horses closer to hers, he lowered his voice. "Do not raise your voice to him; do not disagree. Do not insult him. Show appreciation for his kindness. Bite your tongue to keep it still. Keep a smile. No matter what you see when you get to camp do not criticize or ridicule; do not show disgust. Be tactful, cooperate. For that he will like you, and you will make him into a friend and protector."

" 'Friend and protector'; two helpless children scalped and murdered. He ordered it . . ."

"That is in the past. If you want to keep your hair and your life, think of the future."

"Why are you telling me all this? What do you care about me?"

"It is not for what you think. I do not do that to women. It is unchristian."

"Will he . . . ?"

"Rape you?"

He hesitated. She searched his eyes for an answer then looked around them.

"Will anybody?"

"If he does not, nobody else will. Maybe he will not. If, as I say, you behave yourself. And when we get there, make yourself useful."

"How long will he keep me?"

"Weeks, months, years . . ." He shrugged. "Who can answer such a question?"

She scowled. "I'll get out of this; you watch, my husband will show up with five hundred soldiers."

He sighed and rolled his eyes. "Whatever you do, do not threaten Chief Ottowa with that!"

ELEVEN

The two days felt like weeks to John Pryor, while he waited for Colonel Moonlight to devise a strategy for the rescue of Jenny, Mary, and the Larimers. Meanwhile Walter and Millicent Armbruster and the other survivors of the Oglala attack topped off their water casks, brought dwindling supplies up to proper quantity, and readied the eleven undamaged wagons to resume the journey to Oregon. John was rapidly running out of patience when Walter Armbruster approached him just inside the main gate.

"We're leaving at sunup tomorrow," said the older man, and offered his hand as Millicent came over to join them. "I truly wish you and your loved ones were coming with us."

"Good things can happen when you least expect them," added Millicent. "You could get them back safe and sound before you know it."

"*I* could. It certainly looks like it'll be up to me."

"What does Moonlight say?" Armbruster asked.

"Words, words, words. Variations on the same old excuse for inaction. He *claims* he's trying to contact Heffernan, the local Indian agent, so he in turn can contact his counterpart up at Wind Cave. Only Heffernan is not around."

"Why don't he contact the other fellow d'rectly? Telegraph him?"

"Who knows why?" He spotted Colonel Moonlight on the far side of the parade ground in conversation with two enlisted men. "Speak of the devil; excuse me, folks. Good luck to you both." He smiled weakly at Millicent. "Maybe it *will* turn out like you say, I'll get them back safe and sound. One's got to be optimistic, right?"

"God bless you, John," she said. "Jenny and Mary'll be in our prayers every night."

He caught up with the colonel as he concluded what he had to say to the men and was starting off toward headquarters.

"Mr. Pryor. Lovely day . . ."

"What do you need with this Heffernan? Why can't you contact the agent up at Wind Cave directly?"

"Whoa, whoa, whoa, let's go into my office, shall we?"

"Let's not bother. I've come to a decision, Moonlight: forget the Indian agents, at least for now. Instead, give me twenty men and we'll go up to the Black Hills, find the Ogalalas' camp and do business."

"Believe me, I'd love nothing better than to wish you luck and send you off, but I can't. Number one, I can't spare two men, let alone twenty. Look around, have you any idea how many able-bodied people I have to defend this place? Forty-eight— not counting two in the hospital. Plus two officers: Captain Fuchs and Lieutenant Bullock.

"Forget Fuchs; the man spends more time prone than upright. If it's not his stomach it's his feet; if it's not headaches, ringing in the ears, pinkeye or inflamed gums, it's his heart or his liver or his gall bladder. The esteemed captain's got more ills and ailments than all the Judeans Isaiah groused about in the Bible. Fuchs is about as useful to me as my hemorrhoids."

"So you've got forty-nine men."

"Exactly. Only about fourteen hundred and fifty short of

fully designated strength. Secondly, it's contrary to army regulations for civilians to command troops."

"I don't have to *command* anybody, your lieutenant can . . ."

"I'm sorry."

"I know, I know, your hands are tied. How goddamned convenient!"

"Oh, it's not convenient at all. Maybe you haven't been listening but our situation here is a nightmare. It's a powder keg
and as we speak the fuse could be burning. If the Sioux or
Cheyenne get wind of how weak we are they'll burn us out in
two hours time. For nearly five years now we've been putting
up a ghost defense. We might as well have paper walls and toy
cannon for all we could do in the event of attack."

"Who's the Indian agent up at Wind Cave?"

"I don't know."

"Somebody must. You can't telegraph him?"

"If I could get through I would. You're talking about the least
reliable form of communication in the West. Wires are in-
stalled, they work for a few hours then our red neighbors cut
them. The Oglalas up there are as clever as the Apaches. They
cut the wire where it passes through the thickest foliage in trees,
then join the ends with a piece of cloth or rawhide. Transmis-
sion's impossible, finding the break can take six weeks. No matter what your personal feelings may be toward the tribes, don't
make the mistake of short-changing them on brains. I could tell
you stories . . ."

"I'm not interested. So that's your final word: You refuse to
give me men, you won't send them under Lieutenant what's-his-
name."

"It's not I 'won't,' I can't."

"Who can help me? And forget about Indian agents."

"They're your best bet."

"If you can't even contact them they're no bet at all. I'm getting out of here."

"Don't do it, son, don't go up there alone. They'll spot you and scalp you and leave you for the circling birds before you get within six miles of their camp."

"I have to try. I have one idea . . ."

"What?"

"With all due respect, Colonel, none of your goddamned business!"

The land tilted up suddenly into the sprawling Black Hills. Out of the plains they rose, a remnant of an enormous domelike formation, sixty million years old. Nearing the area with her captors, Jenny marveled at the towers and pinnacles grouped and challenging the heavens.

They arrived at the camp shortly before sunset. She counted more than thirty tepees and among the first sights to greet her eyes was that of a little girl playing with an antelope-skin doll in its cradleboard. She was about Mary's age. Jenny thought of Annie, reduced to a limp rag with her stuffing removed. And Mary and Sarah and Willis.

Her heart heavied; how could she ever face John and tell him what she'd done? *How she alone, and over Mary's objections, had contrived her death?*

The camp was a squalid eyesore in a well-trampled and sunburnt meadow nestled between the hills. Cookfires abounded. The Oglalas' tepees looked not at all like those seen in paintings and book illustrations. Most of these were filthy and ragged, as were the women and children. Dogs scampered about trying to steal meat; small boys played fetch with them; Jenny watched a squaw kick a puppy that strayed too close to her bowl of some kind of stew. The creature ran away yelping.

Moving in among the tepees the odor of rotten meat assailed her nostrils, mingling with those of human and animal excrement and other unidentifiable stenches. She could imagine what the tepee interiors smelled like. Jumping Bear came up beside her.

"Remember everything I told you, Jenny."

"Yes, yes, it's just common sense."

"Now I must tell you about the tepee. What is proper. If the flap is open, a friend may come in. If closed, he should announce his presence and wait for the owner to invite him in. A woman always enters the tepee *after* the man."

"No surprise there."

"Inside, the guest place is to the left of the host. A woman always sits at the left.

"When invited to eat, guests bring their own bowls and spoons. And you eat all that you are given. You never, never walk between the fire and another person; you pass behind the sitters.

"A woman never sits cross-legged like men. You sit on your heels or with your legs to one side. When the host begins to clean his pipe it is the signal for the guests to leave."

"Yes, yes. . . . What is that?" She pointed to four sticks supporting what looked like a canvas bag.

"A cooking pouch, made from the lining of a buffalo's stomach. It lasts three or four days before it becomes soggy and soft from the heat. Then you eat it."

"*You*, not me."

He sighed. "Are you forgetting so soon?" He pointed off to their right. "That's a skewer stand. You hang skewered chunks of meat on a wet rawhide strip and angle it over the fire."

"What is that?" She pointed to a frame with a piece of hairy material stretched on it. And gasped. "Not . . ."

"Yes. A white man's scalp, trimmed and being stretched, while fresh."

"Oh my God . . ."

Ottowa came up with Pawnee Killer and Four Hawks. The chief seized her rope rein. "Get down and come with me."

She glanced at Jumping Bear who nodded all but indis-
cernibly. Still Ottowa caught it. Envy soured his expression.
Jumping Bear seemed not to notice. Jenny's glance shifted back
and forth between them. Jumping Bear was no chief, he had no
power, but he had no fear of Ottowa. And was likely invaluable
to him and the other chiefs in their dealings with the whites. Ottowa started away, waving his hand for her to follow him. She
hesitated. He turned suddenly furious.

"Pinda-Lick-o-Ye!"

"What?"

"Pale Eyes," translated Jumping Bear. "Go!"

She followed Ottowa to a tepee that stood about twenty feet
tall: taller and bigger around at the base than others near it. Like
them it was made of sections of buffalo hide sewn together. At
the top, where two large flaps were supported by slender poles
open to let out smoke, she counted twelve thicker poles. The
two sides of the hide covering were joined by a vertical series
of wooden pins. The door flap was open and on one side the
cover was pulled up about two feet for ventilation. Ottowa
stopped outside the entrance.

"Clea-to-ka."

"Would you mind speaking English?"

"Clea-to-ka!"

He gestured her to follow him inside. So he'd decided to
stop speaking English to her, which meant he expected her to
pick up his language. As if she'd bother.

As Ottowa ducked inside she looked off to the southwest, to
where Beaver Creek coming down from the northwest emptied
into the Cheyenne River. The rising hills prevented view of river
and creek and the plains beyond. But in her mind's eyes she saw
them again.

Was John following? Not alone, God forbid! With soldiers—perhaps nowhere near five hundred, but a force strong
enough to intimidate Milk Eye and his children scalpers. Come

riding into the camp and demand her release. No bargaining, no trading for goods, just get on a horse and ride out surrounded by her rescuers, all guns loaded and cocked and not a single Oglala foolhardy enough to interfere.

When would this fanciful, farfetched rescue take place?

Ottowa yelled at her from inside the tepee. She ducked in. The rolled-up section of the cover didn't seem to let in so much as a breath of fresh air. Or let out any of the overpowering stench of body odor. Her eyes began watering and it was all she could do to keep from gagging. A fire smoldered in the center of the dirt floor; at the rear were two beds placed end to end. Four more beds were arranged in the same manner, two on each side.

Firewood was stacked between a corner lifting pole and one of the three tripod poles that gave the structure its shape. There were also back rests, buffalo robes, and cooking utensils. Beyond the fire, where the rawhide tie that bound the tripod poles at the top descended to a wooden peg in the ground, was a large kettle in which floated chunks of meat.

She had yet to taste buffalo but it had to be much like beef— probably gamier. Milk Eye went straight to the kettle and, dipping in his dirty hand, brought forth a quantity of the contents. He blew on it wetly, ate some—rolling it about in his mouth to cool it—and offered the remainder to her.

Her first instinct was to politely decline; but Jumping Bear's warning came back to her. If she was to cooperate she should start right away. She held out her hand and into it he poured what was left of the stew.

"*Sen-aba-de-o-ma!*"

She ate. Surprisingly, it was rather tasty, although it badly needed salt. It *was* gamier than beef. On second thought, it was quite like the venison the emigrants had been served in the mess hall at the Fort Kearny stopover.

The emigrants. By this time those who'd survived the attack

had to be well up into the Laramie Mountains on their way to
South Pass. On their way to a new life.

A woman came in: chocolate brown with little slits for eyes,
she was so short and fat that she was almost perfectly round.

"*Heyatawin*," said Milk Eye proudly. "*Tawicu.*"

She went to him and rubbed her arm against him. A
welcome-home kiss? Then she came to Jenny, reaching up to
touch her hair. She let her: more cooperation. The woman then
ducked out. They could hear her calling. Four other women
came in. Milk Eye kept repeating *Tawicu* as each one in turn had
to feel Jenny's hair. She had assumed that "*Tawicu*" was the first
woman's name, but it now became obvious that it was their
word for squaw.

So he collected wives, did he? Like the Mormons. Jenny
looked about at the six beds. And they all slept here. Such privacy. Where did he plan to put her? Surely not near the fire in
the middle of the floor. Then it dawned on her.

"*Tawicu?*" she repeated, and pointed at each of the women
in turn. He nodded.

"*Tawicu.*" He pointed at Jenny.

TWELVE

Before Jenny could get a word out, the last wife came in: a tall,
rawboned, miserable-looking woman with hair so black it
looked blue. In a rage, she flew screaming at Jenny and pushed
her over before Milk Eye could intercede. When he finally got
hold of her she struggled, broke free, and whirled on him, beating him with her fists and trying to knee him in the groin. She
set up such a din his other wives—standing dumbstruck—had
to cover their ears.

Jenny had picked herself up. She started toward the woman

but two of the others grabbed her arms and pulled her clear, jabbering warning.

"Wacawin. *Tawicu* . . ."

So this was the shrew of his harem: Wa-ca-win, whatever that meant. Jenny gingerly felt the base of her spine, trusting that nothing had cracked. The lacerations crisscrossing her back were still raw—it was fortunate she hadn't landed flat in the dirt, what with her dress torn in two clear down to her waist.

What a madhouse! She'd love to stride up to the vixen and slap her so hard she'd leave a black and blue mark. That would calm her down and make her mind her manners! Milk Eye finally got her under control and pushed her outside. The others followed obediently. The situation made it necessary for them to converse in English.

"*Tawicu* means 'wife.' "

"I gathered that. She's no wife, she's a wild animal."

The second it came out she realized she shouldn't have said it. But it didn't upset him; he smiled; he looked almost apologetic.

"She is like a rattlesnake when she is angry. Screaming and striking out. Maybe you had better stay away from her for a few days."

"How do I do that? Oh, it'd help if I stayed in another tepee."

He grunted. She got the impression that he may not like the suggestion but it did make sense. It likely would be easier on him.

"I will decide later. Now we will eat." He indicated a stack of wooden bowls, each with its own spoon. "Give me a bowl. You take one. We will talk."

While they ate, he instructed her.

"No one will harm you if you do as you are told."

"As you order."

"Yes."

"Do you intend to rape me?"

He seemed not to understand. "Can a husband rape his wife?"

"It's commoner than you think. All husbands are not paragons."

"Para . . . ?"

"And who says we're married?"

He thumbed his chest. "Me."

"It may have slipped your mind but I already have a husband."

"He is dead."

"He is not. If he was, how would you know? You wouldn't know him if you fell over him."

"As good as dead. You will never see each other again."

"You'll be surprised."

"Oglala marriages are simply made."

"I don't doubt it; if there's mutual agreement on the part of both parties."

"Mu . . . ?"

"Never mind."

He belched. She averted her head as the fumes came at her. "Among our people a boy meets a girl in front of her tepee. He throws his robe over her and himself, and standing in front of her family, embraces her and whispers with her."

"And if she doesn't like him?"

He lowered his eyes. "She . . . refuses to be embraced under the robe."

"She ducks out from under."

"Yes."

"In other words, she *can* refuse him. And no one is hurt. You already have six wives. That's enough for Brigham Young. Mustn't be greedy. I may be your prisoner but according to your own customs, I don't have to be your wife."

"I am a chief. If you refuse to marry me it will look very bad."

"You'd lose face. A shame."

"I did not bring you all the way here just to look at the fire in your hair. I brought you to be my wife."

"Maybe you should have . . ." She paused. She couldn't say "asked me first"; if he had asked, she would have refused him back at the wagon train, and probably been scalped and hacked to pieces on the spot!

"What?" he asked.

"Nothing. This meat is quite good."

"It is antelope."

"I thought it was buffalo."

"I do not eat buffalo; it is too stringy, it sticks in my teeth."

"I'm full. I'm very tired. Chief Ottowa, will you have somebody show me to where I can sleep? Undisturbed?"

He understood every word. He stared at her at length before responding. When he finally did, it wasn't really a response. He simply got up and pushed her outside ahead of him. It was getting dark, the cookfires were dying, the dogs rested. Ottowa pointed at a tepee much smaller than his own. Feeling all eyes on her, she crossed to the entrance flap. Inside it was filled with stacks of buffalo robes, meat packed with salt in baskets, and additional baskets filled with fruit and other foods.

She made room and made a bed out of four robes on top of each other and a fifth one to pull over her against the chill of the oncoming night. Lying down, she pulled her "quilt" up to her chin. Her back was very sore; she turned on her side. A familiar figure came in: Jumping Bear.

"I saw you leave his tepee. So this is where he put you."

"He wants me to be wife number seven." Jumping Bear chuckled. "It's not funny! How do I protect myself against him?"

"Think, Jenny; if he wanted you, he'd take you. Wouldn't he? No, he is a chief, he must behave like a chief."

"Or lose his precious face . . ."

"Exactly. He *loves* himself; *he* is much more important to him than any of his wives and children."

"He has children?"

"At least thirty. He is very proud, much too proud to risk losing face. But, it is not that bad. I do not think he will force you to submit to him. True, you have refused him, but that is all right, as long as nobody else hears about it. Another thing, he brought you here, he is responsible for you. You are his; so no one will bother you."

"You really think so?"

"Not unless they're drunk."

"Oh, God. . . . Will you do something for me? Get me a knife. You're the only one who can. I certainly can't ask Milk Eye. Please, Jumping Bear."

He grimaced and shook his head. "If I got you a knife, or if you got one from anybody else and he finds out, who will he accuse?"

"But I've got to be able to defend myself. I promise it'll never leave this tepee, it'll be just for when I'm sleeping."

"Forget a knife, forget any kind of weapon. My own tepee is just across the way, I will keep an eye on your front entrance."

"All night? Every night?"

"Jenny, I will do what I can to protect you; I just do not think you will need protecting."

"You're a man, you wouldn't understand. Apart from all your friends who attacked us there's Waca . . ."

"Wacawin. Flower Woman, his number one wife."

"They're numbered?"

"His . . ."

"Principal wife."

"Yes, she rules his tepee. Oh, every warrior rules his own, but she . . . he . . . lets her."

"What you mean is he's henpecked." He didn't understand the term. "Ironic, he rules the roost, she rules him. Her brain is cracked, you know, he should keep her tied up for his own safety. What a handful!"

"She *is* high-spirited."

"You can tell him for me, Jumping Bear, if she and I tangle— and we will—I won't hesitate to break her neck."

"Better you keep out of her way."

"That's what he said. As if I could."

She was supporting herself on one elbow. He sat cross-legged by her improvised bed, his knees supporting his fore-arms. It was almost pitch black; she could barely make out his features. She had paused to let her anger abate. She pondered.

"Do not try it, Jenny."

"What?"

"Escaping."

"How did you know I was thinking about that?"

"What else would you be *thinking* about? He chose you, he saved your life. That is why you've made it this far. For you to attempt to escape would be slapping his face. He has left you alone, he is letting you sleep alone. He has given you your life. And you would repay him by insulting him? Degrading him in the eyes of his people?"

"You miss the point. I don't belong here; he kidnapped me!"

"He could have killed you."

"He has no right to do anything to me!"

"Shhhhh. You are his prisoner. Keep that in mind and please do not try to escape. There are better ways to get free . . ."

"Name one. Listen to me, what if you were to ride to Fort Laramie, talk to the colonel there, tell him I've alive, I'm here . . ."

"You want me to be a traitor to my people?"

"To save my life."

"Your life is not in danger."

"Of course it is!"

"Not if you behave like I told you. You have already seen what cooperating can earn you—this place, privacy . . ."

"Watch, when Wacawin . . ."

"Flower Woman," he corrected Jenny.

"When she finds out I'm here she'll burn it down. She's crazy."

"She makes a lot of noise, but there is a limit. If she bothers you, that is one thing; if she tried to harm you, that is going too far. He will protect you."

"From what I've seen, against her he has trouble protecting himself."

"How is your back?"

"Don't change the subject."

"This is taking us round and round a circle. I brought you this. . . ." Out of his belt he got a small pouch. Unfolding it, he held it close so that she could see its contents in the darkness. It was a salve. "We call it the healing herb; your wounds should be gently rubbed with it."

"It smells like comfrey."

"It comes from a flower that grows by rivers and in moist places. Many different colors: bluish-purple, yellow, red, even white."

"Comfrey."

"It is very good. Let me rub it into your wounds. You will sleep better and they will heal faster."

She let him apply it. He was surprisingly gentle. It was soothing; when he was done she lay back down on her side.

"I must go now," he said. "You sleep. Like long-claws."

"Long . . . ?"

"The grizzly bear. Deep, like he sleeps in the white season. When you get up, go straight to Ottowa's tepee. He will like that."

"Report to him." She snickered. "The only thing is, if I stay clear of him, it'll be easier to keep away from her."

"I am sure she is beginning to get used to having you around."

"I'm sure you're wrong. Thank you, Jumping Bear, for the salve, the good words, for being a friend when I need one. Good night."

She slept. The door knocker sounded.

"Yes?"

"It's me."

She opened her apartment door to John. He shoved in a bouquet: daisies, yellow poppies, zinnias, carnations, and in the center a single, large, shimmeringly red rose, dominating like a queen over her throng of handmaidens. He came in, held her, kissed her tenderly.

"It's been soooo long," he murmured.

"A whole day." She laughed and led him into the parlor. "Where's Mary?"

"Agnes Longstreth is keeping an eye on her. Mary and her two girls play together. Jenny, do you realize this is the first time it's been just us two in the daytime?"

"Sit. Let me get a vase for these; they're lovely. . . ."

She arranged the bouquet in her best cased-glass vase. He sat on the divan, watching her.

"Oh, for a picture of that. The beautiful arranging the beautiful."

"I'm not beautiful. My nose is too pointy, my eyes too far apart. They're frog green instead of soft and light like . . . like . . ."

"Emeralds?"

"*Anything* but the color they are. I'm skinny as a rake, I have freckles . . ."

"You do not."

"Look closely, you'll see them."

"Come here. I don't see a one." He held her hand. "I love you, Jenny Sanders; and Mary thinks you're queen of the universe."

"I adore her."

"How do you feel about the other Pryor?"

"He'll do." She jabbed him playfully. "I *do* adore her, John. She's so quick and bright, sweet, unspoiled . . ."

"Oh, she's spoiled. I should know, I'm responsible."

"That's balderdash, whatever balderdash is."

She excused herself to make tea. Minutes later she was back. The afternoon sun slanted down onto the moquette rug. As she sipped, the impression came that the world outside was watching them, waiting expectantly for what was to come, the reason he'd dropped by. She was so happy she glowed; she could feel it all over. She eyed him over the protection of her cup as he sipped his tea. How she loved him! In his embrace her heart went wild. When he kissed her she wanted to faint. Only whatever would he think if she did? John Pryor, like most men, did not find delicate flowers attractive.

But why didn't he propose? Why come so close so often and stop? Back off? He wanted to; all the signs were there like flashing stars. She knew she was the only girl he was seeing. He insisted he loved her. She'd been held and kissed by others who told her they loved her, but this was wholly different: It was genuine. And his eyes when he said it—she wished they could hold that look forever.

Holding his hand, she could feel the heat in his blood, as if mere contact sent his temperature rising. And when he held her close his heart outpounded her own.

In a dozen ways he betrayed how he felt.

Why didn't he propose?

He set down his tea and took her cup from her; he held both her hands.

"Jenny, there's something I must say."

"That serious?"

No, she mustn't make light of this of all moments; only she was suddenly so nervous. She must get a grip on herself. He cleared his throat and went on quietly, solemnly.

"About Mary . . ."

"What about her?"

"She's six now, not exactly a babe in arms."

"And?"

"I know you love her, and she's crazy about you."

"I think the intensity of fondness is equal. What are you trying to say, darling?"

"She's not your average six year old. There's nothing 'average' about her. She's high-spirited. She's fiercely independent for one so young. She has my temper. At times it's like trying to control a tigress. She can be almost intimidating. Oh, maybe not that bad, you *can* reason with her, but she doesn't take discipline . . . graciously."

"Who does at that age?"

"I did, believe it or not. Of course, boys do have the strap to contend with. I don't know where Mary gets it; Norma was nothing like her. Of course, Mary *is* adopted . . ."

"John?"

"Yes?"

"Has it occurred to you that maybe the only thing Mary needs is a mother? Oh, to the devil with it! I have a question for you."

He gaped as she got down on her knees and clasped his hands. . . .

She woke up choking. Flames licked at the base of the tepee cover. Smoke curled thickly upward, filling the tepee. Still choking, her eyes burning, she staggered and clawed her way through the stacks of buffalo robes and piles of food. Coughing, stumbling, falling, she crawled toward the entrance flap. From her improvised bed it was only a few feet away. Now it seemed yards. Reaching it, feeling about, she dug her nails into the cover searching for the flap . . .

Finally finding it. The strings hung untied but the flap was tightly closed. She pushed with her fists, then her shoulder, but it would not give. She fought for air, her nostrils stinging, her lungs on fire.

She passed out.

THIRTEEN

The first sight to meet her eyes was the darkened sky. The stars stared down indifferently. Her chest burned; acrid smoke ascended her throat, lanced into her nostrils. She could hear beating. She turned toward the sound. Men were beating small flames with blankets. Too little effort, much too late. Smoke curled from the blackened remains of the tepee and its contents.

The Oglalas milled about. Ottowa stood close, looking down at her out of his working eye. Beside him was Jumping Bear, knife in hand. It was he who had cut away the entrance flap and saved her. Somebody had fastened it from the outside; that had to be it, inside she couldn't budge it. Jumping Bear had to have noticed how it was fastened when he cut it open.

Ottowa barked a command. Jumping Bear translated.

"Sit up."

He helped her up. She looked about. Flower Woman was nowhere to be seen. She'd started the fire. Who else? Again Milk Eye spoke. Jumping Bear gestured. She got to her feet without his assistance. Breathing was painful, every inhalation aggravating the burning sensation assaulting her lungs and throat.

"Keep breathing deeply," said Jumping Bear. "In a few minutes it won't burn as much."

"My lungs feel like rags. And my throat's so raw it feels shredded. Thank you, my friend. Oh, thank you!"

Impulsively, she seized his hands and pumped them. Milk Eye pushed between them, separating them, glaring first at one then the other. Jumping Bear flared and began speaking rapidly.

Milk Eye considered his words before nodding. Jumping Bear kept pointing at the rubble of the tepee. The only word Jenny caught was *Wacawin*.

Once more she looked about her. So this was the hell-hag's first try. There would be others. Even if Milk Eye was too dense or too stubborn to figure it out, Jumping Bear was doing his best to incriminate Wacawin. Would the old man punish her?

Jumping Bear was still speaking, sounding very insistent. Was it about calling her to account? If it was, Milk Eye didn't appear eager; yet he had to do *something* to discipline her. For attempting to destroy his property, if for no other reason. Jenny thought: he'd beaten her for throwing away the sacred ceremonial pipe. Surely attempted murder was a far greater crime.

She was thinking like a white. At that, what did it matter if Milk Eye punished Wacawin or not? He wouldn't order her executed; whatever he did—if anything—she'd survive to try again. And keep trying until she succeeded.

"Oh, John, John, John . . ."

Her first words since regaining consciousness stopped Jumping Bear midsentence. He and Milk Eye stared at her, then Jumping Bear spoke.

"It is still many hours till dawn. We will find another bed for you."

"You're joking. If I close my eyes I'll never open them."

"That is stupid talk." He smiled. "I told you I'd keep an eye on you."

"Thank God. You were just in time."

"I know, I am sorry that you passed out before I could get inside."

"How did she 'lock' the flap?"

He grinned. Almost admiringly, Jenny reflected. "She sewed it with rawhide. A neat job. Lucky for you I sharpened my knife just yesterday."

Ottowa interrupted with a flurry of words, confronting Jenny. She interrupted him.

"I don't know a word you're saying and you know it! Speak English or don't talk to me at all!"

Jumping Bear understood, as did Ottowa. Most of the others might not have realized what she said but her tone was unmistakable. Everyone looked appalled. Ottowa's face darkened in shock, until he caught himself.

"You dare talk so to me and I will cut your throat. Cut you to small pieces and feed you to the dogs!"

"I'm . . . sorry. . . ."

"Out of my eyes!"

She hesitated, then walked off. Jumping Bear followed.

"A-i-i-i, *why* did you do that?" he rasped.

"He infuriates me!"

"So you scream at him? Make him look foolish in front of the whole camp? He *will* slit your throat, you know; you keep on like you are going and you will force him to. And you want him to punish Flower Woman? Oh, he was planning to; now you can forget it. He will do nothing for you who yells at him, insults him with her tongue that is like a knife in the hand of a crazy Arapaho. Jenny, Jenny, Jenny."

"I'm sorry. Truly. It was stupid . . ."

"You must apologize, make amends, do *something*. . . . For now, come to my tepee. I will fix a bed for you."

She stopped short. "I . . ."

His worried expression gave way to anger. "What, are you

afraid I will rape you in your sleep? Do not be stupid! I could
have done it before, when I rubbed your back. You have no
choice, Jenny."

She couldn't argue anything he'd said. She no longer cared
if the hell-hag got punished; in the wink of an eye she had alien-
ated Ottowa. She'd never seen him so upset. Far worse than
when he accosted her after she'd thrown away his precious pipe.

"I talk too much," she muttered.

"What?"

"Nothing."

<hr>

FOURTEEN

John Pryor washed his hands of Colonel Thomas Moonlight.
He decided that he could hang around Fort Laramie until the
Platte froze and be no closer than he was right now to working
out a rescue plan.

He could not continue to sit on his hands waiting. Over
Moonlight's protests, which grew louder and more vehement as
John's fifth day at the fort wore on, he resolved to ride the well-
over-two-hundred miles to Wind Cave.

There he would discuss the situation with the resident Indian agent and together they would develop a plan of action.
Why the agent operated out of Wind Cave instead of Fort Sully
was a mystery to John, nor could Moonlight explain it. Thomas
Heffernan, the local Indian agent, was lodged at Fort Laramie.
Unfortunately, he had to pick now of all times to be away, although even had he been available *he'd* get no more cooperation out of the colonel than had John.

John speculated on what sort of man the Wind Cave Indian
agent would turn out to be. Would he have backbone? Would
he button on his authority, confront the Oglalas, and bargain

with them? Were two helpless innocents worth the risk of upsetting the fragile truce between red man and white?

More to the point, would the warriors who'd attacked the
wagon train even be up there? John had seen them ride away in
that direction, but what if they were simply throwing any would-
be pursuers off their trail—starting out in one direction and
once out of sight turning the opposite way? He recalled Moonlight's assertion that the Oglalas were spread practically all over
the map.

Colonel Thomas Moonlight. He might have sympathized
with him for his "tied hands," if Moonlight hadn't whined so
about it. *I can't, I'm sorry.* Right: the sorriest sonovabitch west
of the Mississippi. He's sorry, and so's the army, the Secretary
of War, President Johnson, the whole damned country!

Colonel Thomas Moonlight: the bigger the mouth, the
smaller the balls.

This area was Cheyenne territory, with some Sioux—the
Oglalas up in the Black Hills and in the Tetons further north.
None of the three tribes was peaceful and a lone man riding
through their hunting grounds had to be as vulnerable as a
woman with a child.

Yet another problem reared, snakelike: John had driven
every conceivable type of horse-drawn vehicle, but rarely had
he actually ridden a horse. Reflecting on it, it had to be close to
three years since the last time. He could ride, but he would suffer for it.

He debated the wisdom of traveling by night and holing up
during daylight. Indians, he knew, avoided moving about at
night; their fear of the dark or superstition, whatever it was that
kept them in their tepees after sundown, could conceivably
work to his advantage. His horse—a feisty roan mare who loved
to run—also gave him an edge. The stableman who'd handed
him the reins assured him that she was grain-fed "from out of
her maw," so that she could easily outrun any Cheyenne or

Sioux ponies, all of which were grass-fed and short on endurance. But with this good news came a warning that over a short run, a grass-fed Indian grulla mustang could "beat the fastest wind."

He didn't fancy being chased by anything with four legs, regardless of what it ate. Maybe hiding during the day wouldn't be a bad idea. The horse would appreciate being spared the sun. He'd have to see.

Leaving his wagon, the oxen, and everything he and Jenny owned in the world, he set out from Fort Laramie before dawn—before reveille and before Moonlight reached for his first cigar of the day. He had no desire to say good-bye to the colonel; he was afraid he might lose his temper and tell him off.

In preparing for the trip the day before, he'd thought about dragging a pack mule behind him. He'd suggested it to the quartermaster, who told him that if any Indians saw a white man heading toward the Black Hills with a pack mule they'd assume he was a prospector, and gold seekers trespassing their sacred lands were fair game for arrow or tomahawk. Around the fourth or fifth day on the trail he might have to cut down on his rations and his water, but getting to Wind Cave as fast as he could travel had to take precedence over amenities and necessities alike.

Setting out, he rode all day with only two brief stops to water the horse. By the time the sun began dissolving into the Laramies, he figured he'd covered at least sixty miles. He based his estimate on landmarks the quartermaster had told him about: mainly the creeks issuing from the mountains. He forded Lodgepole Creek, Horse Creek, and Bear Creek; he stopped for the night on the south bank of Chugwater Creek. He could have gone on at least four hours longer but hurrying the pace would be too hard on the horse and could deplete her at the end of the run when, in the heart of Oglala Territory, he might very well need her at top speed.

There was another reason for not overdoing it; it came swiftly to mind when he dismounted and tried to sit.

He kindled a small fire in a cleft in a ledge, concealing the flame, hoping that the smoke would not be visible at a distance, in the moonlight. He ate salted venison, drank the vilest coffee he'd ever tasted, and downed one of the six hard-boiled eggs the quartermaster had given him just before he left. Not only was the egg filling but it helped dispel the foul taste of the coffee. Rolling up in his blanket, he lay down with his pack for a pillow and thought about Jenny and Mary.

If they were still alive, what condition were they in? Had all the warriors had their way with Jenny? Could she still walk? And what about Mary? Did they rape children? He wouldn't put it past them. *He'd make them pay in blood!*

"Sure you will. Big talk, Pryor. Who do you think you are, Kit Carson?"

But considering the situation in its entirety, the worst of it was not knowing what was going on with Jenny and Mary. And naturally assuming the worst. On the other hand, Jenny was no ordinary woman. She had guts to match her fire, and was as bright as the North Star. She'd know how to play one against another, how to conduct herself in their midst. She could ascertain who she could trust and who not. She'd master their taboos and avoid them like the pox. She'd adjust.

She could be the sweetest, most charming, most thoroughly likable individual in the crowd. Unfortunately, she could be a spitfire, and when her fury took over, uncontrollable. He chuckled mirthlessly; could it be that whoever had abducted her was regretting it mightily?

If that were the case it could lead to one of three things: let her and Mary go, kill them, or turn them over to another. Poor Mary only complicated an already badly tangled situation. How did the Indians treat captive children? The more he thought

about both their situations the more frantic with worry he became.

Nearly sixty miles. Roughly 160 more to Wind Cave. Three
days? Possibly, providing he could find it without too much
wandering about.

FIFTEEN

Chief Ottowa, for the time being, was too busy to avenge
Jenny's insulting outburst. Led by all three of their chiefs, the
Oglalas threw themselves into preparations for the annual
gazing-at-the-sun dance. Virgins were sent out to select the sacred tree. Elders cut it down, stripped it of its branches, and carried it back to camp.

The Sun Dance, the most important dance of the year, was
sponsored by a pledger, an individual whose need for a spiritual
favor was deemed to be greater than any other's. This year,
Makatoźanźan—Clear Blue Earth—a middle-aged warrior
badly crippled in battle, asserted to the chiefs and elders that he
had been ordered to assume the role of pledger in a dream.
Kangi—Raven—a revered elder and Makatoźanźan's cousin,
supported his petition for preference among those who requested the coveted role.

The Sun Dance was conducted over one entire day. A good-
sized lodge, facing east, was specially built for the ceremony.
The tree selected by the virgins was set in the ground outside
the lodge. In the fork of the tree sacred objects were placed: a
bundle of brush rendered sacred by Kangi, a tomahawk that had
been rendered sacred by the elders, a tomahawk that had killed
twenty despised Cheyenne, a war bonnet worn by the now-
deceased great chief Catka—Left Hand. The participating war-

riors danced facing the tree for hours, staring at one of the sacred objects, gradually hypnotizing themselves.

But the most bizarre part of the ceremony was the *o-kee-pee*,
a torture rite witnessed inside the lodge by the men only. Jumping Bear described for Jenny what she would be missing.

"Young warriors volunteer and Makatoźanźan selects those
who will take part. Dancing the torture rite is one of the great-
est honors a warrior can earn."

"They volunteer to be tortured?"

"Eagerly. They fight for the privilege. First they must fast
and purify themselves."

They stood near Jumping Bear's tepee surrounded by the vi-
brant colors of tepees, robes, and blankets. The people swarmed
like bees, caught up in the excitement. The air fairly bristled
with anticipation; scores of dogs scampered about barking,
adding to the human clamor.

"What is the point?" Jenny asked.

"One and all seek powerful visions."

"Being tortured gives them visions?"

"Torture, fasting, purifying themselves, and dancing around
the ceremonial post until they collapse in a stupor; all con-
tribute. Of course the torture is the most important." He turned
her around, touching under one shoulder then the other. "Here
and here slits are made and pegs inserted under the skin."

"Lovely."

"They can not wait to be cut."

"Was it done to you?"

"I have never volunteered."

"Don't you think it's disgusting?"

"I do not question any of our people's practices. No one
does. The Sun Dance, like other rituals, is very old."

"So are the rack and the iron maiden. Go on."

"After the pegs are inserted, strings hanging from overhead

posts are attached to them. The warriors strain against the pull of the strings until their flesh tears, freeing them."

"Good God."

He grinned. "You disapprove? That is one way; sometimes buffalo skulls are suspended from the pegs. The volunteers hang dead weight. The added weight of the skulls helps tear them free. But it takes longer."

"That's enough. You're making me nauseous. So that's why half the warriors have those scars on their backs. Why so many missing fingers?"

"The scars are medals of bravery and endurance."

"Unbelievable . . ."

"You should see Chief Ottowa's back. When he was younger he went through the ritual three years in a row. Most faint in a few minutes. When they come to, they drag themselves to the *cho-di-ah*, a masked warrior. He chops off one or two fingers with his tomahawk."

"Delightful."

"Relax, you will not be allowed to watch any of it. I told you, no women allowed inside the lodge."

"How disappointing."

"You can watch the second half, outside; everybody does."

"More torture?"

He grinned, amused by her sarcasm. "You will see."

"Not me, I'll just shut myself up in your tepee till the whole silly spectacle is over."

He shook his head. "Chief Ottowa would not approve of that. He will expect you to watch. It is everybody's sacred duty— even children. It is no 'spectacle,' Jenny, it is the fire that hardens the metal in a warrior's spine."

She scoffed and dismissed this, waving both hands.

Two days later, all the preparations completed, the *o-kee-pee* was performed in privacy in the big lodge. Late in the afternoon the bleeding and mutilated participants staggered forth into the sunlight. A space had been cleared in front of Kangi's tepee. The crippled pledger Makatoźanźan sat beside the revered elder. Jenny watched with Jumping Bear. He pointed to a ten-foot center post.

"They have to run around it."

"Dragging those buffalo skulls, I know . . ."

"Only until they tear the pegs from their flesh."

"I'm closing my eyes."

"This is the climax of the whole ceremony. You want to miss it?"

"If it's so amusing to you, how can you carry on so about honor and courage? Look at them, most can barely drag one leg after the other."

"You will be surprised; with everybody watching, they will get their second wind."

"Three cheers."

Around and around the center post staggered the volunteers, battling to keep from fainting. One after another collapsed, and to Jenny's surprise and disgust their friends ran up to them and dragged them around the circle until the buffalo skulls finally tore free.

Out of nearly twenty men, only two had their burdens pull free of their backs and remained conscious. They continued staggering around the post. Jenny watched as finally Ottowa and the other two chiefs came out of the crowd and stopped them. The Oglalas cheered and whooped.

"They have beaten it," murmured Jumping Bear.

"Do they get ribbons?"

"They will be designated by the chiefs and elders as candidates for future leadership. It may be painful, but it is worth it."

Amazing, she thought. Brains, skill, talent for organization, even courage, meant nothing compared with the ability to withstand pain. Just as appalling was the realization that these people put no limits to the self-torture inflicted on their protectors, the most esteemed members of the tribe.

If this is what they did to themselves, what would they do to her—a detested enemy—if Milk Eye turned on her? She watched him escort the two survivors inside the ceremonial lodge with his fellow chiefs. Up to now he had not even looked in her direction. But just before disappearing inside he paused and turned back. Their eyes met across the dusty open ground. Like the stinging quirt days earlier, his good eye struck. In it, dire warning. Now that the Sun Dance was over he would deal with her.

Jumping Bear noticed. And grunted.

SIXTEEN

The ancient geological upheaval of the Black Hills rose up to four thousand feet above the desolate sea of prairie grass. Towers and pinnacles trapped thunderheads, imbuing the hills with a climate all their own, according to the quartermaster. A strange place they were, a site of legend and myth and rumor that stirred the imagination and struck fear into the heart of any white man foolish enough to venture into them. Skirting them would add another hundred miles to John Pryor's mission; cutting east and coming down to Wind Cave was out of the question. The time wasted at Fort Laramie nagged his conscience; every additional day, every hour Jenny and Mary remained with the Oglalas added to the danger. Crossing over into South Dakota, he found and followed Hell Canyon Creek into chilly late afternoon, the sun setting off his right shoulder. He had pushed the mare hard since the fort shrank to a speck and disappeared from view. She was willing, but beginning to show signs of losing her remarkable stamina. Climbing into the hills only hastened it.

He reined up, dismounted wearily, and walked the horse about to keep her legs from stiffening. He fed and watered her before hobbling her for the night. Gathering firewood, he was preparing to light it when ahead and to the east he caught sight of a series of small white clouds rising one after another.

Smoke signals!

Oglala or Cheyenne? Either tribe would treasure his scalp. He felt the tiny hairs at the back of his neck rising. Should he stay put and hope they were just "talking" and not on the move? He was trying to decide when instinct prompted by his mounting fear warned him to look behind him.

More signals. And he was squarely between them. Had the ones to the south caught sight of him leaving the plains? Were they now warning the others about the white trespasser? He thought about it. Why go to all that trouble for one man?

But something *was* up. Was fighting about to erupt with him trapped between them? At this time of day? Could they be preparing for a battle at dawn? Apart from the little he'd picked up on his last trip West he knew next to nothing about Indians in general. Reflecting on this, still crouching by his pile of sticks with a match in his hand, his heart began churning.

Less than thirty yards away, from the other side of a huge boulder perched perilously on the hump of a ledge, a large puff of smoke arose.

He swallowed. Hide! Where? He cast about. Behind him, at least forty paces back, a crevice yawned wide enough to back the horse into. Once inside it, they'd both be out of sight, so dark was the interior.

Could he make it back to there without being seen? Or would he be safer where he was, with the boulder between the signalers and him?

Yet all they had to see was the horse standing out in the open nibbling grass. As he was debating what to do, a brave stepped out from behind the boulder. John held his breath as he watched the man kneel to adjust the lacing on his moccasin. Then the brave looked up, jumped up, pointed at him, and shouted.

SEVENTEEN

Two more braves appeared. One nocked an arrow to his bow, but not before John got to his saddle and pack on the far side of the pile of sticks. He snatched up his Navy Colt and fired in one motion as the arrow came whirring his way. It ripped his sleeve just below his left shoulder, scraping, drawing blood before lodging in the ground behind him. He scarcely felt it.

His shot had struck the brave in the throat. The bow clattered to rest as the brave set both hands to the wound. For an instant it looked as if he was choking himself. Then he fell headfirst into the grass.

His companions ducked behind the boulder. John glanced about. No cover within ten yards. Colt upraised, aiming at their concealment, waving the gun back and forth to cover both sides, he duck-waddled forward and snatched up the Henry. It was fully loaded: sixteen shots. But it had a lever action; both hands were needed to fire it and lever another cartridge into the chamber. He shoved his pistol into his belt and backed off the way he'd come, looking warily left and right.

One of the signalers peered out from behind the boulder at the left. John saw the bow ready to let fly. John fired and missed. It would be a Mexican standoff. They'd stay put, he'd find cover; together they'd sit it out, waiting for one side or the other to try something foolish out of impatience.

He looked over at the dead brave lying face down not six feet from where his horse had resumed grazing. She swished her tail contentedly then lifted her head to look his way, as if to ask "what now?"

A thought occurred. Neither brave appeared willing to risk looking around the boulder to check his movements. Which meant that any action to bring matters to a quick conclusion had to come from him. If he could sneak far enough around to see behind the boulder, get a clear shot . . .

He started to his right, head down, keeping low, moving faster and faster, following a circle at least 100 yards in diameter. He threaded between rocks, pausing now and then to risk raising his head for a look at the boulder. But he had yet to move far enough around to be able to see behind it. When eventually he reached that point and straightened for a look, to his surprise no one was there. Only a heap of smoldering grass and the blanket they'd used lying bunched up alongside it.

Sweat started across his upper lip. Had they jumped down to come after him? Or had they anticipated his moving and themselves moved around front of their cover? However they'd managed to vanish, they hadn't made a sound, even with the breeze obligingly blowing toward him.

He moved forward. He gauged he was now three-quarters of the way around the circle he had set for himself. Pausing, preparing to slip sideways between two outcroppings, he instinctively turned for a look behind him.

They were following! He could not see them, could hear nothing, but they were there. The slight twisting sensation in his gut and his heartbeat noticeably speeding up confirmed it. Slipping between the outcroppings, he pulled back behind one and waited, Colt cocked and upraised. *Could* he ambush them?

"We shall see . . ."

He drew further back behind his concealment. This made good sense. Let them slip through as he had done, continue on, and offer their backs for a target.

He waited. The shadows stretched, the air grew chillier. Now and again the wind tested its strength, swirling among the rocks. In the west the sun lost itself behind clouds the color of chaparral peas. He watched as gradually it burnt through, erasing the purple with blazing gold. He waited. What were they up to?

This wasn't working. It had seemed so simple, even after they guessed what he was up to and turned him into the hare. Had they themselves taken cover somewhere back up the circle route, suspecting he was readying an ambush?

"Damn!"

Slowly, apprehensively, he eased back around the outcropping, passing between it and the one nearly butting up against it. Stealthily retracing his steps, his gun still in hand, he came back to where he had a clear view of the campsite.

The corpse was gone!

Horse, saddle, pack: gone!

EIGHTEEN

"Tawicu!"

Milk Eye rudely poked Jenny's breastbone with his gnarled index finger. He had ordered her to his tepee after castigating Jumping Bear for his temerity in taking her under his wing. Jumping Bear had taken his dressing down with an air of affected unconcern, managing to hide his grin from the chief's good eye.

Now Jenny stood before Milk Eye in his tepee while his six wives watched them and whispered behind their hands. She would have glowed in embarrassment had the whole business not been so ridiculous. He simply had to dominate the stage. He did not speak, he declaimed. Everything he did he performed. He seemed to delight in putting himself on exhibition and most of the time ended up looking foolish. Jumping Bear understood his type. He maintained that the older every chief got the more he substituted intimidation for persuasion and bluster for wisdom.

Milk Eye had ordered a bed built. It was set as close to the center of his tepee as the fire and pole tie and peg permitted.

Jenny wondered if, when she rejected him, he would force himself on her. And decided that, unfortunately, he would have to or risk demeaning himself in the eyes of his wives. Which in itself was ironic; one would imagine they'd be jealous of the captive intruder in their midst. Still, they weren't jealous of each other—why should they be of her?

Of course Flower Woman was wildly jealous. Whenever Jenny's eyes met hers she could see the simmering hatred igniting the older woman's stare. Had Milk Eye punished her for the attempted murder? Even tongue-lashed her? Jumping Bear's opinion came back to Jenny; likely the chief had done nothing to the arsonist after she, Jenny, lit into him in front of half the tribe. Now, with the Sun Dance behind them and life restored to normal, he would probably turn his attention to avenging his wounded dignity against his insolent "guest." Put her in her place, force her to live with him, sleep with him. He would break her like a horse; he would teach her humility, make her submissive, compliant.

He would try!

"You will live here from now on. Not with Jumping Bear, not with anyone else. *My* wives live in *my* tepee."

"We've already had this conversation," murmured Jenny. "I told you before, I say it again: I . . . am . . . already . . . married. Bigamy doesn't appeal to me."

As she expected, the word was unfamiliar to him. The only reason she dared say it. He let it pass, unwilling to show his ignorance in front of the others. Jenny bridled the impulse to throw up her hands. What was the use? Why delude herself? Clearly, if she didn't do as he dictated she'd end up in even deeper trouble. These people were savages; they were as quick with a knife as she was with an insult.

She was nineteen, he had to be in his mid-seventies. What could he do but lie beside her and fondle and fumble and fail, pretending he was assaulting her. Still, a few men his age fathered children. She sighed. He eyed her icily.

"What?"

"Nothing."

"*Uśi maya ye.* I command your attention. *Uśi maya ye.* Say it."

"*Uśi maya ye.*"

"Learn it. Learn to speak our language like you speak your English." Again he jabbed her roughly. "*Winu.*"

"*Wee-noo.*"

"*Winu!*"

"*Winu.*"

"Captive woman. *You are a winu. Hiyapo.*" She stared. "*Hiyapo:* come forward."

"*Hiyapo.*"

He continued instructing her in conversational words and phrases before becoming bored and ordering everybody outside.

"I wish to walk with my wives. With all of you. You, Jen-ny. *Tawicu!*"

He simply had to show off his trophy! Flower Woman had stepped up beside him while the others trailed behind. Before they started out he jabbered something to Flower Woman. She bristled and snapped back. He responded in the same tone and pushed her away so hard she nearly fell.

"*Hiyapo!*" he commanded Jenny.

She moved forward and took Flower Woman's place beside him. Women at their cookfires, children playing, warriors and older men in conversation, all paused to look at Ottowa and his wives.

Jenny wondered where his children were. She had yet to see one, not that she was especially interested. Ottowa held up the parade while he ducked inside the tepee and put on his ceremonial headdress. Then he started them forward. He nodded greeting to everyone they passed, the consummate politician out for his afternoon stroll among his constituents.

Suddenly there was a commotion at the rear of the line. Jenny and he both looked back. Flower Woman was pushing the others aside, trying to get back to the front of the line. The upraised knife in her hand caught the sun. Scowling furiously at Jenny, she began screaming.

She threw herself forward, brandishing the knife, and would have stabbed her had not Ottowa reacted with surprising speed for his age. As he thrust himself in front of Jenny, down came the knife, stabbing his forearm. Blood surfaced, spurted. He bellowed, knocking the knife from Flower Woman's grasp and using his injured arm, sent her sprawling. She scrambled about, retrieved the knife and came at him. Two burly warriors came to his rescue, one wresting the knife from her while the other pinned her arms.

Glowering, Ottowa accosted her and, as Jenny looked on, ordered her back to the tepee to await his return. Flower Woman wrenched free and backed off glaring, firing her eyes at Jenny, before swinging about and striding off. Jenny winced; she'd never seen such fury!

By now she was trembling. She looked at the sky and then at Jumping Bear standing talking to another man in front of his tepee. Both had witnessed the episode; Jumping Bear's expression mingled sympathy and concern. Jenny's glance drifted to the other man. She started slightly. He had Flower Woman's face, although he was dressed like a warrior and carried a rifle.

Now Ottowa was speaking to her rapidly in Oglala. She couldn't understand but his words weren't intended for her.

Everyone within earshot listened attentively. His tone made it sound like an apology. His expression looked apologetic.

His wound was deeper than she'd first assumed, his arm and hand gauntleted with blood. One of his wives offered a strip of hide torn from the hem of her skirt. Another snatched it from her and ripped one end. Then she began bandaging his wound. Jenny pushed her aside, removed the strip, and winding it around his arm just above the wound, made a tourniquet. When she was done she tightened it with a stick, stopping the bleeding. Then she bandaged the wound itself with a second strip of rawhide.

He grunted approvingly and held his arm up for everyone to see. Jenny suppressed a snicker. He appreciated his wound, it gave him a chance to show off his manliness. But his eye showed that it was extremely painful.

"*Wacawin wacap!*" he bellowed. "Flower Woman is a stabber," he translated to Jenny. "*Mitawicu! Mitawicu!*" He pointed at Jenny, nodding emphatically. Everyone whooped and cheered. So wide was his grin it almost joined his earlobes. "I have told them that I have taken a new wife!"

"Mmm. . . ."

She looked about. His assailant had vanished, though not in the direction of the tepee. She hadn't gotten far, Jenny was sure. And doubtless along about now, Flower Woman had to be more determined than ever to keep trying until the detested *winu* was dead.

Summer lengthened. Day after day the sun over the parched land blazing furiously, bringing insufferable heat. The people sweated, the dogs slept, and the Black Hills seemed to shrivel. Milk Eye chose Jenny's bed for his sleep.

Like all the Oglalas he slept naked. He would climb into the bed, wrap around her and nod off almost immediately into painfully loud snoring.

He did not bathe. Water seemed to him to be as dangerous as poison oak. His stench resembled that of a skunk. He wore it continuously, although sometimes it was more severe than others. He didn't bathe, didn't wipe himself after a bowel movement, didn't cleanse his mouth after eating. He was beyond repulsive. Lying with him in bed brought nausea to Jenny's stomach until sleep rescued her.

Her lord and master was also capable of an old man's erection. She would grit her teeth, clear her mind of him, of his stench, of where she was, and submit without a murmur. Back to John she would despatch her thoughts, back to their bed and his arms and his musky smell when he was aroused. And when her assailant had satisfied his lust and rolled off her, she mentally checked off one more night in her captivity.

For all the good counting did her.

And she prayed that in time the novelty would wear off and he'd tire of her. She no longer talked back to him, no longer courted his disapproval or displeasure. She played the game according to Jumping Bear's rules: biding her time, mastering their language as well as she could, and cooperating with Milk Eye. All this demanded a degree of willpower and patience that she never would have realized was attainable. But she managed it.

She waited for John, for the army, for something to happen to end the nightmare.

On the days Milk Eye went out hunting, she sought out Jumping Bear just to talk. To hear a friendly voice. She generally found him either in front of or inside his tepee working on his weapons or playing games or talking with warrior friends, including Icamani—Walks Alongside—who, as Jenny suspected from the striking resemblance, was indeed related to Flower Woman. He was her younger brother.

On this particular afternoon, however, Jumping Bear was more interested in discussing something else.

"What did you do to Chief Ottowa's wound?"

"Napewastéwin . . ."

He smiled. "Good Hands Woman."

"She tried to wrap it with a piece of hide Heyatawin tore off."

"Heyatawin, Woman on the Ridge."

"She took it from the hem of her skirt. It was filthy. I snatched it away."

"With the others watching?"

"Who cares about any of them? I made a tourniquet before bandaging it with a separate piece of hide. After, I washed the wound with clear water and put on a clean bandage. Now it's healing beautifully."

"Very good; if he had left it as it was he could have become . . . what is the word?"

He was sharpening his tomahawk with a stone rubbed with bear grease. He kept testing the edge with his thumb.

"Infected," she replied. "It would have. He's so dirty; he never goes near water. His hair is a filthy mat. And it stinks."

"Most older men do not bother to clean themselves." He grinned. "They can not seem to smell it."

"In his case because he's a chief, I'm sure." Jumping Bear didn't understand. "Back through history kings, emperors, some great people, even women, refused to bathe. Although at least they covered up their stink with perfumes or powders."

"What did he say when he showed you his wound healing?"

"Believe it or not, he was actually grateful. As if he thought I'd worked some kind of magic."

"Be careful, you will make Wiyaka jealous."

"Who?"

"Wiyaka—Eagle's Tailfeather—our *wapiya*, a sacred man. A healer."

"Why didn't Milk . . . Ottowa go to him right off?"

"It was not life threatening; warriors do not consult the *wapiya* unless they suffer a life-threatening wound. It is not considered manly."

"Of course, I'm not thinking."

He held the tomahawk, edge up, for her to test its sharpness. She obliged him.

"Very good."

"You are catching on, Jenny. Make life a lot easier for yourself. Is being nice to him so hard?"

"Aren't you forgetting something? He murdered Mary. Let's talk about something else."

"How is Flower Woman treating you?"

"She stays away, but she's plotting something, scheming. I feel it: woman's intuition. She won't be satisfied until I'm dead."

"If you think about it, it is the best reason for letting him sleep with you. In the dark, she is afraid to attack you—she might injure him."

"Definitely."

"So at least at night you are safe. Stay away from her during the day."

"We still all of us eat together; a tepee is really terribly tiny with eight people crowded into it. I watch where she sits and then sit down as far away from her as I can get. He doesn't seem to notice. But she does hate me with a passion. She can't even look at me . . ."

"Without cracking her face—an Oglala expression. Hatred makes deep lines in the face, right? Cracks."

"Tell me about her brother."

"Icamani."

"Is he a close friend?"

"Not really. But very close to his sister. He idolizes her . . ."

"Are you implying I should worry about him as well?" He

rubbed his chin and avoided her eyes; he seemed to be avoiding answering. "I should, right?"

"He is not a bad man, not wild like her. Not when he is sober."

"And when he drinks?"

"How does any man become when he is drunk?"

"Some are worse than others."

"I am afraid he is . . . very wild."

"Crazy."

"I guess you could say."

"Oh my God . . ."

"Just watch out for him."

"Why didn't you warn me before?"

"I . . . did not want to worry you."

"I'm sure."

"Jenny, do not worry about him."

"You say he idolizes her; he'd do anything for her, right? Even kill; especially kill. She hates me!"

"I do not think she would ask him to hurt you."

"Does she have to ask? If he's as devoted to her as you say he'll jump at the chance."

"He has not yet."

She had gotten up and was pacing the short distance the walls permitted. She sighed.

"Only because he hasn't been drinking." She turned to look at Jumping Bear and decided, from his expression, that he agreed. "So that's it. Once he gets his hand on liquor and gets drunk I'm doomed. Dead!"

"You are exaggerating . . ."

"Oh, he'll do it, all right; she's tried and failed twice already and Ottowa hasn't even bawled her out, not that I know of. If this Ic . . . Ic . . ."

"Walks Alongside."

"For him to try is the same as her; nothing'll happen to him. Of course at that point what difference would it make to me, the corpse? Face it, I'm a lowly *winu*, no better than a dog you play with one day and roast and eat the next. Even Ottowa has no real reason to protect me. If he did, everyone would question it."

"It is not that bad . . ."

"I think it is. He orders me about, gives me all the dirty work; he practically ignores his other wives."

"He is hard on you because he wants to bring you into line."

"Where do the warriors get their liquor?"

"From traders passing through. Or at nearby trading posts."

"Where's the nearest trading post?"

He shrugged. "I guess at Wind Cave. There is one up the line on Battle Creek."

"This is great good news; now I have this crazy man to contend with."

She paused to ponder, debating whether or not to approach Ottowa. What *could* she do to protect herself? Icamani would jump at the chance to do his beloved sister's dirty work for her. What was he waiting for?

"Somebody will hand him a bottle. He'll fill up with courage and come after me, just you watch!"

"That is enough!" He lowered his voice. "I am sorry. Do you want me to talk to him?"

"What good will that do?"

She could feel tears coming. She lowered her eyes and turned her back on him.

"I can't take much more of this; it's not just the threat, it's Mary, it's this life, living like an animal. The filth, the stinks; the dogs behave better than the people. All they do is argue and fight and treat me like dirt. How much am I supposed to take? How much could anyone?"

He had gotten up, he put his arm around her. "It will not be forever."

"Not much . . ."

"Shhhh. You are very brave, you have the heart of a warrior. It takes all and gives it back. You are an unusual woman."

"I'm a child, I'm nineteen."

"A woman."

She stopped sniffling and feeling sorry for herself and gazed at him. "I guess I am. I *was* a child when I married John, when we left Cincinnati. Right up until the attack. From that point on I started growing up."

"You did, I watched you."

"I did, didn't I?"

He nodded. "A woman. I am proud to know you. And do not worry about Flower Woman and Walks Alongside; Ottowa will not let them or anybody else harm you."

He sounded as if he really believed it; she only wished she could.

NINETEEN

The Indians left John with his weapons, the cartridges in their respective chambers, and seven sulphur matches. Upon reflection, he figured he was lucky he was still upright and unscathed. And though they may have stripped him of his dignity, he still had his wallet.

He got his bearings. Beaver Creek lay to the west just over the Wyoming line. To the north, possibly dead ahead, was Wind Cave. Only how far? Twenty miles? Fifty?

It wasn't the distance that worried him, but the fact that he was deep in hostile territory and in sacred land—the place of the Sioux spirits. Increasingly, white men were invading these Black Hills looking for gold. The Sioux resented their intrusion, and if he were to come upon any more of them they'd take him for a prospector right off, ignoring the fact that he wasn't carrying so much as a trowel. They assumed every white man venturing into the hills was after gold. Who would believe he was the exception?

What had surprised John was the ease with which the Indians had vanished, as if the sky had sucked them up: corpse, horse, and all. He had no idea which tribe they belonged to— only that they weren't dressed or painted like the Oglalas who'd attacked the wagon train. *Those* had worn paint, but whether for war or merely decoration he had no way of knowing.

Today's attackers had worn breechclouts only, not even jackets against the chill night air. They also wore knee bands to which metal disks were attached, but other than a wide red sash worn across the chest and shoulders, the ends draped down the back, the disks were their only decoration. The only resemblance between them and the Oglalas was their hair: Both wore it in long braids tightly wrapped with cloth at the ends.

It was getting much colder and the sky had turned to the gray that powdered the yolk of a hard-boiled egg. The change brought a desolate feeling: Discouragement threatened. Losing his horse and gear changed everything, reducing him to walking and wasting time he could ill afford to squander. No food, no water, except whatever brook or stream he would come across. Night coming on. With no blanket, trying to sleep would be useless. Even though the encounter with the signalers had exhausted him he resolved to keep on.

Assuming he could even find it, he knew little about Wind Cave other than what Moonlight had heard. The colonel described it as a collection of shacks huddled around a single brick building, where he'd no doubt find the Indian agent.

So much depending on a man he'd yet to even meet. Did the law require him to help in such situations? Not that whites being kidnapped by Indians was unique, but *shouldn't* the army take charge? There was no official law out here in the wilds, the army was it. The man waiting in Wind Cave would no doubt be sympathetic, but was it *his* job to help?

Moonlight implied that it was—but now that John reflected on their discussion of it, he hadn't actually said so, only touched on an agent's general duties. Indian agents issued supplies and paid out annuities to hostile tribes—bribed them, was how the colonel put it. Indian agents mediated disputes between the tribes and the whites and, at least theoretically, saw to it that both sides lived up to the treaties they signed.

If a given agent's Indians trusted him, if he was sympathetic and was honest in his dealings, relations could be smooth. But greedy, mediocre, and downright dishonest men dominated the ranks. Every agent's principal responsibility was to keep the white man off Indian lands; whoever the agent was in Wind Cave he didn't seem to be succeeding in the Black Hills. Still, he was all but powerless; red men and white did pretty much as they pleased. And the pay was no inducement to capable, honest men. The government paid Indian agents less than village postmasters. Little wonder thievery, cheating, and double-dealing were the norms.

Walking on through the darkness, the millions of stars pricking the cobalt heavens and the moon monitoring his slow progress north, he thought about his next move. If, for whatever reason, the agent flatly refused to help, unfortunately, he was in no position to threaten, demand, or otherwise pressure him to act.

If that was the way things turned out, what would he do next? Buy a horse and continue on to Fort Sully? Demand help there? What made him think the colonel at Sully would be in any better position to help than Thomas Moonlight? Sully's commander could well have even fewer men at his disposal.

He rested for nearly an hour by his watch, sitting on a flat rock out of the wind, removing his boots to massage his aching feet. The temperature was still dropping. He recalled the stifling heat coming up the plain, the burning air, both he and the mare bathed in sweat from sunrise to dark. He missed her: her desire, her spirit. And now he had no one to talk to. He looked himself over. His clothes were filthy, he stank; some imposing figure he'd present walking into Wind Cave. Yet the Wind Cave agent should know where the tribes under his jurisdiction were located. He must keep tabs on their movements. Hopefully Jenny's and Mary's abductors weren't too far away.

His boots restored, he resumed walking. The wind traveled with him, and the moon. He followed the North Star. About two hours later, the stars began to fade, their pulsing brilliance gradually draining away, and in the east, the sky assumed the blush of a ripening peach. The sun came up gloriously, flooding the hills, chasing the chill from the air. Rounding a boulder as big as a house, he was starting up a sandy slope when a familiar smell struck his nostrils. Ten paces further and to his ears came a soft sizzling sound. He climbed through a pile of rocks, coming out the other side to the sight of the timber-framed adit to a mine. Two men sat cooking their breakfast in front of it. Horses and burrows were hobbled nearby; picks, shovels, and other tools lay about. There was a stack of small crates and two water casks. There was also a ratty-looking tent.

The shorter of the two miners was done frying the bacon and was now breaking eggs into the grease. John's stomach awoke.

He licked his lips and gestured. "Good morning . . ."

"Howdy, pilgrim."

The little man had to be well under five feet tall, a runt who might easily be taken for an undernourished nine year old were it not for his beard, his mostly missing front teeth. It struck John that his clothes hadn't been off his body in months. They looked stuck to his skin, even his pant legs.

His companion was two heads taller than he, as broad as a wagon seat, and looked strong enough to pick up the boulder he was sitting on. In contrast to the little man he was cleaner, tidier, more concerned with his appearance. He was also clean-shaven. A small metal mirror hung from the front tent pole. They greeted John warmly, despite their puzzled expressions. He told them what had happened. The little man's name was Roy; just Roy, no last name offered, none asked for. His partner was Grady Means "of California by way of Gadsden, Alabama." They interrupted John's explanation to offer him breakfast. He went on with his story between sips of scalding coffee from a dented cup.

"We seed them smoke signals," said Roy. "They was Tetons."

"What were they up to?"

"Just jawing, keeping scattered bunches of 'em in contact. For the past week they been busy working up a buffalo surround."

"Surround?"

Means nodded. "They collect about seventy-five or a hundred braves and divide them into two columns. They gallop in and converge on the herd, yelling and waving blankets. The idea is to turn the lead buffalo back into the herd."

"Makes 'em plumb crazy," said Roy. "They gets all confused and begin swirling 'round in a circle. Then the Injuns charge 'em with bows and arrers and lances. Gets pretty dusty and pretty bloody afore they're done. Serious buffalo huntin' starts about now and keeps on till fall. Dead o' winter when the heavy snows is down they pick it up again."

It was all very interesting but only delayed discussion of a more important subject.

"How far to Wind Cave?"

"No more'n five mile from here." Roy pointed directly north then moved his outstretched arm slightly to the east. "They's signs."

"I've been told there's an Indian agent there."

"Lincoln Hammer," said Means, nodding.

"I've got important business with him."

They eyed him questioningly but he pretended not to notice. The whole sorry affair was nobody's business, not anybody
who wasn't directly involved. Moreover it was becoming harder
and harder to think about. Every time Jenny's and Mary's faces
came into focus before his mind's eye, it revived his grinding
fears for them—and honed his expectation of the worst.

"What sort of fellow is this Hammer?"

"Good man, so everybody says," answered Means. "We've
never met him. He's honest, conscientious. He drinks—but who
wouldn't with his job? Talk about thankless . . ."

"Speaking o' liquor," said Roy, "would you like a snort?"

"No thanks."

"You tem'prance?"

"No, it's just a little early."

"Me and Grady never been tempted to temp'rance."

John went on. "Hammer goes out and talks to the tribes?"

"He's all the time parlaying," said Roy. "And knows 'em all
'round these parts. Which are mainly the Sioux: Tetons,
Hunkpapas, Sans Arcs."

"Oglalas . . ."

The two miners exchanged glances. John caught his breath.
There had to be Oglalas!

"I followed Oglalas's tracks up here. They took off this way.
I followed their tracks until the wind blew them away. It's been
so dry . . ."

"Dunno about Oglalas," said Roy. "They could be, exceptin'
the only Oglalas I heered of is down 'round the North Platte,
near Blue Water."

John could feel the palms of his hands getting clammy. His
upper lip began beading with perspiration. "Are you saying
there are no Oglalas in the Black Hills?"

"There could be, Roy," said Means. "Could be any tribe. They all move around so . . ."

Roy agreed. "Restless buggars." He grinned, showing his gaps. "Itchy feet. Like white folks."

"You think I can get a horse in Wind Cave?"

"Ask Hammer. You should be able to buy one from one o' his personal Injuns."

"I have to." John's hand strayed to the bulge in his back pocket reassuring him that his money was still there.

"Tell Hammer your tale o' woe," Roy went on. "He's church-people, good-hearted, so they say."

By now the sun had freed itself from the distant Coteau des Prairies and was at work bleaching the last of the night from the cloudless sky. Sight of the sun lifted John's heart. The weather had been kind all the way up the plains and now he was only five miles from Wind Cave and the help he needed in the person of Lincoln Hammer. He thanked Roy and Grady for breakfast, took a few minutes to borrow Means' razor, then went on his way.

For perhaps the hundredth time since leaving Fort Laramie, he thought about Jenny and Mary. What were they doing at the moment? Were they well? Unharmed? Were they at least free to move about? Were the Oglalas leaving them alone?

There was a false hope. Why abduct them if not to abuse them or hold them for ransom? Had they harmed either? He worried about Jenny. Her patience had as short a leash as her temper. Would she risk attempting escape with Mary there? Would she risk it *because* of Mary? What choice would she have if their lives were in danger? Only how would she get away? And if she did, where would she go? Without horses, without food.

What it came down to was that he didn't know what to think, didn't know how to figure it. It had become like a tangled ball of knitting. Why torture himself?

All he could really do was hope and pray that everything would turn out all right and that for the present they were holding their own.

"I'm coming, Hammer. . . ."

═══ TWENTY ═══

Milk Eye got into the habit of lecturing Jenny daily on everything from her behavior to the Oglalas' ways. He was particularly insistent that she master the language. She was sure it was his way of reminding her that she would be around—if not permanently—for a long time.

With Jumping Bear's help, she had mastered the talent, even art, of biting her tongue, bridling her sarcasm, and avoiding even verbal conflict with anyone. She took taunting from women and children and snide remarks from Flower Woman with aplomb and patience. Jumping Bear lauded her. Even Milk Eye was impressed at her complete turnabout in attitude.

Milk Eye was done with today's lecture and she got the feeling that he was beginning to get bored with her; the novelty had worn off. He'd captured her, seduced her, conquered her . . . what was left to be done with her? Was the time approaching when he would tire of her completely and turn her over to someone else? Trade her for a knife and two blankets?

Jumping Bear had repeatedly warned that this could happen eventually and it could help if she warmed up to him. Only that she couldn't do; not Mary's murderer, not the way he raped and abused her. Cooperating to stay alive was one thing; kowtowing to him, offering to be his slave quite another.

They were within a stone's throw of the nearest tepees, with the smell of smoke, of human sweat and rancid meat coming toward them on the breeze, when loud shouting erupted out of sight behind the nearest tepee. Two warriors appeared, struggling with a rifle. Both looked drunk to Jenny. The one with the rifle broke free. . . .

He turned and began firing at her.

TWENTY-ONE

In all, seven shots came winging in the general direction of Jenny and Milk Eye. Fortunately for both, the first six shots were wild, not one coming within six feet of either of them. But the seventh shot plowed into Milk Eye's forearm. He had raised his arm to shield his eyes from the sun to see better. Jenny dropped flat between the first and second shots.

"Get down!" she yelled at Milk Eye.

He threw her a haughty look of refusal; at once she understood why: He wasn't the target and he knew it. When the seventh round hit him he bellowed, as much in surprise as pain, spinning and waving his arm. By this time their assailant's companion had wrested the rifle from his grasp. Trying to retrieve it he stumbled and fell. He looked even drunker than the other man—which, Jenny decided, was what saved her life.

Though not Milk Eye's arm. It was not the arm Flower Woman had stabbed earlier and it didn't bleed as copiously. He had dropped to his knees. His free hand started for his wound.

"No! Don't touch it. Wait, *ahpe* . . ." She tore a strip from the hem of her skirt, tying it loosely above the wound. Then she found a stick and inserting it in the knot fashioned a tourniquet. He turned it until the bleeding stopped.

"The bullet will have to come out," she said. He sputtered

in Oglala, nodding vigorously. "Who was that shooting? The sun made it hard to see his face."

"Icamani." He grunted. "Wacawin's brother."

"Lucky he was drunk." Milk Eye flexed his arm gingerly. "Don't move it, I think the bone's broken." She pressed his arm close to the wound; he winced, sucking a breath in sharply. She relieved the pressure of the tourniquet a couple of turns. "It's broken, it'll have to be set in a cast."

"Cast?"

"We'll swath it in mud; it'll dry solid and keep the ends from shifting about inside there. Clay is even better, it won't break as easily."

It wasn't until she examined his wound more closely that she saw that the bullet had passed nearly through his forearm. She found it lodged in the flesh on the side opposite the point of entry. Milk Eye slowly doubled his arm and picked the slug out as if removing a bug. There was little blood.

"Clay?" he asked.

"Yes. Otherwise, the bones may knit out of line. You'd end up with a crippled arm."

He frowned at this. "Not me, I am a chief!"

"Can Wapiya set it and put it in a cast?"

He considered this, then shook his head. "He sprinkles powder and dust, he chants, he dances with his rattles and the drummers; he does not touch bones or bullet wounds."

"First I'll bandage your wound to keep the clay out of it, prevent infection."

"In . . ."

"Sickness in the blood, the flesh around the hole. It has to be kept clean."

"Ahhhh . . ."

His eyes said he was impressed; his interest in her was rapidly reviving. She didn't mind taking care of him, she liked playing nurse. At one time she had wanted to become a nurse, but something happened. Young people change tracks so easily. She'd help a stray mongrel if it were hurt. Anything living if she could. Even a blood enemy. Even a murderer.

She ran into Jumping Bear later in the day. He had contracted a large blister on the top of his great toe.

"From my moccasin. I was so mad I threw them away."

"You shouldn't walk around barefoot. If it breaks dirt'll get in."

"Infection. That is all you seem to worry about."

"It's worth worrying about; you can lose any part of you that gets infected—eye, finger, arm, great toe. I suggest you keep it bandaged."

"How is your other patient?"

They sat behind Jumping Bear's tepee out of sight of the others. It had become their secret meeting place, the nearest thing to privacy they could find without leaving camp or going inside the tepee. For the latter choice it was much too hot in daytime. Brutally hot for the end of August.

"He'll live," said Jenny.

Jumping Bear chuckled. "Maybe Icamani will not. He may have been drunk but that is no excuse, not to Chief Ottowa. I hear he was furious."

"When it happened, he seemed more surprised than anything else."

"Well, he was furious when he told the other chiefs. Any Oglala who tries to kill another Oglala can be banished."

"Even if I'm the target? It *was* me he was aiming at."

"Chief Ottowa does not seem too sure of that."

"Of course he wouldn't; he's the center of the universe; the world revolves around him; the sun shines only on him. So what happens now? What *will* he do to Walks Alongside? Of course, Flower Woman put him up to it . . ."

"I do not think so. She did not have to; it was—how would you say it—a privilege her devoted brother was all too eager to exercise? It was also rash and stupid.

"I heard something else, Jenny. Chief Ottowa is telling everybody that you have special healing powers. You are . . . gifted."

"Oh, dear."

"What is wrong with that?"

"Wapiya. The healer. Suddenly, just like that I'm his rival? He'll love that. Oh dear, oh dear . . ."

"Wapiya does not set bones, he does not remove bullets."

"What difference does that make? He's the great healer; now he'll see me as his competition. I've enough people against me without him."

"Only Flower Woman and Walks Alongside. Chief Ottowa is on your side. For certain after what you did."

"I didn't do beans."

"You set his broken bone in a cast. Very shrewd, using clay . . ."

She looked both ways and inched closer to him. She lowered her head. "Can I let you in on a little secret?"

"Of course."

"Promise you won't tell a soul?"

"Jenny, would I do *any*thing to make life harder for you? What is it?"

"The bone wasn't broken."

"But . . ."

"I pressed his arm near the wound. Of course it hurt. I told him the bone was broken, his arm had to be placed in a cast so it'd heal properly."

"The bullet *missed* the bone? How?"

"There are two bones in the forearm. There's a space between them." She took his arm and pressed at the spot. "It passed through without touching either."

"But why did you . . . ? Wait, I see! It was a chance to show off your healing powers. And it worked. He thinks you have magic in your hands. Clever . . ."

"I wonder. I still worry about Wapiya. At the time I didn't even think about him."

"Stop worrying so much. You are back in Chief Ottowa's good graces. He will be your champion!"

"Shh."

"Only do not be surprised if from now on everybody comes to you with their breaks and their wounds."

"Seriously, do you think he'll punish Icamani? Even though it was unintentional?"

"I think he will have to take some action, everyone expects it. Look at the blister on my toe."

"What about *her?*"

"How do *I* know? You think I can look inside his head like a hollow tree? What happens will happen. Now look at my toe, please."

"It's a blister. A big blister. It's fairly hard but it'll break."

"I will break it."

"You'll leave it alone, it'll break itself when it's ready."

"When will that be?"

"When the new skin is all formed under it."

He got her a piece of rawhide. She bandaged his toe.

He made a face. "It feels funny."

"Ignore it. Keep it on. We'll have a look in a day or two."

The same admiration she'd seen in Milk Eye's eyes she now saw in his. "You are as good as Dr. Gentile," he said.

"Who?"

"He came to the mission to treat the children. He painted our throats and pinched us all over and dosed us with the foulest tasting dung I have ever swallowed."

"Milk Eye'll be looking for me, I'd better go. Remember to keep that bandage on." She stood up.

"I would not worry about Walks Alongside."

"I've heard that before."

"The situation was not like now. He is sobered up, now he will have to . . . to . . ."

"Face the music?" He didn't understand. "Pay for his sin. Unless Milk Eye's in a forgiving mood."

"Jenny . . ."

"What?"

"Do not call him Milk Eye."

"It's just a pet name."

"If he overhears you he will ask everybody until he finds out what it means. When he does . . . You *do* remember how mad he got when you threw away his sacred pipe. His bad eye is an imperfection. He is a chief, he is supposed to be perfect; to his way of thinking he *is*. I guess because he cannot see his eye. But the rest of the world can. Do you really want to remind him of that?"

"You're right, I should be more careful."

She left thinking she'd stop calling him that.

But only out loud.

TWENTY-TWO

Two days later life in the Oglala camp took an unexpected turn. To everyone's surprise, Flower Woman went missing. Search parties were sent out but she was nowhere to be found. Meanwhile Milk Eye continued to avoid Jenny. No one could fathom what had become of Flower Woman. Jumping Bear offered a theory.

"He killed her."

Jenny scoffed at this. "I don't believe that for a second. If he wanted to kill somebody it'd be Walks Alongside. As far as I know he hasn't even reprimanded him."

"I say he killed her. Think of what her death would accomplish. Number one, it would punish her devoted brother. Much worse than anything done to Icamani directly. Chief Ottowa decided that *she* was the cause of it all. She had already stabbed him, now she shoots him—with her brother's gun."

"That doesn't make sense."

"It makes great good sense to an Oglala chief. Besides, what does he need with a hornet in his tepee? He already has five other wives, plus you. She has got him thinking, 'what will she do next?' Why give her a third chance to kill you? Next time she may kill you both."

"He could divorce her."

"Pushing her out the flap would not get rid of her. No, she had to be killed."

Jenny shook her head. "He couldn't, he wouldn't have the strength. His knife wound isn't completely healed yet; then there's his bullet wound. His cast isn't even cracked."

"Maybe he did not do it. Maybe he asked a close friend to help him out."

"Pawnee Killer and Four Hawks?"

"They would be happy to help. The whole thing would not take more than an hour. The whole camp is asleep."

"Not the guards."

"They know where the guards are, know how to slip between them without being seen.

"Now you mention it he does seem different since Flower Woman disappeared."

"How?"

"He is smiling more, he is more relaxed; it is like a burden has been lifted from his shoulders."

"There you are. Yes, he had her killed. As easily as you kill a mosquito. In his day, he has spilled blood like you spill kettle water. He would not hesitate. . . . Do not look so. Smile, you should be relieved. You should be celebrating!"

"You don't celebrate murder, not even of your worst enemy."

"You are not Dakotah. Or one of your bluecoat soldiers."

"It sounds feasible, I'll give you that. But it's too easy. I think she's alive and she'll be showing up back here any day."

"Tell that to Walks Alongside, he has gone into mourning."

She wondered. Could Jumping Bear be right? It sounded bizarre, but what wasn't bizarre here? And if that had been what happened, it would definitely make life easier for her.

TWENTY-THREE

A ball of birds rolled down the sky, speckling the sun, lending it briefly a tattered look. As tattered as John Pryor's hopes. He had arrived in Wind Cave to be told that Indian agent Lincoln Hammer was "out in the field."

The source of this information was a scruffy-looking ancient affecting a beard badly in need of trimming and clad in ragged bib overalls. The man sat with his chair tilted against the front of Wind Cave's lone brick building, in the shadow of the overhang, whittling and chewing a wad of tobacco—which, when he rested his jaws, rounded his cheek to the size of a billiard ball.

"When is he due back?" John asked.

"Hard to say. He spends most o' his time out visiting the tribes. That's his job and he takes it serious."

The chips flew; a string of tobacco juice shot from his mouth, spattering the board sidewalk. Wind Cave was small but was not the jumble of shacks Thomas Moonlight had described. Neat frame buildings faced each other across a wide street in typical western-town fashion. The old man ceased his whittling, snapped closed his jackknife, and pointed across the way.

"Over there is the Dakota House, only hotel in town. Rooms are a buck a night."

"Thank you. Would you do me a favor, Mr. . . ."

"Horton. Cleanth Horton, after my granddaddy."

"If you should happen to see Mr. Hammer when he does come back, would you tell him I'm looking for him? John Pryor. It's terribly important I see him. A matter of life and death."

"That a fact?" One frazzled eyebrow curved upward. "Tell me about it, I'll tell him."

"Just please tell him I'm looking for him."

John started across the street. So Hammer was away; yet another disappointment, more delay. He stopped and looked over the Dakota House. There was no sign, no indication that it was anything but a private residence. It looked too small for a hotel—he guessed no more than six or eight rooms—and a firetrap. He glanced up the street. At the end of the row of buildings on the opposite side stood a tent with the side facing the street rolled up and tied. He could barely make out the word BAR painted on the top. He headed for it.

The bar turned out to be a plank set across two rain barrels, with matching eight-foot-tall bookcases crammed with jugs and bottles behind it. Two men were drinking. The bartender hummed to himself as he polished a glass. John eyed his stock. The majority of bottles bore no labels, and the few labeled bottles were brands unfamiliar to him. His thirst encouraged him to take his chances. His taste buds would judge the quality.

"Whiskey, please."

The bartender appeared about to burst his vest buttons. It was an expensive brocade vest designed for a much slimmer individual; his oversized head sat on his shoulders with no visible neck between. His hair was parted in the center and pomaded flat on both sides; the strands surmounting his forehead on either side twisted into matching curls.

"Five or ten cents?" he said.

"Ten."

The taste was acidulous and the fire went down like a lead

ball. But it warmed and began to relax him in seconds. He was wringing with exhaustion, not just from walking all night but mostly from the strain of the separation, and the growing anxiety that went with it. Now this. Hammer could be away a week, even longer. He called over the bartender and introduced himself.

"I've come all the way from Fort Laramie to see Lincoln Hammer. I know he's out of town—just my luck—I'll have to wait however long it takes before he gets back. Could I ask you a few questions about him?"

"Such as?"

"What's the longest he's usually gone?"

"One time he was away to somewheres down near the Bozeman Trail for nearly a month."

"Good God . . ."

"But most times less than a week. It's important you talk to him, eh?"

John sighed wearily, finished his drink, rapped the glass for a refill. He couldn't keep it a secret forever. "My wife and daughter were kidnapped by Oglala Indians. They're somewhere in the Black Hills. I need Mr. Hammer's help."

Sympathy spilled down the man's face. The two other patrons had overheard and moved closer. They looked like brothers to John: both about the same height, both slightly overweight, although not in the bartender's class, and no more than four years separating their ages. Both wore identical hats and suits with railroad watches dangling from chains slung across their midriffs.

"You're sure it was the Oglalas?" said the bartender.

"Definitely. That's about the only thing I know for certain. A war party attacked our wagon train about twenty miles east of Fort Laramie and rode off with Jenny and Mary toward here."

The bartender looked at his other two customers. "Sounds like Hinhanska's boys. Could be Icabu's."

"Could be Ottowa's," said the older brother.

"What are those names?" John asked.

"White Owl, Drumbeater, and Bloody Sky," said the bartender. "The Oglalas' three big chiefs."

John's heart quickened. "And they're somewhere in the Black Hills?" All three nodded. "Where exactly?"

The bartender's frown bunched his little mouth. "That's hard to say. The Black Hills have to be at least seventy-five miles north to south and nearly that far west to east."

"But Hammer must know where they're camped."

"He might," said the younger brother. "But all the tribes move around a lot."

"I know, I keep hearing that."

"It's so," said the bartender. "They never camp in the same spot two summers in a row."

"Hammer has to know their chiefs. . . ."

The three nodded. The older brother spoke. "I'm sure he's had dealings with them. He knows every chief of every tribe; he's been here six or seven years."

"Eight," his brother corrected him. "I remember when he came to town. It was the spring of fifty-seven. He came from down near Durango in Colorado. The Bureau of Indian Affairs reassigned him to Dakota Territory."

"I hear he's capable and conscientious," said John. "A good man."

"For sure he's a good customer," said the bartender, winking and grinning at the others. "As far as agenting, he leans a little too much toward the savages. As far as I'm concerned, they don't deserve spit, not the way they treat white people. Oh, not that the Oglalas would mistreat your wife and child. No, they're kindly toward women and children."

His tone sounded somewhat lame. The others nodded, agreeing; solely for his benefit, John decided. They obviously knew nothing firsthand about Indian treatment of captives.

There was a weighty silence. No one seemed to know what to say next. Finally the bartender spoke.

"How about one on the house, Mr. Pryor?"

"No thanks, any more and I'll pass out. I've got to get over to the hotel and get some sleep. If any of you see Mr. Hammer before I do, would you please tell him I'm here?"

"We will," said one of the brothers.

The others chuckled. John reacted, puzzled.

" 'Hotel' is good," the man said. "A dump half the size of a dog house. Make sure Lyle Tupper gives you a wool mattress."

"No straw," said his younger brother. "His straw mattresses got bedbugs big as your thumbnail. They'll chew you to death."

"And don't eat there," said the older brother. "Mrs. Tupper is three-quarters blind; she doesn't know salt from pepper or sugar from either. Her husband'd eat the heels off his boots par-boiled, so she's got it in her head that guests'll eat anything that won't walk off the plate."

"Then where do visitors in town eat?" said John.

"Callahan's," chorused all three.

"Next to last building on your left, the far end of the street," added the bartender.

John checked into the Dakota House. He insisted on a wool mattress; Tupper insisted just as strenuously that all the wool mattresses were in use. John started for the door. . . . Tupper managed to find a wool mattress.

Luck flowered among the weeds in the wasteland of John Pryor's dilemma. He'd resigned himself to waiting at least a week for Lincoln Hammer to return. He was elated when Wind Cave's resident Indian agent came wheeling into town in his buggy around noon two days later. The bartender drew John's attention to Hammer's arrival. John threw down a quarter and hurried up the street, catching up with Hammer as he wound his reins around the hitching post in front of the brick building. John introduced himself as the agent got his carpetbag out from under the seat and immediately began detailing his reason for coming to Wind Cave.

"The Oglalas took Jenny and our seven year old, Mary."

"You don't want to talk about this in the street, Mr. Pryor. Come inside. Make it fast—if I don't get something strong inside me in the next sixty seconds, my throat'll crack like glass."

The centerpiece of Hammer's office was a solid oak curtain-top desk, at least six feet wide, that looked as if it weighed a thousand pounds. On the wall above it was a map combining the Dakota, Wyoming, and Nebraska Territories, with his jurisdiction outlined in red ink.

He got a jug of whiskey down from the closet shelf, uncorked it, and blew dust out of two jam glasses.

"A fellow over in Buffalo Gap makes this. It's not half bad. Takes a little getting used to; take care you sip it."

The product of Buffalo Gap made the whiskey in the tent bar taste like the finest available imported spirits. John assessed Hammer as the agent questioned him. The man was an accomplished drinker and a fiercely dedicated one; his gravel voice, the distended veins in his eyes, the mottled skin covering his nose, the sorry condition of his teeth, gave him away. Could he stay sober long enough to help him? He watched as Hammer threw down half a glass of whiskey in a single gulp. Finishing off what remained, he refilled his glass with a slightly trembling hand. He was preparing to resume drinking when John reached out and caught his wrist.

"Can we talk first?"

"Sure." He set down the glass but did not take his eyes off it, licking his lips in anticipation.

"What can you do?" John asked. "Is it possible to get a cavalry troop from Fort Sully?"

"Not a chance. Colonel Nelson Galsworthy's got fewer men

than your friend Moonlight. Barely enough manpower to keep the place swept."

"Damn . . ."

"Let me finish. Last week Fort Randall welcomed the first replacements in the whole territory in nearly five years—two whole troops. With officers, that's more than four hundred horse."

"Great! How far is Fort Randall?"

"It's not exactly the next town over. Would you mind if I drink?" He didn't wait for permission. He didn't "drink" in the accepted meaning of the word—he attacked his whiskey. Setting down the empty glass he pointed south-southeast.

"Randall is about two hundred miles as the crow flies. Across the Cheyenne River and straight on."

"Could you send the commanding officer a telegram?"

"No lines."

"The Indians cut them?"

"No. There just aren't any; never have been. Mr. Pryor, I sympathize with your situation. I'd be some heartless bastard if I didn't. I know you're going through hell wondering what's happening. I'm willing and able to help get them back safe and sound.

"But these things are always tricky. They have to be handled . . . delicately. It has to be done right the first time and, unfortunately, there are no shortcuts."

"What if we were to approach the Oglalas directly? I mean just us two, no cavalry?"

"Waste of time. You'd get your hopes up only to have them dashed. They'd know we were coming before we got within twenty miles of their camp. They'd squirrel away your wife and daughter and you'd never get to see them, much less get them out of there."

"But if we bargain with them . . ."

"They won't even consider bargaining."

"Look, I'm willing to give them whatever they ask. Goods, money . . ."

"Strangely enough, what you offer isn't that important. It's all, you might say, symbolic. They know they've got you in a corner and you're forced to play according to their rules. Unless you can show you've the strength to back up your demands . . ."

"Troopers . . ."

Hammer nodded. "They'll swap you your wife and daughter for two blankets and a decent horse if you've got a hundred men with Spencers sitting their saddles behind you. Now, it'll take us at least six days to get to Fort Russell . . ."

"Four," rasped John.

"It's more than two hundred miles . . ."

"Four."

"Well, at least six getting back and up into the hills and find the Oglala camp." He used a pencil to take them from Wind Cave to Fort Randall and return to the Black Hills on his map. He swung a multiple circle around the area where the Oglala camp *might* be, acknowledging that he couldn't be absolutely sure of the location. "But I've heard rumors that that's where they're spending the summer."

"When's the last time you visited them?" John asked.

"Not this past spring, but the one before. I've got a lot of ground to cover. I rarely see the same tribe twice in one year, unless there's a crisis of some sort. Like this. Don't get discouraged. I know it's nerve-wracking and time's vital to you. But like I said before, there are no shortcuts. It can't be rushed. At least we'll be putting the wheels in motion."

"Finally."

"I suggest we both get a good night's sleep and meet here at dawn. In the meantime I'll talk to some of the Sioux and see if I can confirm the Oglalas' exact location. Where's your horse?"

John told him how he had come to lose his horse and gear.

"You should be able to pick one up here in town for under fifty dollars, if you're good at dickering."

"Money's no object."

"Money's always an object. It could turn out to be the only ransom that'll interest the Oglalas."

"There's one thing I don't understand. If we show up at their camp with a hundred troopers to back us up, why do we have to resort to bargaining?"

"That . . . ," said Hammer, leaning forward, "is how the game is played. Take two warring European countries. They meet to thrash out a cease-fire or a truce. They despise each other but treat each other as equals even if they're not. If the U.S. government doesn't at least make a pretense of treating the Indians as equals we'd never get anywhere trying to do business. It's all about pride.

"Now how about another drink? I'm having one."

John took that for granted. His thoughts flew ahead. Hammer wouldn't be driving his buggy to Fort Randall, a horse would be much faster. And the most a horse could carry with gear and other necessities would be two jugs tied together with a foot of rope between and slung over its rump behind his saddle.

That helped.

But could Hammer last two weeks, perhaps even longer, on only two jugs?

TWENTY-FOUR

Not unexpectedly, Chief Ottowa announced that henceforth Jenny would be his number one wife. He seemed quite sure that Flower Woman wasn't coming back. Jumping Bear observed that Ottowa had to be one of the few who would actually know this. Jenny wondered if he would resumed forcing himself on her. He did not, at least not that night.

Life in the Oglala camp went on as September beckoned. The insufferable, relentless heat shortened everyone's patience. Everyone's anger fired too easily. Domestic shouting matches and brawling abounded, children bickered and squabbled, even the dogs picked on each other. Milk Eye refused to let Jenny treat anyone's wounds or illnesses, preferring to reserve her talents for his exclusive use. His job no longer in jeopardy, Wapiya was pleased. Milk Eye evidently understood the value of diplomacy. Jumping Bear and Jenny discussed it in their private place.

"For all his pettiness, Chief Ottowa is a wise man," said Jumping Bear.

"Also infuriatingly childish."

Jumping Bear grinned. "Because he is a man? Or because he is Indian?"

"There are so many like him around here. Oh, not you, not really."

"What does that mean?"

He was chipping flint, shaping it into an arrowhead. A slow process, time-consuming, considering how swiftly an arrow could be nocked and released. And gone forever. But Indians, at least these, were not as short on patience as were white men.

"You have your childish moments," she said. And sobered. "I'm so sick of all this, I don't know how much longer I can stand it. Worst of all is the filth; everyone, everything is so dirty. Returns at Dawn and Woman on the Ridge are forever picking lice off themselves. They look like monkeys in the zoo."

"Everybody has lice. Chief Ottowa does."

"You don't."

"On second thought, most warriors do not. I guess because we are more active than he is or the women."

"They don't bathe, don't bathe the children . . ."

"If we were camped near water they would. The nearest water is quite a way off."

"Why didn't they make camp closer to it?"

"Too many rocks. A flat, grassy area is always best."

"Lice make people sick, you know. Don't they know that?"

"Lice can make white people sick, not Oglalas. We are tougher, we can throw off a lot of sicknesses. Things that put you and others like you in bed."

"Having to sleep in the same tepee with them, knowing the place is crawling with lice and bedbugs is disgusting. And you can't tell me they don't have diseases."

"I did not say that, only that they have stronger resistence than white people. Dr. Gentile always said so. Many times. And kept on painting our throats, pinching us, and dosing us with that dung in the yellow bottle."

He had notched the end of the shaft in which the arrowhead would be inserted, but first the head itself had to be finished. For this a piece of bone was used to snap tiny chips out of the edges to make the barbs so difficult and painful to extract from flesh.

Jenny went on. "I've never seen a people so outrageously superstitious. They believe the wildest things. The hills and mountains are the backs of huge animals that died long ago; the sun and wind are spirits."

"Our 'superstitions' are our religion, Jenny. Are not white people's superstitions their religions?"

"I'm religious—at least I believe in God. But I'm not superstitious."

"Not even a little?"

"Not even a little."

He grunted, accepting this, although clearly not believing it. "One good thing I have noticed you're getting good at lately."

"There's got to be *some*thing."

"Your attitude. You are much more pleasant, you are cheerful. Few of our women are cheerful."

"From what I can see they've little reason to be. Believe me, it's only a mask. It was your suggestion, remember?"

"I know, but you do it well, so well that the men are beginning to talk about you. You have gotten a new name for yourself around the camp. Tana-win."

"What does it mean?"

"Real Woman. They respect you, Jenny. Because he does. Because you know how to act."

She grunted and changed the subject. "I notice the nights are starting to get colder."

"We are coming to the end of summer."

"Jumping Bear, seriously, I've got to get out of here. I can't stand it."

"Please do not try it. You will be rescued, ransomed."

"When? How? John has no idea where I am."

"The army knows, the agent in Wind Cave does. At least that you are somewhere in these hills."

"Then why don't they come?"

"They will." He patted her arm consolingly. "You will see." He stopped his work, leaned close and lowered his voice. "Chief Ottowa knows."

"I don't follow you."

"Knows they are coming. I am sure he has already decided how much he will demand for your ransom."

"Ha! He'll be lucky to avoid the hangman."

"Nobody is going to hang him. Whatever happens for now, you have to be patient. Do not try to get away. You will be caught, brought back, and that could be the end. You have gotten into Chief Ottowa's good graces. It took a while but you did it. You can see for yourself how different he is treating you lately. You try to escape and it will infuriate him; in his eyes you will be the worst sort of ingrate. A traitor to his friendship. Worse than that, he will lose face."

" 'Face' again."

"Jenny, any chief's face is terrifically important to him; it is how his followers see him. How his friends do, and his warriors. With us, respect is everything. For him to lose it, for you to strip him of it, is unthinkable. It is playing with fire."

"Mmmmm . . ."

"Are you listening?"

"I'm listening, only I'm fast reaching a point where I don't give a damn."

"You had better!" He softened his tone. "If you want to go on living. Do you want your husband to show up here and find you gone? Buried under a pile of rocks like Flower Woman? Hand me that shaft, would you?"

TWENTY-FIVE

Zebediah W. Hornbecker—and he introduced himself using his middle initial—was an intinerant trader. He roamed the Black Hills and the Badlands to the east. He trailed three burros loaded down with brass and copper pots and kettles, jug whiskey, knives, scissors and shears of every type. He carried axes, hatchets, shovels, picks, mattocks, crow bars, buck saws, two-handed crosscut saws and a hundred other tools, cooking utensils, devices, trappings, contrivances, and paraphernalia.

He did not offer firearms or ammunition for trade. The government forbade such traffic, although many of his fellow traders flouted this dictum.

Zebediah W. Hornbecker was far from impressive-looking. He was no more than thirty. His hair was long and as light as Willis Larimer's. He was muscular, well-built, and about six feet tall. He was also as homely as a neglected mud fence. His face was deeply pitted and riddled with acne, his huge nose nestled in the center of it; his eyes were as beady and red as a shoat's. His all but lipless mouth looked like a puncture. At first sight of him, Jenny wondered why he bothered to shave; a beard would have concealed a good portion of his homeliness. But shave he did.

He was garrulous, happy-go-lucky, well-spoken, brimming with confidence, and trusting almost to the point of being naive. To roam hostile Indian territory all by himself . . . any man had to be either ingenuous in the extreme or as blazingly courageous as a missionary alone in the jungles of Africa.

He was also the first white man she'd seen since the massacre. Could he help her get away? While Hornbecker warmed up the Oglalas crowding around his laden burros, she discussed it with Jumping Bear. The two of them watched from sufficient distance to ensure that they wouldn't be overheard.

"You are not thinking, Jenny. How could he possibly help you? He is risking his own neck every time he rides into a camp. The tribes deal with him and he rides out unharmed. But he has to live with his heart in his throat—some drunken fool might cut his throat or stab him in the back just to show off to his friends or his woman. Now, do you really think he would stick his neck out for you? For any white captive?"

"You have a point . . ."

"Not 'a' point, the only point. Forget it. Watch him go out of his way to avoid you."

"He wouldn't go that far . . ."

"He will. He will act like he does not even see you. He is not going to play hero; he knows he could end up getting you both killed."

"Let's go watch."

"If you promise me one thing."

"Don't try to take him aside," she said. "I know. I won't . . . I guess."

"You will not, period. I am on your side, Jenny, you should know that by now. I tell you this for your protection. And for his. If Chief Ottowa, if anybody, thinks for two seconds that you two are cooking up a scheme to get you out of here . . ."

"All right, all right! I understand."

"Do not be angry."

"I'm not, I'm . . . frustrated."

"My friends, everything you see is for trade. Only no buffalo robes. Beadwork, quillwork, your beautiful jewelry, knife handles, rawhide in any form, bull rawhide belts, shirts, skirts, moccasins, dresses, mittens—with or without hair. Blankets, tools and utensils, headdresses, pipes with or without decoration, any carvings, decorated lances, arrows, tomahawks.

"Whatever you want to trade. Zebediah W. Hornbecker offers the merchandise and the fairest deals of any trader in the territories!"

"Whiskey!" shouted a man and the word was taken up in a chant.

"For medicinal purposes only," called out Jumping Bear when the crowd quieted down.

Hornbecker laughed. "You speak excellent English, brother." He came through the crowd. "What can I . . ." Sight of Jenny stopped him. He almost spoke to her but caught himself and turned his attention back to Jumping Bear.

"What did I tell you?" Jumping Bear whispered.

"What can I offer you? Hornbecker went on. "What do you need? What have you got to trade?"

Everyone was staring at Jumping Bear. "I do not need a thing."

"Everybody needs something. How about a jug of fine whiskey?"

"No whiskey. Nothing." Jumping Bear's friendly expression deteriorated into a frown.

Hornbecker took the hint. "Who else? Let's do business

here. Step up, show me what you've got, look at what I've got and we'll trade, trade, trade!"

Jumping Bear and Jenny left. She hadn't seen Milk Eye. He must be somewhere in the assembled crowd. She wasn't eager that he see her with Jumping Bear, so they rarely got together other than in their private place behind the tepee.

They headed back there.

TWENTY-SIX

John bought himself a thickset, big-boned pinto with a bald face: sturdy, strong and, in Lincoln Hammer's opinion, over-priced. But John couldn't be bothered quibbling. He felt comfortable on "Baldy's" back, although he missed the stolen mare—did her new owner appreciate her as much as he had? The sun was just beginning to whiten the slate sky when he and Hammer rode out of Wind Cave toward the distant Nebraska border and Fort Randall.

They reached Buffalo Gap around ten in the morning. Hammer insisted that they stop off at his favorite distiller's place to pick up a couple of jugs. Half an hour after they left town they forded the south fork of the Cheyenne. John hoped to average at least fifty miles a day. The first two days would not be a problem but by the fourth day both horses would be fortunate to cover half that distance.

In talking to Indians Hammer was told that Oglalas in the Black Hills had indeed captured a white woman, but no one seemed to know anything about her daughter. Responsibility for the deed fixed on one of the tribe's three chiefs.

"Bloody Sky," said Hammer. "Ottowa."

"Do you know him?"

"Well. He's pushing eighty, but his conceit makes him think

he's half that age. He struts around, blowing off, boasting, and bullying anyone who'll put up with it. He's sneaky, deceitful, and lies in his rotten teeth. If he were white he'd be a politician. He's the one who did the actual kidnapping."

"He's got more than that to answer for; people died in that attack, and he led it. He should be arrested and hanged for murder!"

"That might be a bit hard to prove, whereas the kidnapping isn't."

"Tell me more about him."

"There isn't much; what you see is what he is: vain, egotistical. He has five or six wives. The tribe's other two chiefs—both much younger—have only one each."

"Pushing eighty?"

"As I say, not in his eyes."

"He sounds like he'll be tough to deal with."

"They all are when they get their backs up. It's his conceit— he looks down his nose at the whole world. His men once stole about forty horses and I had to go talk to him. At the time they were camped down near Hot Springs. We talked, just the two of us; he denied even leaving the camp, let alone leading the rustling party. In the end I had to ring in the army that time, too."

"What did they do to him?"

"Nothing, nobody could prove a thing. And not one of the horses ever showed up in the area. All army-branded but not a one was ever found."

"He got off scot-free."

"No witnesses, how could we accuse him? He knows how to protect himself; very careful, very clever. You've got to treat him with kid gloves, and Lord is he ever in his glory when you do."

"I'll 'treat him with kid gloves,' I'll blow his goddamned head off!"

"That would be very helpful in recovering your wife and daughter. John, you must understand something. It's critical to the whole fragile setup involving 'them' and 'us.' The Indians know that they're gradually losing everything: their hunting grounds, the buffalo, their freedom of movement, their power, their influence, most importantly their ability to stand up to the white man. They resent it. Deeply."

"I know . . ."

"You don't, you've no idea. They're a much prouder people than we are." He paused to bring both jugs around to his pommel and drink from one. "They know the sun's going down for them. That in the long run they're helpless against our sheer force of numbers. You might compare it to fighting a retreating action, in that they'll do anything they can to make life difficult for us, in hopes of slowing down the process. To their way of thinking, every wagon they burn, every scalp they take delays extinction by a few minutes, right?"

"Extinction?"

"Absolutely. They're convinced that that's what the Great White Father in Washington is aiming for. Not peaceful coexistence, not relocation. Genocide. So when the time comes and we're sitting across from Ottowa and his fellow chiefs dickering for your wife and daughter, don't be fooled by his smile, his friendly manner. He hates the sight of us, and he'll do everything in his power to make negotiating as difficult as he can."

"Mangy bastard!"

"I suppose."

"Suppose?"

"Tell me, what would you do if you were in his moccasins? Wouldn't you feel the same?"

"Who's in command at Fort Randall?"

"Colonel Virgil Truscott. Good man; a bit long in the tooth for the job but a spotless record."

"What's his opinion of Indians?"

"John, no post commander out here has any love for any of the tribes. All the warm admiration and respect for the noble savage is back East."

"You're not exactly an Indian-hater."

"I try very hard to tread the narrow line of impartiality. It's the only way for an Indian agent. Drink?"

"No thanks."

Hammer corked the jug and restored both jugs to his horse's rump. He was riding a trim-built sorrel with a blazed face. John could see from the way he sat his saddle that he much preferred his buggy.

"I wouldn't accomplish much if I didn't play the soul of diplomacy. I've worked hard to win their trust and I deal with them fairly and honestly. Oh, save the medal, I figure it's just the only way to do the job."

"Does Ottowa like you?"

"Of course not! I'm white."

"Obviously his antipathy doesn't extend to white women. God, I hate this! Imagining the worst: abuse, torture, the pain and suffering!"

Hammer reined up and placed a hand on his arm. "Don't do that to yourself. I can't tell you they're living high on the hog, but they're not being harmed, not as long as he has them. He's as practical as he is shrewd. They're bargaining chips. You sure you don't want a drink? I don't know why, but I'm thirsty as a bear this morning."

"Don't drink any more, Lincoln, I mean it. You could get drunk, fall off and break your neck."

Both had stopped. Hammer was reaching back for the jugs again. He hesitated, brought back his hand and studied John archly.

"I *have* fallen a couple times." He forced an embarrassed smile. "I'm a drunk. There are worse things a man can be. It's the job: the thanklessness of it, the pointlessness, the knowing you can't win. All you can do is put off the bloodshed if you're lucky. Worst of all is the loneliness. My wife couldn't take my being away so much. She left me, went back to Charleston."

"Why stick with it?"

"It's past too late to change horses, I guess."

"You're not exactly ancient."

"I'll be fifty next May. Can we talk about something else?"

They got onto the subject of Oregon and its promise, John's belief that all this was only a bump in the road. He'd be reunited with Jenny and Mary, they'd resume their long journey and complete it. Hammer gushed encouragement until his enthusiasm began straining the limits of probability.

It was late afternoon; rain threatened, thunderheads stacking up rapidly to the east and heading their way. The were fording Horsehead Creek. Hammer pulled up splashing beside John.

"I quit." John eyed him questioningly. "Drinking. Here, now, bull by the horns."

"Just like that?"

"Just like that." Side by side they charged up the opposite bank. "With you here I can do it. I mean it, not another drop. When I get back to Wind Cave the first thing I do, even before I unpack, is take the pledge. I'll wear the ribbon and all. Proudly!"

John beckoned. "Give me the jugs."

Hammer reached back, took hold of the rope connecting the two jugs and started to lift both. Then paused. John could hear the sloshing, one was full, the other, three-quarters. Again he gestured.

"Give them here, Lincoln."

Hammer released the rope, the jugs settled back into position, bouncing lightly off his horse's flanks as it shifted about restlessly.

"I will, I will. Only not right away. It's too fast, it's like . . .

like a bucket of ice water dashed in your face. Oh, I'll quit, all right. I swear by everything I hold dear. Only I'll need time. Just a little . . ."

John grunted, heeled his horse, and sprinted forward.

═══════ TWENTY-SEVEN ═══════

Night. Ottowa sat with Hinhanska and Icabu in the latter's tepee while his wife slept nearby. Zebediah Hornbecker had left that afternoon, having stayed over the night before, business with the Oglalas was so good. Since the trader's departure, worry appeared stamped on Ottowa's face. It deepened the crow's feet crowding his eyes and around his mouth and the furrows lacing his forehead. But in meeting with his fellow chiefs he made a pretext of joviality in an effort to create the impression that he hadn't a care in the world.

"You asked for this meeting," said Hinhanska. "What is so important that it cannot wait until morning?"

At thirty, Hinhanska was the youngest of the three leaders. He wore a new ghost shirt with fringed hem and cuffs and similarly designed vee neck. Around his middle were slender alternating blue and red bands and above them, up to and over his shoulders, red speckles abounded, with small blue and red circles at the top of his chest on either side. Around his neck he wore several varicolored bead necklaces and a half-necklace that came around his nape, started down inside each shoulder, and terminated in pear-shaped copper disks. His hair at his hairline stood straight up while at the sides it hung loosely down to the middle of his chest. Hoops depended from his earlobes. His copper-hued face showed no paint.

Icabu wore his jet-black hair piled high in front and tightly braided at the sides down to his waist. He, too, wore several necklaces but instead of a ghost shirt had on a blue army shirt with unadorned epaulets and button breast pockets. He was approaching forty. His nose had been badly broken and the fragments left to heal without any effort at restoring their normal shape. But for his nose, he would have been reasonably handsome, with his high cheekbones, piercing eyes, and well-formed chin. However, he looked sallow. He suffered all sorts of illnesses. When one ran its course, invariably another took its place. Something in his system made it impossible for him to enjoy even as short a time as two weeks of good health. It was Ottowa's opinion that he wouldn't last out the year, although he'd been making the same observation for the past six years.

Hinhanska went on, getting out his pipe, stuffing it with green tobacco leaves and lighting it with a stick thrust into the embers of the cookfire.

"We are listening, Ottowa."

"My friend," said Ottowa. "I owe you a favor. You found my best horse, the best I have ever owned, when it wandered off last spring. I have not forgotten that."

Hinhanska's eyes widened expectantly. "Now you want to give it to me?"

"No, something better. Better than six fine horses."

"What?"

Icabu also leaned forward, his curiosity similarly aroused.

Ottowa cleared his throat. "I want to give you Real Woman."

The two chiefs exchanged glances; both were puzzled.

"Why?" asked Icabu.

"I am bored with her."

Hinhanska puffed and studied Ottowa through the smoke rising from his bowl. "If that is so, why not scalp her, cut her throat and bury her where you stuck Wacawin?"

"Yes, yes," added Icabu, "save that hair . . ."

Ottowa bristled. "I had nothing to do with Wacawin's death."

Icabu smirked. "How then do you know she *is* dead?"

"Never mind Wacawin, I am talking about the *winu*, my captive woman."

"We understand." Hinhanska narrowed his eyes and shook his finger slowly. "*Ahpe, ahpe,* the trader Hornbecker left here this afternoon. Is that not so, Icabu?"

"Forget Hornbecker," said Ottowa. "He has nothing to do with this."

"No, no," said Hinhanska. "He is important. He leaves here and goes to another tribe. Maybe on the way he stops at Fort Sully or Fort Rice. Or meets bluecoats on the road. And tells them that you, Ottowa, are holding a white woman."

"That is stupid talk," growled Ottowa.

"Only he is right," said Icabu. "It has finally dawned on you that you can not have the army coming here to trade for Real Woman."

Ottowa sneered. "Stupid! Why not?"

"Because of what you did to her child." Hinhanska nodded, agreeing. "Real Woman will tell on you. You did not think of that before, but now . . ."

"Now," said Hinhanska, "Hornbecker will spill the kettle on you, they will come running."

"This is *che-ba-na*, nonsense!" Ottowa burst. "Out of the kindness of my heart, owing you a favor, I offer you, Hinhanska, my dear friend, a gift. And you thank me by accusing me?"

Hinhanska smoked. "I do not want your 'gift.' Neither of us does. It is a handful of hot coals."

"If you are smart," said Icabu, "you will get rid of her fast. Before sunrise. Before they show up here. Your mistake was in letting Hornbecker leave. You should have cut *his* throat and buried him with Wacawin."

Ottowa flared. "Stop all this talk of throat-cutting, you are both wrong!"

Hinhanska smirked. "Are we? Your face says otherwise."

He shrugged. "All right, if you do not want to kill Real Woman there are others ways of solving the problem."

"I have no problem!"

Both laughed. Ottowa was suddenly furious. He got to his feet glaring at them.

"You are fools. Both of you. You make me sick with your stupid suspicions!"

"Thank you for your gift, Ottowa," said Hinhanska. "But no thank you. You got yourself into this, get yourself out."

"Fast as you can," added Icabu. "Before the bluebacks come riding in here rattling their swords. Get rid of her."

"Give Wacawin company in her grave," said Hinhanska, and laughed.

Ottowa scowled and stormed out seething.

"Killing Real Woman's child was a foolish thing to do," said Hinhanska. "He should not have let anger fog his brain."

Icabu snickered. "It was not anger—it was old age."

"I hope he takes your advice and saves that red hair. That is a prize. It would look grand on a war shield. Or mounted with golden eagle feathers on a war bonnet. Or decorating his horse's mane."

TWENTY-EIGHT

A small wedding. As she walked down the aisle Jenny had wondered if he'd actually go through with it. For it was she who'd proposed. He'd reacted with mild shock, but recovered, accepted, then proposed. So *her* impulsiveness in the face of *his* hesitancy ended up in *their* marriage . . . however roundabout the route to it.

A small wedding. Only eighteen guests and no honeymoon.

Agnes Longstreth offered to take Mary overnight and husband and wife took an inexpensive room at the Queen City Hotel. It was small, the ceiling unusually low. The one window was painted permanently shut; the distinctive odor of mothballs pervaded the room; the bed turned out lumpy and was embarrassingly loud; the walls were paper thin. Not the most promising setting for a night in heaven. But it turned out to be just that.

From the moment he set her down after carrying her across the threshold neither said a word until morning. What was there to talk about? The minister tripping and turning his ankle coming out to begin the ceremony? The organist dozing off before the recessional? The singer misplacing her sheet music to "At Thy Sweet Voice"? All were more amusing than annoying. And who gets married without a slip or two? Why let little things ruin the most joyous day of one's life?

Now he held her beneath the cool sheet and opened his heart without words—his expression and his touch proclaimed his devotion. And their new life opened like a rose in a sudden burst of sunlight. The future waited to be challenged. Oregon!

The simple brushing of his hand across her cheek, her shoulder, her thigh, or any part of her made her want to cry out with joy. And when she seized him, she told herself she would never let him go. They were inseparable forever. Night would fade, morning would creep over the windowsill, the new day would consume everyone, and still she would hold him, her husband, her love, her life.

She awoke. Familiar stenches assaulted her nostrils. She looked upward at the smokehole. Escape! She must, she was in mortal danger. From Ottawa, from Walks Alongside, everyone around her. She sat up. The others were still asleep, as was he. She could dimly make out his outline lying beside Returns at Dawn Woman: Anpagliwin.

Escape, yes; to stay meant death. Don't bring Jumping Bear

into it, he'd down the mere idea. Get away without Jumping Bear's help. Even if he offered—which he could hardly do—why put her only friend here in jeopardy?

Escape as soon as possible after darkness fell. Give herself the longest possible time before the camp awoke. Surely she could find her way back to the site of the massacre and follow the trail to Fort Laramie.

Only would that be wise? They'd expect her to retrace her steps. Sarah Larimer had done so and look what happened. Where, then, if not west out of the hills and south, back down the plain? The opposite way? From what she'd heard from Jumping Bear, going north one would be moving even deeper into Sioux territory. It was the heartland of their nation.

She'd have to dodge Indians in every direction. Travel by night, hide during the day. Water wouldn't be a problem, but what about food? She had no weapon, although she could probably steal a knife. What would she do with it, kill a rabbit? She didn't know the first thing about trapping any creature, and doubted if she could bring herself to kill it if she did catch one.

Fish? How do you catch a fish with only your hands? She could eat berries, other fruit. What berries? What fruit? All the Oglalas ate was meat, any animal they could catch or shoot and every part.

Starving to death on the trail had to be the least of her worries. . . . Get out tomorrow night. Steal somebody's knife just before sundown and hide it. If she couldn't bring herself to kill an animal, even if starving, it would come in handy to defend herself when they caught up with her. . . .

TWENTY-NINE

The rain fell in a deluge. John and Lincoln Hammer kept on, although the quagmire slowed their progress. The Indian agent still made no move to dispose of his whiskey. He appeared to have conveniently forgotten about it. The man's personal demon was no concern of John's—except if he was too drunk to function when it came time to face the Oglalas.

Rain guttered in the brim of John's hat and sluiced down onto the pommel of his saddle, the overflow from the cistern of his soul. So it felt. It battered and drenched him, sinking into every inch of blood and nerve.

What had Jenny or he ever done to merit such misfortune? All they asked was to be left alone to make their way to the northwest. What did they know or care about the conflict between the two races? Suddenly Jenny and Mary were pawns in a bloody game. And it fell to him—with the help of God, the bureaucracy and the army—to get them safely off the board. It was beyond daunting, the prospect overwhelmed. . . .

Neither horse seemed to mind the weather; it did keep the dust down. It curbed their sweating and cooled them—a welcome break from the merciless heat. John scanned the heavens: the immense ash-gray canopy out of which the deluge descended. He and Hammer had to raise their voices to make themselves heard even though they were riding side by side. John said no more about the whiskey. Instead he got onto the subject of his frustration with Thomas Moonlight. Hammer knew the colonel only by reputation. Like most men, Moonlight was a mix of good points and bad, strengths and weaknesses.

"Did he mention that before the war he was a soldier of fortune?"

"Him?" John snickered. "Oh, I'm sure he doesn't lack

courage under fire, it's just that I got the impression he's by the book: all rules and regulations, not exactly another Quantrill."

"He had a good military record in the war."

"Good for him."

"You can't really blame him, John; blame your timing. Your wagon train should have passed through there back in May. Moonlight left Fort Laramie on May third with Jim Bridger and five hundred troopers."

"Five hundred . . . ?"

"I know. By the time you got there, he was down to around fifty men. Departmental Headquarters moves troops around practically at whim. A rumor that Indians have moved can change flags all over the map. Anyway, back in early May Moonlight set out to surprise a bunch of Cheyennes in the Wind River Valley. It was his chance to be a hero and maybe get his long-coveted brigadier star. It was still cold, snow still on the prairie, not enough grass for the horses. He searched for over two weeks, traveling nearly five hundred miles . . . and couldn't find a single Cheyenne. He came back to Laramie and a few days later, still fuming, he hanged two Oglala chiefs."

"What for?"

"Because they were handy. Hanged them without a trial. They turned out to be friendlies. It was the second of four or five blunders. To make a long story short, by the time you met him he was on his way out. He may even be transferred by now. Not that his personal problems influenced him to stay out of this; what he told you was the truth, he just doesn't have the manpower."

"I bleed for him."

"Last June Major General Dodge and Brigadier Patrick Connor, with Washington's blessing, decided to move the friendly Brulés and Oglalas eastward to Fort Kearny."

"We stopped there."

"Everybody on the Oregon Trail does. The brass wanted to

prevent the Oglalas and Brulés from joining the hostiles up in the Powder River country. Only neither was too keen on moving into Pawnee country. Would you want to live in your mortal enemy's backyard? On the way to Horse Creek the Indians turned on their escort and killed a captain and four men.

"Colonel Thomas Moonlight was sent out to catch up with them. He did, only they outsmarted him. They got away, running off most of his horses in the process. His brigadier general's star was slipping further and further from his grasp."

"I don't understand, how could he be so successful back east and such a failure out here?"

"Different jurisdictions, calling for wholly different approaches to dealing with the enemy. Out here it's raid and run, slaughter and destruction for a few hours, peace and quiet for six months. The army has yet to establish an overall strategy for dealing with the Indian problem—it's all but impossible to frame one . . . artillery's useless, infantry's worthless. It falls squarely to the cavalry—and in an area twice the size of the whole U.S. east of the Mississippi. Try covering that with fifteen thousand men."

"How many Indians?"

"The official estimate is close to three hundred thousand. It's like a forest fire that covers miles and miles. You beat out one blaze, up pops another. You wind up running around like the proverbial chicken."

Night was coming on rapidly, like a blanket thrown on a bed. The storm showed no signs of letting up. They camped. Lighting a fire was impossible, neither tried. They ate cold rations. Hammer got respectably drunk—without once mentioning swearing off. They curled up sopping in their blankets and neither slept a wink.

THIRTY

The storm slowed the run to Fort Randall. John and Lincoln Hammer arrived four and a half days after leaving Wind Cave, their horses as exhausted as they were. The foul weather had given Hammer a cold which he liberally dosed with the handiest medicine available. But it failed to curb his sneezing.

Fort Randall was the first in a chain of military installations along the upper—the so-called "Little"—Missouri and, according to Hammer, was destined to be the base of operations for most of the Sioux Expedition. During the Civil War it was one of the principle forts garrisoned by ex-Confederates, so-called "Galvanized Yankees." John and Hammer discovered it crowded with cavalrymen when they rode in. John found this heartening; in a sense he and Hammer would be offering Colonel Truscott the chance to play the knight in shining armor. An assignment irresistible to an officer.

"We'll ask him for a full column," murmured Hammer behind his hand.

They had dismounted and started up the steps to the colonel's office. John could see that the layout of Fort Randall differed from that of Fort Laramie. Randall was built around a nearly 400-foot-long parade ground, and appeared neat and orderly. No outbuildings could be seen, and the impression of haphazard, even careless administration, was absent. Randall looked much more military than Laramie.

Colonel Virgil Truscott sat at his desk talking to a major. Hammer touched John's arm, keeping them outside the door, out of the colonel's line of sight while the noncom manning the desk at the front door strode in, saluted sharply, excused the interruption and announced that two civilians were waiting to speak with the colonel "on a matter of grave urgency."

Truscott excused the major, the two exchanging salutes, and

summoned John and Hammer. The office was spotless, the desk cleared, papers in the stacked in and out boxes tidily squared. The colonel looked pressed and polished, not a single gray hair out of place. His salt-and-pepper handlebar mustache displayed dagger-sharp ends and was as perfectly shaped as a bird's wings. Between sneezes, the bleary- and puffy-eyed Hammer explained why they'd come. John watch the colonel's expression change from interest to concern to sympathy.

"The Oglalas . . ."

"Yes, sir," said Hammer.

"Are you absolutely sure, Mr. Pryor?"

"Absolutely."

"Forgive me, but how are you able to distinguish one tribe from another?"

"I can't. Colonel Moonlight at Fort Laramie identified them after I described them."

"Tom Moonlight. We were together at Chickamauga. Good man. He's run into a streak of bad luck, but let's not get off on that. Shall we look at the map?"

His wall map was rolled up. He pulled it down. On either side of it hung framed photographs of Presidents Lincoln and Johnson. Truscott indicated.

"Here are the Black Hills. Where did you track them to? Roughly?"

"Actually, I didn't. I was five days behind."

"Trying to get help from Colonel Moonlight," said Hammer. "He didn't have it to give. Maybe I can help here." He got up and joined the colonel at the map. "There are grassy areas here, here, all over this area. They're camped for the summer in one of them. I'll get back to that. First, their chiefs are White Owl, Drumbeater, and Bloody Sky. Bloody Sky's the culprit."

"How can you be so sure?"

"The Sioux around Wind Cave confirmed it. Colonel, they know . . ."

"They do."

Hammer cleared his throat, sneezed, excused himself and went on. "Sir, we don't want to waste your time. If I may I'll get right to the point? In my capacity as Indian agent for the Department of the Dakota I'd like to formally request that a column accompany us back and into the Black Hills. The same Indians who identified Ottowa—Bloody Sky—say that his people are encamped right about here. So it's not as if we have to roam all over the the hills searching. I know you'll want the request in writing and as soon as your clerk can make out the form I'll sign it."

"Whoa, slow down. What you'll need is half a squadron. Sixty-four men. Four troops of sixteen files—more than enough to throw the fear of God into them."

"But nobody knows how big the tribe is," said Hammer.

"How many warriors? How many attacked your wagon train, Mr. Pryor?"

"Between thirty and forty."

"Sixty-four men armed with Spencers, seasoned veterans all, will be more than enough for the job. They'll be your biggest bargaining chip." Truscott sat on the edge of his desk swinging one leg and flipping aimlessly the pair of immaculate white gloves tucked in his belt. "This type of . . . situation is, unfortunately, not uncommon these days. But it should hearten you to know that the majority of captives are eventually freed unharmed."

" 'Unharmed?' "

"Well . . ."

"It's going on a month since my wife and daughter were taken. I really can't believe they're still unharmed; my only hope is they're still alive."

"I understand, sir. I personally believe they are. The Sioux don't abduct women and children to kill them. They're too valuable."

"No question, but that doesn't mean they won't torture or otherwise abuse them."

"Sir, they're savages but they're not stupid. Torturing a captive you later intend to give over for ransom would be at the very least shortsighted."

"Let's just not get into that."

"As you wish. What sort is this Bloody Sky, Mr. Hammer?"

"He's smart enough to know their value."

"There you are," said Truscott to John.

Where was that? John wondered. But sarcasm wasn't called for; not on top of the offer of sixty-four men. They'd be enough. All that was left now was to get back to the Black Hills as soon as possible. His heart lifted; it could be all over in five days, the three of them reunited! He'd ask whoever commanded the detachment for an escort to take them to Fort Laramie. A reasonable request. He couldn't wait to see the look on Moonlight's face when he introduced Jenny and Mary. But of course, by that time Colonel Do-nothing would likely be long gone, if Hammer was right.

He stood up. "Colonel, I can't begin to tell you how grateful I am. How relieved."

"Please, that's one of the things we're here for. To protect you emigrants and to help however we can. Billings!"

The noncom came in saluting smartly. Truscott returned it less than halfheartedly. "Get hold of Captain Schmidt. He may be in chapel. I want him here pronto. And send in the officer of the day and Lieutenant O'Hara. And get Corporal O'Flynn to escort these gentlemen to my quarters. You both look like you could use a few hours sleep. Then we'll feed you."

Corporal Damien O'Flynn was all freckles, teeth, and irrepressible good humor.

"This is a fine looking facility," murmured John.

"Looks good from the outside. Enlisted men's quarters is something else. 'Specially in summer. Buildings is so overrunned with rats and other critters most o' the lads sleep out-doors." He laughed and lowered his voice. "They just finished fixing up the colonel's office. You shoulda' seen it, and him so personal neat and clean. It was so rundown and ratty it was worse'n the guardhouse. Captain Schmidt was sitting there one day talking to the colonel and three bugs dropped from the ceiling onto him—ask him. Lads call this place Fort Shithole."

Hammer suggested they sit on the steps of the colonel's house and wait for him to complete preparations for the expedition. "Expedition" was what Hammer had taken to calling the rescue mission before they even arrived. John didn't care what anybody called it as long as they got started.

Petunias grew in boxes attached to the veranda railing. Up close the colonel's house did not look that impressive. Boards needed replacing and a paint job was definitely in order. One front windowpane displayed a diagonal crack. John wondered if "rats and other critters" frequented the premises.

"Hungry?" Hammer asked. "I am. Thirsty, too."

"When are you not thirsty?"

"During the storm the other day. Notice I didn't take one drink?"

"You were afraid when you opened the jug rain would get in and dilute it."

"That's unkind, John. You sure seem in a buoyant mood. You should be, things are really looking up."

"I wonder what sort of man Schmidt is; if he's any good. God willing, he's not a loudmouth who'll talk us into trouble with your friend Ottowa."

"You notice Truscott didn't hesitate to assign him. He must trust him. Let's wait till we meet the man before we pass judgment."

"I'm not passing judgment. God, I'm tired."

"Do you want to stay overnight? Get to sleep in a bed?"

"No, no, no, we've got to be on our way before sundown.

Lincoln, Lincoln, is this real or am I dreaming? We're finally beginning to see a glimmer at the end of the tunnel."

"Indeed we are. Let's have a drink on that. A toast to unqualified success!"

"Why not?"

THIRTY-ONE

Captain Oscar Schmidt tried his best to make his men, John Pryor, and Lincoln Hammer think that he was a martinet, but couldn't quite bring it off. Hammer put it accurately in a nutshell: The man's bite was no match for his bark. Schmidt was in his forties. He had been wounded at First Bull Run, had recovered, and had fought with distinction at Fredericksburg and under Sherman in the Carolinas and elsewhere before being transferred west. He wore all his medals on every article of clothing above the waist except his undershirt. Stern and strict though he tried to be, he could not help looking slightly comical. His strut was too pronounced; he forced his voice too low, causing it to crack occasionally; he scowled too fiercely and changed his expression from a mild look to cruel, from wry grin to bullying, too swiftly. As if he were trying on different masks.

But for all his failure to inspire respect, if not fear, his men didn't dislike him. Nor did John or Hammer. They stood to one side watching as he ordered his troopers to line up beside their mounts for final inspection before riding out. Colonel Truscott had emerged from his office with other officers to watch. Officers and enlisted men on all sides stopped what they were doing to see the performance.

With Lieutenant Strothers by his side—both mounted on wide-chested stallions whose meticulously brushed coats positively gleamed in the sun—Captain Schmidt moved down the

line, snapping curt orders and returning saber salutes with a
white-gloved hand. Firmly seizing the spotlight, the captain
put on a great good show, so impressive it drew spirited applause
from a group of bare-chested enlisted men shoveling manure
in front of the stables. Schmidt glowered, but Colonel Truscott
grinned before stepping forward and returning the captain's
parting salute.

Off they rode following the trail John and Hammer had
taken coming down, Schmidt inviting the two civilians to flank
him at the head of the double line. The sun was high and hot,
the weather held no discernible threat of change. With luck, the
rain would stay away and they'd come within sight of the Black
Hills on schedule.

"Oglalas," murmured Schmidt. "And the colonel tells me no
more than forty warriors attacked your wagon train."

"Maybe not even that many," said John.

"How long ago?"

"Sixteen days."

Schmidt pursed his fat lips and joined his eyebrows above
the bridge of his nose, plunging into thought. John eyed him,
then Hammer, who was also studying the captain. They looked
at each other as they waited for him to go on. A smile started at
the corners of the Indian agent's mouth. John sighed. What pro-
found observation would be forthcoming? Where had the man's
mind gotten to?

"Wouldn't it be marvelous if we could wipe out their whole
camp? Like John Chivington did to those Cheyennes at Sand
Creek back in November last year. Men, women, and children—shot and bludgeoned to death. Remember how he re-
ported it, Mr. Hammer? 'Unnecessary to report that I captured
no prisoners.'"

"I remember," said Hammer. "I also recall Chivington was
court-martialed."

"True, but acquitted."

"Are you planning to massacre the Oglalas?"

"Not necessarily."

"Not at all," snapped John, turning the captain's head sharply. "This is a rescue mission."

"Your wife and daughter, I know, I know. Please, don't think for a split second that I'd jeopardize them by acting rashly."

"I should hope not."

"You surprise me, Mr. Pryor. The Oglalas capture your loved ones, putting them in mortal danger, and you're not bitter?"

"It's hardly a black and white situation. The whole purpose is to get Jenny and Mary out of there alive. Which, as I see it, means no shooting. You don't harm the Oglalas, don't even threaten to; at least not until Jenny and Mary are safely away. Then, as far as I'm concerned you can do as you please with their chiefs and warriors."

Schmidt's smile narrowed his eyes. "Their squaws bear children, boys who grow up to be warriors."

"Captain Schmidt," said Hammer. "You have your opinions and you're entitled to them. Our views may not coincide but we're likewise entitled to *ours*. But John is right, this is wholly and completely a rescue mission—not retribution."

Schmidt pulled his sword, holding it by the hilt and blade, catching the sun on it. "Gentlemen, would you believe I've yet to pull this sword in battle against savages? I know I will, but I haven't yet. They're here all around us, men, women, children, for one reason only: to be wiped from the face of the earth. Not pushed into Canada, not collected on reservations and put to farming. Eliminated."

"Like the buffalo," said Hammer.

"Unfortunate analogy but true. The buffalo one can respect, even admire."

John made no effort to suppress a groan. Schmidt was so busy pressing his case with Hammer he failed to notice. So this was how it would be? The man had blood in his eye before they even found the camp. John looked past the captain at Hammer. Could Hammer control him? Did he have the authority? He'd heard about Colonel J. M. Chivington. Two thirds of the Cheyennes killed were women and children. The crowning irony was that the tribe was peaceful; they held a treaty they were abiding by. Chivington had trumpeted his victory to the newspapers, covering his infamous actions with a carefully woven fabric of outright lies, claiming that he'd completely broken up the tribe and now emigrants and settlers would no longer be molested by them. It was a sickening display of the sword, indiscriminate slaughter for which the man was awarded full exoneration.

And at posts scattered all over the territories were hundreds of Chivingtons. Their presence made the difficult job of Indian agent even harder for conscientious souls like Lincoln Hammer. Now it turned out Schmidt was one of them.

"Captain . . . ," said John.

"Sir?"

"I appreciate this effort to rescue my wife and daughter beyond any words to express it."

"It's our job."

"Please, let me finish. I'm grateful, I'm relieved. At last I'll get them back. I'm sure we will. But it has to be done without any blood being shed."

"Mr. Pryor . . ."

"You're in command. You're responsible. How you do it is all up to you. But if anything goes wrong, if fighting breaks out putting my wife and daughter in danger, I'll hold you responsible."

"John . . . ," began Hammer.

John held up his hand, stopping him. "We go in, Captain, we talk, we make our deal. We get them out of there. When Mr. Hammer and the three of us ride away you'll be free to do as you please with their chiefs and warriors. But not until then. Understood?"

Schmidt was staring at him coldly; he licked his lips but nothing came out. Hammer spoke.

"What he's saying . . ."

"I heard. You threatened me, sir. Mr. Hammer heard, so did Lieutenant Strothers. You did, Claude," he added, turning to the lieutenant behind him.

"What I did was warn you. Fair warning, Captain. Now why don't we just drop it. For good. The last thing we need is to ride in wrangling among ourselves."

"I warn *you*, sir, this goes into my report."

"It should. Along with my reason for touching on it."

They rode on, John heeling his horse out ahead.

"I can't say I blame you," said Hammer as he rode up beside him. "But I think you're overreacting. He's just blowing off steam. He wouldn't have the guts to do what Chivington did. Not with us along."

"Why did Truscott pick such a man?"

"He's teaching him to swim by throwing him in the river. Schmidt's new out here, yet to fight his first skirmish. He told you that himself."

"So my wife and daughter are to be put in even more danger while he learns the ropes, is that what you're saying?"

"No. Just that windbags shouldn't be taken seriously. When we come face to face with them he'll pull in his horns."

"I sincerely hope you're right."

"I am."

John drew his Colt from his belt, hefted its more than two-and-a-half pounds, examined its octagonal barrel and the creeping lever ramrod attached to it. "Because if you're not, if he does anything to keep us from getting Jenny and Mary out of there, he's dead!"

* * *

Four days later, they rode into the Oglala camp. Lookouts posted on the highest hills saw them coming from ten miles distant. Hinhanska, Icabu, and Ottowa were already seated on blankets near the center of the patch of open ground where the survivors of the Sun Dance torture had dragged themselves around until they collapsed. Surveying the setting, John was surprised; drawn up in a line at the edge of the circle behind the chiefs were less than twenty warriors.

"Where are all the warriors?" he asked Hammer. "Watching us from hiding?"

"No. Out buffalo hunting. Before the season ends."

Schmidt seemed pleased to see so few warriors. He and his men remained mounted as John and Hammer got down and approached the chiefs. Behind them the women and children had gathered to watch.

John took a deep breath.

This was it!

THIRTY-TWO

Hammer began negotiations. His heart beating wildly, John gave up looking around for Jenny and Mary and turned to eye Captain Schmidt directly behind him. He was trying to look his sternest. How long would he keep control? The troopers made an impressive sight with their sheathed sabers and shiny, new, seven-shot Spencers.

"Great Chief," Hammer addressed Ottowa. "We have come to bargain for the release of your two prisoners: the red-haired woman and her daughter."

Confusion slid down Ottowa's face erasing his pleasant ex-

pression. Up came his hand stopping the Indian agent. He consulted with his fellow chiefs before responding.

"Red-haired woman? Daugh-ter?"

"Jenny and Mary Pryor, the wife and child of this man, John
Pryor. We're prepared . . ."

"*Ahpe.* Wait. I do not understand."

Hammer patiently repeated what he'd said. John sighed in-
wardly. So this was how it was going to be: They first had to
dance around the candle. Again he looked around. Where were
they hiding Jenny and Mary? Were they even there? He recalled
Hammer mentioning that the Oglalas would see them coming
from far enough away to give them ample time to hide them.
Only where?

Ottowa spoke. "We have no red-haired woman, no child
here. We have no captives. Oglalas do not take white captives.
It is wrong, it can only lead to trouble, blood spilling. It is for
Pawnee dogs to take captives."

"Hold it right there," snapped Schmidt, his left hand settling
on the hilt of his saber.

"Keep out of it, Captain!" barked Hammer.

Schmidt scowled but held his tongue. His men seemed to
be getting restless. John sighed. It was all falling apart, and so
soon. . . .

"No captives," Ottowa repeated. Hinhanska and Icabu
agreed, shaking their heads in denial. Behind them, the warriors
stared impassively. "Search the camp if you like. You will find
no whites here: no captives, no prisoners. None of us has ever
seen the two you describe."

"What you have heard is false," said Drumbeater. "Whoever
told you such a thing is a liar."

John's heart sank like a stone. Were they being truthful? How
could he be absolutely sure? So much time had elapsed, they
could have left here the day after they arrived; they could have
taken them away and given them to another tribe miles from here.

Hammer was now engaged in earnest discussion with all three chiefs but clearly was getting nowhere. He finally gave it up.

"As you suggest, Chief Ottowa," he said. "We will search the camp."

"Why?" snapped John. "They're not here."

"My turn, Mr. Pryor," said Schmidt.

"Keep out of it!"

The captain drew his saber. The unfamiliar sound breaking the temporary silence stiffened the warriors standing behind the chiefs.

"Put that thing back!" burst Hammer.

Ottowa got to his feet. The disagreement appeared to amuse him. He held up his hands, calling for attention. The crowd quieted, he asked if anyone had seen a "red-haired woman and her child." Some shook their heads. Others looked at each other questioningly and began mumbling. The chief leered.

Someone laughed. John, his frustration building and stoking the fire of his anger, could not see who. Others were grinning. He exploded, lunged, seized Ottowa by the throat.

"I'll kill you!"

Schmidt got down quickly. With Hammer helping, he tried to pull John off the chief. The warriors reacted, pulling knives, raising their tomahawks. Sharp clicking sounds were heard as troopers levered and aimed their rifles. Strothers joined the captain and Hammer, finally loosening John's grip. The two warriors right behind Ottowa started forward. Pulled by Hammer, John staggered backward as the two Oglalas swung their tomahawks. One narrowly missed his shoulder. Hammer shouted.

"Don't shoot! Don't shoot!"

Schmidt was turning purple. Again he jerked out his saber, and together with Hammer and Strothers, crowded in front of John to keep him from reaching Ottowa a second time. Slowly the warriors lowered their tomahawks.

"I'm sorry, sorry," said Hammer to the chief. "He . . . lost control."

Ottowa's hand had gone to his throat, touching it tentatively with the tips of his fingers.

"Filthy liar!" burst John.

"Shut up!" Hammer shouted, whirling on him. "Let's get out of here."

"What about the search?" Schmidt asked.

"Out, I said!"

THIRTY-THREE

Jenny fell asleep, irreversibly committed to getting away the following night. She'd be prepared—food, knife and all. As soon as darkness fell she'd go. No. Wait until everyone was asleep. With luck, she'd make it out of the hills before the sun came up. From then on it would be hare and hounds.

Her sleep was undisturbed. It was still dark out when she awoke. Ottowa was standing over her. His other wives were still asleep. He ordered Jenny to get up and follow him outside. The sun, as yet unseen, sent a lemon glow up over the hills crowding between Elk and Boxelder Creeks. He gestured her to hold out her hands. He whipped out a length of rawhide and tied her wrists.

"What are you doing?" she gasped.

"Shh, hold still."

Everyone still slept. Not everyone: Pawnee Killer and Four Hawks came loping up as if reporting for duty. He spoke to them, so rapidly she failed to catch a single word.

"Why have you tied me? What's going on?"

Across the way Jumping Bear emerged from his tepee, looked over, saw what was going on. His face darkened.

"What are they doing?" she called to him.

He shook his head sadly, offered a grim look of sympathy and ducked back inside. Pawnee Killer had left. He returned, bringing three horses. Vapor issued from their nostrils. They fussed and whinnied, pawing the earth. Ottowa patted the single black mustang's rump.

"Get on," he said. "You are leaving."

"Why? Where?"

"Do not ask questions. Pawnee Killer and Four Hawks will take you. It is a long way. If you give them no trouble, if you do not try anything foolish, they will untie your wrists when you stop to rest. That will not be until the sun hangs from the top of the sky."

"This is crazy . . ."

She caught herself. Why bother objecting? And asking him to explain made no sense, he wasn't about to enlighten her. Where *were* they taking her? Far enough so that no one would see them kill her? No. He'd mentioned stopping to rest at noon. No need to take her that far just to dispose of her!

"Jumping Bear!" she shouted.

He stuck his head out.

Ottowa snapped at him irritably. "This is none of your business!"

Again Jumping Bear looked her way sympathetically before vanishing inside. They got up on their horses. Ottowa gave final instructions. This time she managed to catch two separate words. The first was *nitas´unka*—your horse. The second, *Siksika*. It was the tribe's term for the Blackfeet, like the Oglala, a tribe of the Teton branch of the Sioux.

She remembered Jumping Bear saying that they were located in the north, but he'd never said how far north. More or less than 100 miles? What difference did it make? And why ask Ottowa for an explanation? Obviously, he had decided to get rid of his healer, send her off to his cousins the Blackfeet.

Why, all of a sudden? She'd done nothing to offend or embarrass him, at least not lately. She'd come to his rescue not once but twice, treating his wounds. He'd said he was grateful. And he was getting to like her, treating her with more respect every day. Why this sudden change in attitude?

Could Hornbecker have something to do with it? Thinking back, Ottowa had changed dramatically since the trader rode off. He took to acting like a man carrying a great weight. Worried that Hornbecker would tell the army he'd seen a white woman in the Oglala camp?

"That's it!" Pawnee Killer and Four Hawks riding ahead and on either side of the trail looked back. "He's afraid."

Neither understood. She went on thinking out loud. "Your fearless leader Milk Eye. Afraid the army will come looking for me and I'll tell the whole disgusting story: how he murdered Mary and the Larimers, beat me, raped me, forced me to do everything under the sun against my will. Oh, would I ever give them an earful! They'd hang him on the spot!"

"*O-ka-ba-le-ah!*"

"Shut up yourself!"

Anger surged. Of course! By getting rid of her he'd escape the hangman! Only why let her live? Could it be that he owed somebody in the Blackfoot camp a favor? Was she to be an outright gift for an old friend? Somebody even older, filthier, crueler than he was?

"Dear God . . ."

Ignoring Pawnee Killer's occasional remarks flung back at her, she analyzed the situation. If Ottowa had delayed this by just one day she'd have left.

"One stinking day!"

What rotten luck! Only why not try to escape now, on the trail? Before they got where they were going? Would they kill her if they caught up with her? No question.

Why hadn't he ordered her done away with? It was the simplest solution. Could it be he really was afraid? He didn't dare order her killed, not after Hornbecker had seen her. Killing Mary and the Larimers was Milk Eye's first mistake. Mistreating her, letting Hornbecker leave camp alive, letting her live, blunders all. And he had to be blind in both eyes not to see that one day, one way or another, she'd leave. Return to John. From then on the whole tribe would be a target for retribution.

On they rode. Around noon of the second day they passed a crude sign made with a burning stick identifying and pointing toward Wind Cave. Like all other white settlements, even solitary houses, the Oglalas gave it a wide berth.

Guilt caught up with Jenny, and as the hours slipped by, it grew until it flourished. If she and John ever did see each other again, how would she explain what happened to Mary? He'd be devastated. He had to be living in hope that both of them had survived. She'd return and shatter his heart. She fingered her locket with Mary's silhouette in it.

Could he ever forgive her? Hardly, not if she told him the truth. Could she ever forgive herself?

Would he leave her? If they never saw each other again maybe it would be for the best. At least it would spare her sight of his face when she told him. And spare him the need to dismiss her from his life.

"Poor John . . ."

"*Ga-sha-neen-na. Sunktanka.*"

"My horse is not tired! Leave me alone!"

She dismissed Pawnee Killer with a sharp movement of her hand. The ends of his mouth turned down, she had hurt his feelings. He turned back, resuming talking to Four Hawks. Poor, poor John: living in slender hope, praying that both of them had survived.

And the guilt grew heavier.

THIRTY-FOUR

Trailing his three burros, Zebediah W. Hornbecker moved slowly down out of the Black Hills, planning to pick up the Cheyenne River and follow it eastward and slightly north in the general direction of Fort Sully. The trader's stomach glowed with satisfaction, his mood was expansive. Business with the Oglalas had been even better than he'd anticipated, well worth the risk to his scalp. He could be proud of himself. He lit up another Pollock's Crown Stogie and puffed contentedly.

"It's a fact, Emmaline, the man with guts is the man who profits. I'm the only trader who dares ride into the Sacred Hills. Making me the only one to do a land-office business with the Sioux, bless their murderous hearts. White Owl, Drumbeater, and Bloody Sky I wouldn't trust as far as I could throw any one of them, but they do let me keep my hair."

Reaching behind him he untied two separate knots and lifted free his banjo. Holding his reins in his mouth he began tuning the instrument. Then wrapping the reins around one wrist, freeing both hands and mouth, he began to play.

I'm just a poor wayfaring stranger, a-traveling through this world of woe;
But there's no sickness, toil nor danger in that bright world to which I go.
I'm going there to see my father, I'm going there no more to roam,
I'm just a-going over Jordan, I'm just a-going over home.

He paused. Two riders were dusting toward him from the south. He reined up. One by one the burrows came to a halt behind him. He squinted under his hand.

"Well I'll be! Reed Samuels . . ."

He was about Hornbecker's age, carrying a belly much too big for his frame, round-faced, as tan as an Indian, and with a smile that appeared permanent. He was a bounty hunter, a career Hornbecker had considered at one time, only to reject as too dangerous. Chasing wanted men, desperate men, was like chasing rattlesnakes; the prey could turn much too easily. With Samuels was a stranger.

"Like you to meet Wilton Benyus, Zeb, from down Amarillo way."

"Pleased to make your acquaintance," said Hornbecker, shaking the Texan's huge hand. "You a bounty hunter, too?"

"Bet your boots," said Samuels. "We teamed up."

"You after anybody I know?"

"We're packing a few wanted dodgers. We're on our way to Hayes."

"We hear bad hombres like to hide out there," said Benyus, "figuring Injuns'll leave 'em alone and whoever's after 'em will be afraid to go into there, they's so many."

"Makes sense," said Hornbecker. "I expect you boys know what you're doing. Reed, do you chase *just* criminals? Or anybody you can get a reward for?"

"What did you have in mind, Zeb?"

Hornbecker jerked a thumb back over his shoulder. "Up there—just follow the main east trail—there's a camp full of Oglalas."

"What's Oglalas?" Benyus asked.

"Sioux," said Samuels. "Go on, Zeb."

"They're holding a white woman captive. I saw her."

Samuels' eyes widened. "Do tell . . ."

"I'm not saying it'd be easy, but if you could get her away from them I'd bet her family'd reward you with enough cash to choke your horse. She's young, pretty, and in good shape, last I saw. A redhead."

"Sounds risky as hell to me," muttered Benyus. "I don't much like doing business with no Injuns."

"Wait, wait," said Hornbecker. "Reed, I seriously think these *want* to get rid of her. You offer two blankets and a bottle and she's yours."

Samuels scratched his chin as he thought. "I don't know, Zeb, Oglalas are pretty mean customers."

"You could probably get a thousand dollars for her, maybe two."

"Wealthy family?"

"I'm sure."

"What's their name? Where are they? Are they settlers, emigrants? What?"

"I can't tell you any of that. I pretended I didn't even see her. But I did, and her family or her husband's got to want her back in the worst way. Besides, it'd be a shame to leave her where she is. It's your chance to be heroes and get yourselves a reward into the bargain. Sooner or later old Ottowa's going to trade with somebody for her. It might as well be you boys."

"I still don't know," said Samuels.

"You'd just have to make a little detour. It's not far from here."

"We prefers to stay out'n any Injuns' way," said Benyus.

"Well, it's up to you, I just thought you might be interested."

"Appreciate it all the same, Zeb," said Samuels.

He touched his hat brim. They rode on. Hornbecker resumed playing his banjo.

THIRTY-FIVE

Schmidt and Lincoln Hammer finally quieted John down, after reassembling to the west of the camp.

"You nearly got your shoulder split," the captain reminded him.

"Bastard . . ."

They agreed to conduct a search, although with little enthusiasm. Hammer raised a valid point.

"We might at least find some clue that they were here. And work from that point."

Four hours later, nearing sundown, Schmidt ordered the bugler to sound assembly, ending the search. He, Hammer, and John discussed their next move.

"Since there'd be no danger to Mrs. Pryor or the little one," said the captain, "I move we put the whole camp to fire and sword. Teach that one-eyed red devil and his cronies a lesson they'll take with them to Hell!"

"And how in the world would that help us find Jenny and Mary?" John asked.

"Must I draw pictures, Mr. Pryor?"

"No sword play, nobody fires a shot," muttered Hammer.

He was visibly upset, his patience by now worn thin. For days John had wondered how a man with his experience could generate such optimism. Reaching this dead end had to be as frustrating to Hammer as it was to him.

"All things considered," said Hammer, "Ottowa was so nonchalant, so sure of himself, there's no question he sent them away."

"Whatever gave you that idea?" burst Schmidt.

"Spare me the sarcasm," said John, fastening his stare on the captain. "Lincoln, I agree, killing and burning them would be stupid. Still, that bastard should be made to pay. Why don't we take him hostage against Jenny's and Mary's safe return? Take all three chiefs?"

"Excellent idea!" snapped Schmidt.

"No." Hammer shook his head. He stood with one leg raised on a rock, looking at the sun purpling the clouds as it lowered. "They'd fight like demons."

Schmidt snorted. "Let 'em, there can't be more than twenty warriors . . ."

"I don't care if there are only two. You try to take their chiefs hostage and it'll end up in shooting. God forbid Ottowa or one of the others is killed. Think about it, boys, we come looking for your wife and daughter, they tell us they're not here, they invite us to look for ourselves, we don't find them. As far as they're concerned that ends it."

"He took them," said John. "He's the one. When they rode away Jenny, Mary, and the Larimers were with them."

"The problem is you never actually saw Ottowa and his men take them," said Hammer. "I don't question that they did, it's the most logical assumption in the world. But that's no longer important, since they've gotten rid of them. Believe me, John, Ottowa won't get away with it. He'll end up swinging."

"Sure."

"But isn't it far more important that we find Jenny and Mary? I've a thought. Why don't we find the buffalo hunters and talk to them? They've no way of knowing we've been here; if we phrase our questions cleverly maybe somebody'll tip his hand."

"Tell us where they were taken?"

"It's possible."

Schmidt scoffed. "It's ridiculous."

"I don't think so," said John, "I say it's worth a try."

Blackfoot tepees differed from Oglala in that they were supported by four poles instead of three and displayed painted designs on the outside. From a distance the camp looked twice the size of the Oglalas' but just as messy, was doubtless just as filthy and, as they drew closer, as noisy.

"*A-ge-wah,*" said Pawnee Killer.

"I can see we're *here,*" said Jenny.

There'd been no chance to escape en route. Neither man left her side further than ten feet and at night they tied her hand and foot before going to sleep themselves. If she was to get away it would have to be from here. And get away she must; John would track her to the Oglala camp maybe, but not this far. Only Jumping Bear had seen them, no one else had been awake. Did he know they would be heading here? Milk Eye had kept his voice down so Jumping Bear couldn't have overheard. And why should the chief tell him?

But Pawnee Killer and Four Hawks would be returning; maybe in time one or the other would let slip their destination. Jumping Bear would get wind of it. Then what? Would he come and rescue her? Risk his life? He hadn't before, why now? If he even left camp by himself Milk Eye would suspect where he was heading, send men after him, order him killed.

No, she was definitely on her own.

They forded a stream. She asked Pawnee Killer what it was called. He refused to say. Milk Eye's instructions apparently covered every detail. The people stopped what they were doing to watch the three of them pass. They stopped in front of a tepee about the size of Milk Eye's. Intricate designs were painted on the exterior in red, blue, and black. A man came out. He was in his thirties; from the way he was dressed it was hard to tell whether he was a chief or warrior. He had a primitive paintbrush in one hand and in the other was a rawhide shield with a half-completed eagle design. There were also feathers attached to it that matched the two in his hair. He wore fringed buckskin trousers and a top without sleeves. His hair hung loosely to the middle of his chest. He was good-looking, although a livid scar broke the otherwise smooth plane of his left cheek.

So this was her new lord and master. Dear God. Would it ever end? Her escort wasted no time, speaking briefly then exchanging her for two knives and a horse—a small, wild-eyed bay with a reddish mane. Mounting up without a word or a glance back at her, the Oglalas left.

"In," said the man, standing aside and holding back the entrance flap.

She entered. "You speak English?"

"Some. I am Cinta Mazza. Iron Tail. I am a sub-chief. You are Real Woman."

"Jenny Pryor. And you're to let me go. Give me a horse, rations, a knife and let me ride out of here."

A smile cracked his face. "Why should I, Jen-ny Pry-or?"

"Must I remind you what the army does to Indians who take white captives?"

"Hang them?"

"Without a trial."

"Some. But even those they must first find. They could not find you in the Sacred Hills, what makes you think they can all the way up here?"

"Their forts are all over. More and more soldiers are coming west. My husband is searching for me, he's getting help from the army. They'll come by the hundreds and destroy this camp."

"I will watch for them."

There was no intimidating this one anymore than Milk Eye. Iron Tail. Stupid name. She couldn't remember what he'd said it was in his language. Did she care? She looked around the interior. It smelled like every other tepee: a combination of sweat, rancid meat, and smoke. But he didn't smell, certainly not like Milk Eye.

Did he bathe? She'd soon know, she thought wearily. Hanging from one wall was a head scalp on a wooden hoop complete with ears and cheeks. At first glance it looked like a giant bat. It would have revolted her back before the attack; now, it didn't even elicit interest.

There was also a war bonnet with what appeared to be ermine skins attached to the crown. On the floor directly opposite, where the base of the tepee had been rolled up to admit fresh air, were a bow and rifle, each in its fringed and beaded buckskin sheath.

He turned from her. She watched in silence as he finished painting the design on the shield, dripping his crude brush into clay pots of varying colors. The he set the shield against a pole to dry.

"It is time," he murmured, avoiding her eyes.

"What for?"

"Bed."

Said matter-of-factly, implying that it should come as no surprise to her. She stared fixedly at him.

"Look at me. So you plan to start off by raping me? You, a respected sub-chief of the great Blackfoot Nation? How disappointing. That you should turn out no better than the lowest Pawnee dog raper of helpless captives."

"Not rape, just fuck."

"Listen to me, Iron Tail. Listen good. If you don't force yourself on me, if you keep your distance, when the army gets here I'll tell them that you treated me well. I give you my word, they will not punish you. Or any of your people. I will tell them to take me out of here back to my husband and that will be the end of it.

"The Oglalas abused me so they must be punished. Severely. Your friend Bloody Sky will be hanged. Do you want to hang beside him? Think about it."

Up came his hand. "You talk too much. Rest your mouth. And take off your clothes, lie down." He got up and moved close, bringing his face within three inches of hers. "I have earned you. I traded a good horse for you. Do you know what a horse is worth?" He held up the splayed fingers of both hands with his thumbs hidden. "Eight buffalo robes. Also two new knives. Now do as you are told!"

Jumping Bear ran a hand down the outside of his left leg, bringing up his fingers dark with blood and dust. He had fallen from his horse while circling the buffalo herd, and grasped the end of the trailing rawhide thong tied around its neck gradually— as it dragged him—slowing it so that he could remount. He had narrowly missed being trampled.

The Oglalas had surrounded a herd of about sixty, then attacked with bows and arrows and iron-tipped lances. Within ten minutes twelve animals were brought down, with only two horses gored and minor injuries like Jumping Bear's to a few hunters. Now the clouds of dust that rose high above the area had settled, the surviving buffalo had run off, and the hunters busied themselves butchering the kill. Special painted markings on the hunters' arrows identified each man's buffalo.

Two men could dress an entire animal in an hour. Hides, meat, organs, and other edible and usable parts would be taken back to camp on pack horses. Some parts, such as the brains and small intestines, could not be preserved. These the hunters ate raw in a victory celebration.

Walks Alongside was removing a tongue close by Jumping Bear. He held it up proudly before tossing it onto the blanket set aside for tongues.

"How is your leg?" he asked Jumping Bear.

"It is nothing." He was working on removing his buffalo's heart.

When the last pack horse had set out for camp with its heavy load it would leave the area littered with buffalo hearts purposely left behind. Like all other plains tribes the Oglalas believed that the mystical power of the buffalo's heart would help to replace the herd's losses.

Every part of the creature not eaten found some other purpose. Most important and valuable was its hide. The thickest hides came from old bulls and went into shields and the soles of winter moccasins. The thinnest hides came from unborn calves and were fashioned into bags. Horns, bones, hooves, hides, and innards were converted into everything from all sorts of clothing, tepees, and furnishings, to ceremonial objects, weapons, tools, and utensils. Even the buffalo's dung was saved to use as fuel when wood was scarce or unobtainable.

Walks Alongside spoke. "Somebody coming." He shaded his eyes. "Bluebacks!"

"What do they want with us?"

"Meat, what else?"

Jumping Bear wiped the blood from his knife on the grass and held it in readiness. Would the next heart it found be a white man's? They watched the files come to a halt, the dust settle, and two officers, along with two white men in civilian clothes, dismount and approach the nearest hunters. They talked.

"They do not want to fight," said Jumping Bear, returning to his task.

"They better not, we are two to every one of them."

"They have Spencers. We could be four or five to one and they would cut us down like grass."

While the troopers remained in their saddles the four moved about, questioning hunters. They finally came up to Jumping Bear and Walks Alongside. Jumping Bear recognized Lincoln Hammer, though the Indian agent didn't seem to know him.

"We are looking for a red-haired woman and her daughter," he said, holding his hand out at the height of a seven year old.

"Have you seen them?" the captain with him asked.

"No," said Walks Alongside.

"Have you?" the other civilian asked Jumping Bear.

He could feel Walks Alongside's eyes on him. He was tempted to tell; for Jenny's sake. But that was one wasps' nest it would be stupid to tomahawk. He would end up paying with his life. It would be cowardly not to speak up but for all the reasons he could not help her before, neither could he now. Despite the guilt. All these thoughts flashed through his mind as he hesitated before answering.

"Have you?" the man asked again.

He was Jenny's husband—John. In his eyes there was great pain; he looked exhausted from the strain of their separation. And he noticed they had asked about her child, not knowing what had happened. The urge to blurt forth the truth assailed him. He quelled it.

"No."

"They were brought to your camp in the Black Hills," said Hammer. "Mother and child. You must have seen them."

Jumping Bear shook his head. "No."

"Do you deny that it was your chief with the one eye and all of you attacked this man's wagon train down near Fort Laramie?" Schmidt asked.

"We have not been out of the Black Hills since we came here last spring," said Walks Alongside. "Only to hunt, and no further away than here."

"I'm not talking to you."

"We're wasting our time here," muttered John. "Let's go." He glared first at Walks Alongside then at Jumping Bear. "But we'll be back. The captain's right, it was your warriors in that attack. You two were there. I'm not forgetting that for a minute."

Walks Alongside snickered. John stepped toward him. Hammer caught him by the shoulder.

"Let's go," said Schmidt.

Minutes later the whites were heading south. Jumping Bear emptied his lungs loudly in relief.

"Now tell me where Pawnee Killer and Four Hawks took Real Woman," said Walks Alongside.

"I do not know! Stop asking."

"You saw the three of them leave."

"So? Ottowa did not tell me. If you are so curious, ask him. Ask Pawnee Killer and Four Hawks."

"You know they are not back yet. They must have taken her a long way."

They watched the troopers vanishing into the landscape.

"Ottowa got rid of her just in time," Walks Alongside went on. "He must have known the army was coming looking."

"He did not say."

Jumping Bear could see the annoyance taking over Walks Alongside's expression. Disappointment that Jenny was no longer within reach of his knife? Did he actually blame her for what happened to Flower Woman? Ottowa, not Jenny, was responsible for that. Jumping Bear grunted.

"What?" his companion asked.

"Nothing."

"I will do it, I will ask Pawnee Killer and Four Hawks."

Jumping Bear sniffed. Ask. Keeping asking until your tongue falls out. With Ottowa looking over their shoulders you'll be the last one in camp they'll tell.

THIRTY-SIX

Long Bull's squaw was preserving buffalo meat by cutting it into thin slices and hanging it to dry on a long thin line of rawhide that stretched from one side of the tepee to the other. Filling the line, she turned to the next phase of the process, pulverizing the jerky with a stone maul and mixing the powdered meat with ground dried berries and fat. The nutritious pemmican

would be stored away in a parfleche where it would keep for
months.

Long Bull and his visitor paid no more attention to Little
Water and her work than did she to their conversation. Long
Bull, a chief of the Blackfeet, had summoned Iron Tail to discuss
the latter's recent acquisition, the white woman with hair like fire.

"She has come to us at just the right time," said Long Bull.
"The perfect time."

He was ten years older than Iron Tail and had been a chief
of the Blackfeet for six of those years. His hair had been trained
to stand straight up from his forehead and was dyed yellow, the
undyed hair at the sides long and loose. He wore a fringed
buckskin jacket and trousers, numerous bead necklaces. He ex-
uded confidence and authority in equal measure. He excelled
at browbeating. Iron Tail, although not lacking in confidence
himself, had always felt uneasy in Long Bull's presence, particularly facing him alone, as now. To himself he acknowledged
that it was the older man's eyes that intimidated so effectively.
They did not pierce, he did not stare; in them instead was a lan-
guid look which some in the tribe described as the calm before
the thunder and lightning.

"I do not like to lose her so soon," said Iron Tail.

"Except for her skin like snow and her hair, what is so different about her? She is a fuck, that is all. She is too pale, she
cannot speak our language, cannot even speak Oglala; she does
not even cook for you."

"I do not ask her to."

"You cook for you both? Is that proper for a respected sub-
chief of the Siksika?" He grunted disapprovingly and began
drawing with his finger in the dust: a long, twisting line desig-
nating the Little Missouri River and a dot near it. "Here is a
most painful thorn in our foot."

"Fort Sully."

Long Bull's eyes glittered. "I see it gone, Cinta Mazza, the river lowlands absent of life. The walls still standing but nothing inside except the rats."

Iron Tail had heard Long Bull describe his favorite dream many times before; his impression of what Fort Sully would look like unmanned never varied.

Iron Tail shook his head. "It is the same old problem, how do we get inside?"

"What do you call her?"

"Chief Ottowa called her Real Woman."

"Real Woman. She will get us inside."

"How?"

"We will offer to trade her."

"For what?"

"Whatever. That is unimportant." He was becoming impatient with the young man's shortsightedness. Not to mention his lack of enthusiasm for the idea. "Using her, we gain entrance. Once we are all inside, we attack. Attack!" Exclaimed so loudly, Little Water started, scowling at him. He pretended not to see. "Kill every blueback. Remove the thorn and from then on move about our lands *as we please!* Your face says you do not like the idea. Or is it that you do not like giving her up?"

"I do not understand why we need to use her. Why not simply mount a war party and attack?"

"Ah, but how much easier if we are already inside, where they cannot shoot at us from behind the protection of the walls? Where their cannon cannot fire at us. Inside, Cinta Mazza!"

"Fort Sully is two whole sleeps from here. They do not bother us . . ."

"They have before. They will again. A thorn, a thorn! They occupy sacred Siksika land, land our fathers took from the Absaroke, from the Cheyenne. Our land! Overrun with whites like the rats that overrun the marshes. We have a sacred duty!"

"Quiet down," snapped Little Water. "You are giving me a headache."

Long Bull waved a finger at Iron Tail. "We need Real Woman. They will be eager to ransom one of their own."

"*They* will shoot us for keeping her captive."

"You did not capture her, she was a gift. Now you want to do what is right, return her to her people. Galsworthy will appreciate that. And that is another good thing: He will look like her rescuer, a hero."

"The colonel is a worthy enemy and no fool."

"Worthy but weak. And that is why we must strike soon, do you not see, my friend? He has few men, maybe only fifty or sixty guns." He pointed eastward. "Their war beyond the hundred rivers is ended, now all the forts on our lands will be getting more bluecoats. We must make our move. Now, Cinta Mazza. Give us Real Woman. Do not make us take her."

"Anyone who tries will feel my knife."

"You would go against all your friends and fellow warriors? Do not be angry. Think about it. Sleep on it. We will talk again."

THIRTY-SEVEN

In many ways, life among the Blackfeet was turning out to be easier for Jenny than it had been among the Oglalas. Despite forcing himself upon her, Iron Tail was not old, not filthy like Milk Eye, and for the most part treated her as an equal. Nor did he have a number of wives to stir jealousy and cause petty problems. Actually, he was a widower. He was demanding when the torch went out, but closing her eyes and submitting, while at the same time sending her mind back to John, proved easier than the same effort with Milk Eye. Or was she getting better at it with time?

Although also Siouian, the Blackfeet differed from the Oglalas in many respects. They were more powerful and therefore more politically influential in the region. They did not wander about with the changing seasons. All told, in various camps, they numbered close to 40,000, and for decades had led tribal opposition to the white man. For twenty-five years after the turn of the previous century they prevented whites, whom they regarded as poachers, from trapping in the rich beaver country of the upper tributaries of the Missouri. At the same time they attacked the invader's forts and also warred against neighboring tribes, capturing horses and taking scalps. They were as single-minded as the ancient Spartans in their quest for military dominance. Fighting was their joy. Other tribes considered them to be the most aggressive hostiles on the northwestern plains.

As it did their allies and their enemies, the buffalo supplied the Blackfeet with everything they needed to stay alive and to fight—from shields, bow backing, and bowstrings to powder flasks and knife sheaths.

They put their trust and their faith in elaborate medicine bundles, which they believed would bring success in war and hunting and protection against illness and disease.

So Jenny found herself among a people who for the most part embraced superstition over logic and intelligence, where every male above the age of thirteen lived prepared to go to war at any time, where killing was man's noblest purpose.

The Blackfeet were planning something. Jenny felt it intuitively. The people's faces—particularly the warriors'—showed anticipation. Either something was about to happen or the chiefs were organizing something; no doubt involving bloodshed. The air silently crackled, like the tension between two enemies when they come face to face. The warriors seemed to be spending every waking minute working on their weapons: cleaning and repairing and polishing their few ancient Henry or Hawken rifles, sharpening knives and tomahawks, making arrows by the hundreds.

She knew better than to vent her curiosity on Iron Tail. She was a woman, it was none of her business. Nor did she care. If there was to be fighting it would be elsewhere, not around the camp.

It was night, they had finished eating. As usual, by themselves—in the brief time she'd been there she'd noticed that they invariably ate by themselves. No one came to visit Iron Tail, nor did he visit others. Was it that he had no friends? Or was he keeping to himself for a reason? Was he still in mourning for his wife? All the tribes observed prescribed periods of mourning for lost loved ones, all such periods differing in length. Milk Eye hadn't mourned five minutes for Flower Woman. Still, how many people mourn those they've killed? Jumping Bear had told her at the time that the Oglalas generally mourned for as long as a year.

Jumping Bear. How was he? What was he doing? She missed him. His presence had made life tolerable. She missed their long talks and his advice. Without him she might not have weathered her ordeal. At least now, thanks to his guidance, she knew a few ways to avoid trouble. Iron Tail offered no such guidance. He appeared to take it for granted that she knew how to conduct herself without any help from him. The tribal taboos were what could get her into serious trouble. Like the Oglalas, the Blackfeet were held firmly in the grip of supernatural powers. All powers from the spirits were tainted with taboos which, if violated, could earn the violator punishment, even torture and death.

The taboos were so many and so bizarre—even absurd—it surprised Jenny that even the true believers themselves were able to keep track of them. A man whose supernatural helper was an eagle could not let another person walk behind him when he was eating, for the eagle would be disturbed by such conduct. A shield thought to have the power to stop bullets and arrows was often stored at least half a mile from camp so that menstruating women would not walk close to it; when the warrior needed the shield he had to walk in a semicircle to the spot where it was located, then return to camp from the opposite direction, completing the circle.

Bizarre, absurd, childish—like fear of black cats or Friday the thirteenth. Jenny had to keep Jumping Bear's advice in mind at all times—don't do or say anything before first considering whether or not it might violate a taboo. Not easy; at times, almost impossible.

Iron Tail crawled in beside her. They were naked. His body coming in contact with her own from shoulder to hip to foot sent a tingling sensation all through her. Her thoughts flew to John. Never did she feel so secure, so free of tension and concern, so safe as when he was beside her. Now he turned on his side, laying his forearm across her just under her breasts, setting his fingers lightly against her rib cage. Then he set her hand against his erection, curling her fingers around it. She squeezed it submissively. It got quickly huge, throbbing and as hard as a spike. Still he did not mount her. Didn't kiss her, didn't even brush his lips against her cheek. He had never kissed her, nor had Milk Eye. It was not their way.

He threw off the blanket. The walls of the tepee struck by the light of the torches outside glowed like a sunset. He pulled her arm, mutely demanding that she get on top of him. He positioned her so that she came slowly down on his member. He held her in his powerful grip and gyrated his pelvis before bucking himself up inside her. She drew a breath sharply at the slight pain. They began pumping—rather, he did.

She relinquished all command of her body, fleeing into the sanctuary of her mind. The tepee dissolved into the tent taken from the wagon and pitched by the tailgate. The cooking odors, Iron Tail's musky smell, the stench of smoke mingled with rotted food—all vanished. John had shaved as was his custom before retiring, and lightly powdered his face with some of her Tetlow's Swan's Down. It was her suggestion that he use it. She loved the fragrance; its subtlety went with his gentleness, his tenderness. He was both the most considerate and intuitive lover any woman could know.

The act itself was climax to lengthy foreplay and preceded afterplay just as long, so that they kept sleep at bay for hours as they enjoyed each other. Within the walls of the little tent, they made their way slowly to a paradise all their own creation. And back, when at last they separated. As they did, the same wish came to her mind that came every night: that it would stay the same forever. They would never grow older, never lose even a hint of the passion of their fulfillment.

And didn't it help that they always, invariably, awoke as they fell asleep? In each other's arms?

Iron Tail awoke her next morning. "Get up. Dress quickly. Someone is here to see you."

THIRTY-EIGHT

John Pryor had plunged into gloom from which it appeared he would never emerge. Captain Schmidt and his men were on their way back to Fort Randall, John and Lincoln Hammer returned to Wind Cave. They shared a bottle in Hammer's office. The Indian agent tried his utmost to be sympathetic but the realities of the situation were not lost on him, as they seemed to be on John.

The problem at the moment was that they couldn't agree on

what to do next. John's mounting desperation showed in his suggestion.

"We kidnap one or two and force them to tell us where they've taken them. Threaten to hang them!"

"That, John, is not only too farfetched to even discuss but think what it would do to my reputation among all the tribes? Think what Washington would think."

"I don't care."

"I'm afraid I must. Long after this is over I'll still be here trying to put out my fires."

John hurled down a second drink, turning his tumbler upside down to prevent Hammer's refilling it.

"You sit here knowing full well *they know where they are. Every mangy one down to the children.*"

"Perhaps."

"You know it!"

"Calm down!"

John had half risen from his chair. He settled back down after taking a huge breath. "Yes, yes, I'm sorry. I seem to forget you're on my side. What I don't understand is how they knew we were coming."

"They didn't know *when*, but Ottowa knew we'd show up eventually."

"He's the one we should grab!"

"We 'grab' nobody. You're aiming at the wrong target, John. We should be concentrating on where they've taken them. I've spread the word around town. It's possible that . . ."

He paused as the door opened and an Indian came in. He was in rags and stunk of stale whiskey. But Hammer greeted him like a beloved brother.

"Sun Toucher! What have you got, my friend?"

The newcomer answered him in some Indian language, if not Oglala. Whatever it was Hammer understood and responded in kind.

"He says that his cousin was out trapping beaver near Battle Creek and saw two Oglalas with a white woman."

"And child!"

"Shh."

"Where were they heading?"

"North."

"Where north?"

"How could he possibly know that? John, will you please calm down. There are any number of tribes up there: the Cheyenne, the Tetons, the Sans Arcs, the Blackfeet. There's just no way to tell how far they intended to take them."

"Can't we follow their trail?"

"What trail? They no doubt steered clear of any towns, settlements, or Indian camps until they got to where they're going."

Sun Toucher cut in. Hammer nodded, then nodded again. John fidgeted, squirming in his chair. It was like chasing a will-o'-the-wisp, getting close only to see it flit away.

"He says that his cousin saw the same two coming back without her."

"He means without *them*. When was that? How many days after?"

Hammer inquired. The man shook his head.

"His cousin didn't say."

"Where is his cousin now? He's the one we should be talking to. Where is he!" he asked Sun Toucher.

Hammer inquired. Sun Toucher responded at length.

"He says he headed south for the winter. He's a *ka-oh-ta-be*, a loner. A hermit, who lives by trapping and trading at posts all over."

"That's a huge help."

"It's a start, John, at least we know which direction they took them."

"Let's head north, make inquiries as we go along the way."

"It's an awfully big territory to cover. We could wander around till the first blizzard. I'll have to think about that."

"Don't think too long. Better yet, don't bother, I'll go alone." With this John turned the tumbler over and refilled it.

"Something else, John. He's not saying 'them,' he's saying 'her.' Your wife."

"They must have taken Mary with her . . ."

Hammer addressed Sun Toucher. He answered briefly.

"His cousin didn't mention a child."

"But they wouldn't separate mother and child. . . . What are you looking like that for?" John gasped. "You don't think something's happened to Mary?"

"I think you're absolutely right: They'd never separate them."

"Oh my God . . . !"

THIRTY-NINE

The flap of Iron Tail's tepee lifted, and in walked Jumping Bear. Jenny gasped and rushed to embrace him. Iron Tail looked on, his expression a mask of indifference.

"Would you please leave us?" she asked.

"This is my tepee . . ."

"Very well."

She took Jumping Bear by the arm and walked outside. Iron Tail followed but for some reason changed his mind and went off in the other direction. They waited till he was out of earshot. Around them squaws were stirring and feeding the cookfires; men, women, and children were relieving themselves, not even covering their excrement before walking away. She steered Jumping Bear toward the nearest edge of the camp. She was still having a hard time containing her excitement.

"How did you find me?"

"I was clever." He grinned and tapped his temple. "You would have been proud of me. Your escort came back and that night some of us finished a jug of whiskey."

"You got drunk."

Back came his grin. It was so good to see him; it was like an angel had dropped down unexpectedly. He went on.

"I knew Pawnee Killer would never tell where they took you, not even if he was tortured. But Four Hawks is not as tough. And he is stupid. I could hold a buffalo with my bare hands easier than he can keep a secret. Get him a little drunk and you can not stop his tongue. And being stupid makes it even looser. Still and all, he knows what Ottowa would do to him if he found out he spilled the stew."

"Which is why you had to be clever."

"I waited till we had finished the jug then got to talking with him. He and I always got along. I pretended I was curious. I asked how the trip was, the weather, if they ran into any Cheyenne, any whites. How you behaved. I asked if you tried to get away. He said no, because *he* warned you. I asked what you thought of the camp when you got there. He said you did not say but in your eyes you were impressed. I asked what you thought of the people. Again, you never said. I asked what you looked like when the chief he was giving you to came out of his tepee. He corrected me: sub-chief Cinta . . . He stopped and smirked and waved a finger under my nose. He said, 'You know I can not tell you. You can not trick me, do not try.' Then he walked away."

"Cinta . . ."

"Mazza. He was more careless than stupid. And he had no way of knowing that I know Cinta Mazza, Iron Tail. Although only by reputation. He is expert with the lance and a famous buffalo hunter. Hunters tell stories to their sons about his exploits. Cinta Mazza. What is funny is that even now Four Hawks has no idea he gave it away. I certainly did not tell him, I was very careful with my face. And I am sure he did not tell anyone else about our conversation."

"And here you are. Thank God you found me!"

His face darkened. "I am afraid it is just to visit. I . . . can not get you out of here, Jenny. For me to even try to trade for you would be unheard of. He is a sub-chief, I am nothing. It is a matter of . . ."

"Status, I understand. How long can you stay?"

"Not too long; I was not invited. I am nobody's guest."

"You're Iron Tail's. But you will come back?"

"Unless he tells me not to. He may."

"Oh." She stopped him and lowered her voice, despite there being no one near enough to overhear. "I belong to the Blackfeet now, right? Not the Oglalas. When I was down there you couldn't contact Fort Laramie or any other fort to tell them where I was. Ottowa would have had you killed."

"Yes."

"But the Blackfeet are different. You can go back and go down to Fort Laramie and tell them now." He thought about this, pushing his lower lip forward and bunching his forehead. "Ottowa would never find out. I'm never going back to him."

"What makes you think that after all this time your husband is still at Fort Laramie?"

"He doesn't have to be, but he must be somewhere in the area. Maybe the colonel there knows where. Even if he doesn't they'll still come and rescue me." He shook his head slowly. "What's the matter?"

"I want to help you, Jenny, you have to believe that. But for me to walk into Fort Laramie would be like rolling a small rock down a high mountain. It bounces along, catches a bigger rock, that catches an even bigger one and before long the whole side of the mountain is coming down. And I could end up buried alive."

He was right. The army would go after Milk Eye, arrest him, hang him.

But his followers would know who'd tipped over the stew. Jumping Bear's departure may have gone unnoticed but his absence could hardly be. When Jumping Bear was seen returning from the north somebody would put two and two together. She had no right to ask him to put his life on the line for her. Better she just drop it.

"Never mind," she said.

He had been standing shifting his weight from one foot to the other, his eyes downcast like a schoolboy called on the carpet. When she spoke he raised his head; their eyes met.

"I will do it," he said.

In that instant she realized he was in love with her. And he would do it, despite knowing it could cost him his life in the end. She'd be reunited with John and back on the Oregon Trail. He'd fill a traitor's grave.

"No."

"Jenny . . ."

"Just forget I asked." They walked in silence for a time. Down a tree trunk directly in front of them a pigmy nuthatch walked, its beady eyes enclosed by a dull gray cap. Fly, little fellow, fly to Fort Laramie, you tell them. . . . "There's something else, Jumping Bear, nothing to do with me. Something is going on around here. I think they're getting ready for war. I don't know whether it's to be against another tribe or some fort, but something's going on."

"What did you hear?"

"I don't understand a word of their language. I . . . wait . . ."

"What?"

"I did hear something that sounded suspiciously un-Indian."

"English?"

"I don't know. You tell me. Iron Tail was talking to Long Bull."

"Chief Long Bull."

"I should say Long Bull seemed to be lecturing him. They kept repeating the same two words. I couldn't help overhearing: They were standing just outside Iron Tail's tepee, I was lying down inside."

"What two words?"

"Sull and Lee. Could they be two names?"

"Neither one sounds Indian . . ."

"They don't, do they? Sull and Lee. Sull Lee."

"Sully."

"What's that?"

"Fort Sully. Down on the Little Missouri." He pointed in the general direction. "It is the fort closest to the Blackfeet. They would love to destroy it."

"You think they might be planning to? The two of them kept repeating it: Sully, Sully, Sully, Sully."

"They could be planning an attack. It would be a good time. They only have a few soldiers protecting the place. It is like that with most of the forts all over the territories. They are weak, the Blackfeet could overrun them, massacre them, burn the buildings."

"Who's the commander?"

"I do not know."

"He should be warned. Yes, yes, one of us should warn him!"

" 'One of us.' Meaning me. No thank you, Jenny."

"You'd be in no danger."

"Not if I do not come back here. But you would. Think about it. I come here. They ride to Fort Sully and the army is all ready for them. No surprise, their warriors are cut down by cannon before they can get close enough to use their few miserable rifles. Ask yourself this, who would warn them if not their white captive? Using her Oglala friend."

"You give them too much credit."

"You do not give them enough. And there is something else. I care about you. Very much. I love you."

"Please . . ."

"I have to say it. I mean it, I do love you. But not your people. I especially do not love your army. Why should I warn our enemies? Put yourself in my moccasins, Jenny." He paused and studied her. "You are disappointed. You hate me."

"Of course not!"

"I love you, but what you are asking . . ."

"All right, all right."

"You are angry."

"I'm not."

"Tell your face. Maybe it is best that I go."

He looked about. He was beginning to look decidedly uncomfortable. Did he regret coming?

"Will you be back?"

"If I can."

The way he said it, his expression, agreed that he would not. He probably didn't dare return. The woman he loved was fast becoming a threat to his very life. What made her think the moment she saw him that he'd come to rescue her? Even assist her in getting away? After all she'd been through, how could she still be so guileless? Blame desperation. Jumping Bear left within minutes. Iron Tail frowned him away. When his horse vanished he came over to her.

"Don't worry," she said, continuing to stare at the spot where Jumping Bear was last seen. "He's not coming back."

"Why did he come?"

"He's an old friend, he was worried about me."

"Was he? Or is Chief Ottowa. He can not have you back!"

"He doesn't want me. We never said two words about him."

"Then what *did* you talk about? Were you planning? For when he tries to rescue you?"

"Of course not!"

"If he does try, he will end up eating dirt. I will make him."
He sent his hand to his knife.

"You're boring."

"What is 'bor-ing'?"

"Forget it, I'm going for a walk."

"I will come with you."

"Alone."

"No! I am not stupid. I know what he has done for you. Tied
a horse for you somewhere out there."

"Has he?"

He pointed. "There, on the other side of Bull Creek behind
those trees."

"Good. You go find it, I'll go for a walk."

FORTY

Captain Oscar Schmidt snapped off his sharpest salute and settled himself slowly and gingerly into the chair Colonel Truscott
indicated.

"No sign of the woman, eh?" said Truscott.

"No, sir. Oh, she was there at one time, but not now. They
got her out just before we arrived."

"Pity." Using a small hand mirror, the colonel was trimming
his mustache with a pair of scissors fashioned to resemble
a peacock. Schmidt watched him snip and snip without
appearing to be cutting a single hair. "Any hint as to where they
took her?"

"None of them'll say. If they know. No surprise there. My
guess is that she's gone to another Sioux tribe."

"No doubt. Mr. Pryor must have been sorely disappointed."

"That's not the word, sir, he was like a crazy man. Only what could we do? I wasn't about to start wandering all over the territories searching . . ."

Truscott set down his mirror and scissors after checking his teeth in the glass, and swung around to face the captain. "There's one thing we might do: send a few men up to Fort Sully. Technically, the area in question is Nelson Galsworthy's bailiwick, not ours. Why don't you mount four men and run on up to Fort Sully? It's no more than a hundred miles: hop, skip and a jump. I'll bet you a bottle of good Scotch Nelson has gotten wind of something about a red-haired white captive."

Schmidt contained a sigh. "Why the devil didn't Hammer bring Pryor over there in the first place?"

"He explained why—Fort Sully's perilously low on manpower. Even if Nelson wanted to go out chasing he wouldn't be able to spare the men. While we, on the other hand . . ."

"With all due respect, sir, don't you think Mr. Hammer has already checked with Colonel Galsworthy, I mean since we were up there?"

"We can hardly assume that. And I do hate just backing out of the thing, leaving it unresolved. No matter how I write it up in the monthly report it'll sound like we tried, failed, and then sloughed it off. I'd hate like blazes to get my name in the newspapers as the officer who gave up the search for . . . what's her name?"

"Jenny Pryor."

"Understand, back East we have to look like we're doing a job out here. And retrieving Jenny Pryor strikes me as particularly ticklish and important. Human interest and all that. Apart from which it galls me to think any tribe has their filthy hands on a white woman, a wife and mother, at that. Yes, by all means pick some men and get on up to Sully. Report back as soon as you get wind of something helpful; anything."

"Yes, sir."

Schmidt got wearily to his feet, lifting himself with the arms of the chair.

"What's the matter, saddlesore?"

"A bit. Four hundred-odd miles in just over a week . . ."

"Hop, skip and a jump, Oscar. I once rode from here straight down to Department of Texas headquarters in San Antonio, over nine hundred miles, in less than ten days. Wore out six horses. You're a cavalryman, Oscar, an iron arse. Back up into the saddle with you and prove it!"

John Pryor and Lincoln Hammer got into a heated argument from which neither was able to extricate himself without leaving lasting bad feelings. Hammer resented John's ingratitude for all that he'd at least tried to do for him. Matters reached a pass where Hammer's resentment outstripped his sympathy for the man. John's frustration became near unendurable. He no longer spoke, he snapped. He didn't question Hammer's judgment as much as he criticized, even demeaned it. He could not understand why a territory, purportedly under the control of the army, was so unmanageable. So out of control. The government could not even keep telegraph wires intact in order to sustain communication between the various forts and trading posts.

The Indians were in charge. Hammer took this much too personally. He had long harbored his own fixed set of frustrations attending the job. And failure to rescue Jenny Pryor only added to them.

The two parted company glowering at each other. John rode north.

Upon leaving Zebediah W. Hornbecker on the road to Fort Sully, Reed Samuels and Wilton Benyus discussed at length the wisdom of locating the Oglala camp in the Black Hills and attempting to deal for Chief Ottowa's prize captive. They had no way of knowing that the woman's husband, the area Indian agent and the army had already descended on the camp, only to leave empty-handed.

Benyus nurtured an unremitting, abject fear of the Sioux. He compared them to the Kiowa and the Comanche in his native Texas, tribes he'd run up against more than once. He counted himself lucky to have gotten away with his scalp intact. His partner shared his reluctance to tangle with the Oglalas but Samuel's avaricious streak continued to vie with his intrinsic caution.

"A thousand bucks, maybe twice that. And probably no gunplay."

"How can you be so sure of that?" asked Benyus.

They had made camp for the night in the foothills, about fifteen miles west of tiny Hermosa.

"Zebediah didn't run into any, he would have said."

"Zebediah didn't try to deal for her. He ignored her like she was the plague. It'd be a whole different plate o' Mexican strawberries for us going in."

"You're forgetting something. They *want* to trade for her. And who better than us? Better than her husband, than the army, than just about anybody. We don't even know the woman, it'll be strictly business." Samuels nodded, adding emphasis to his assertion.

"You really think those Injuns'll just hand her over, knowing we'll be passing her on to her husband, who no doubt at this very minute is running around with the U.S. Army? Reed, them Injuns'd be petrified the soldier boys'll go running up into them hills and massacre 'em."

"There's a way around that. We just tell her husband when we hand her over that we got her someplace else," said Samuels.

Benyus snorted. "That's stupid; what does she do in the

meantime? Stand by and keep mum? Woman's got a tongue in her head, asshole. And she ain't about to let them Injuns off'n the hook."

"Who you calling asshole?"

"You don't see nobody else around here, do you? Reed, it's a hot potato. I say we stick to our original plan: look for Rudy Smollett and Willie Joe Meeks. Either one is worth twenty-five hunnert iff'n we catch 'em. I say we forget captives."

Benyus got out the packet of wanted dodgers and thumbed through them. "Here's Willie Joe. Last seen in the vicinity of Hayes. Which, if you remember, was where we was heading when we bumped into your friend."

"All right, all right. It just seemed to me a quick ride up into the hills could net us a quick profit. Fifteen stinking minutes palavering and . . ."

"Reed, Reed, Reed, just drop it. Tomorrow sunup we'll turn around and get back on our 'riginal route. To Hayes. And Willie Joe and whoever else might be holed up there that's in this bunch o' wanteds."

Iron Tail pushed into the tepee. Jenny had come in earlier to get out of the biting wind. The skies looked bruised, the few clouds rushed from north to south. They looked fat with snow. How much would fall, how cold it would get would be known by dark.

"We are going," said Iron Tail.

"Where?"

"Always questions."

"Tell me!"

He shrugged. "You will find out anyway. Fort Sully."

"You're taking *me* to Fort Sully? What for?"

"To trade with your people for you."

"Really!"

"That makes you happy? Good. Be happy."

His tone was taking on a sinister edge. What was going on? Why the sudden burst of charity? Were they really planning on trading for her or was it something else?

"What?" He stared inquiringly.

"Do you actually intend to trade me for horses, guns, or whatever?"

"Do you want to return to your people? Then shut up and start packing. Warm things and pemmican. Never mind water, there is plenty on the way."

"It's going to snow."

"So? You will not freeze."

"How long to get there?"

He pretended he didn't hear. He was through answering questions.

Mary dead. Killed somewhere along the way. And Jenny kept alive.

"Mary dead . . ."

John shook his head as if trying to rid his mind of the thought. She . . . was . . . dead. And Jenny alive, somewhere up ahead. He got down from his horse, stretched his aching body, and surveyed the land around him. He had no idea where he was. He had a compass, thrust into his hand at the last minute by Hammer. He'd been heading north as straight as fence wire, but what he really needed was a map. All that he knew for certain was that Wind Cave was about thirty hours behind him.

The air had turned bitter cold; the sun sent down no warmth, despite its brightness. And here he was, fumbling in the dark. To this point he had yet to encounter a single human, only two houses. Both were a mile or more distant, too far out of the way to detour to make inquiries. Too far off Jenny's trail for anyone to notice her passing.

The possible consequences of his rashness, leaving Wind Cave so ill-prepared, began taking on clarity. He had no idea where he was heading, no idea how far he'd have to go, where to begin making inquiries, how to deal with the Indians, didn't know two words of any of their languages. . . .

"Fool!"

He was that; it was far more likely he'd end up yielding his scalp and his life before getting within miles of where she was being held. One against an entire tribe? What he really needed was a miracle. Start with a little luck for a change: meet someone coming the other way, red or white, whom he could question. Someone who just may have spotted them heading north. Jenny's hair would help. And even if whoever he ran into hadn't actually seen them, perhaps he'd heard about them from someone else.

The only trouble with that was that people were so few and far between up here. It was too late in the year for trapping. The hardiest mountain men sat out the winter, but they were in the higher mountains to the west, not these hills.

He could be the only white man for thirty miles in any direction.

On plodded the horse. He glanced overhead. The sky was darkening, the few clouds accelerating, pushing south. The wind lanced his exposed flesh like sharpened steel. Tonight would be bitter cold. Would it snow? It was threatening to.

"Jenny, Jenny . . ."

No moon, no stars; night so dark it was like a robe. And very cold. Ottowa wrapped his blanket more tightly around himself and shifted his aching bones, starting arthritic pain in his joints. He leaned forward. Pawnee Killer and Four Hawks did likewise. Ottowa had summoned them to a perfectly round hill about a hundred yards from camp and within a few feet of where Flower Woman's corpse had been placed and covered with rocks.

"He will kill me if someone doesn't stop him," he murmured. "It is so, I saw it in a vision. And Wiyaka confirmed it, so it must be true. It could be a day, it could be a week, but he will do it. He blames me for his sister Wacawin's unfortunate death. It seethes in him like a fire reduced to embers that refuses to die. And it will be in him until he makes me eat dirt. Last night I woke out of a sound sleep with a sharp pain in my back. Here." He jabbed the area with his thumb. "I dreamt that he sneaked up behind me. He raised his knife . . ."

"He is the one who must eat dirt," said Four Hawks.

"I am not afraid of death, but is it not a terrible thing for an innocent man to give up his life to satisfy another's delusion?"

"We will stick close to you," said Pawnee Killer. "If he comes within four paces . . ."

"Oh, you must not kill him." The two stiffened and stared. "Not in front of everybody, not without . . . provocation."

"The threat to you is provocation," said Pawnee Killer. "It will be done away from the camp."

"Yes, yes, I should have thought of that. Maybe arrange it so that he vanishes into the air."

Four Hawks nodded. "Like Wacawin vanished."

"The same. I leave it up to you, my devoted friends. Oh, it feels good already to know such a great burden will come down off my shoulders. I will be freed of worry. To sleep without dreaming of a knife in my back . . ."

"We are pleased to help in this matter, great Chief," said Four Hawks. "It is an honor."

"A privilege," said Pawnee Killer.

"My honor, my privilege, to have such good and loyal friends." Ottowa yawned. "I must go back, I need sleep. There is no need for haste. Plan well before you deal with him. And be careful. He is clever, vigilant. At night is best, don't you think?"

They nodded.

"You two go on back, I will be along. First I must pay my respects to the bones and spirit of my poor dead wife." He shook his head sadly. "I miss her so."

He started away. Then came back. "I just had a thought, an idea for entrapping him. Listen to this . . ."

FORTY-ONE

The Blackfoot war party moved through the freezing cold, heading southeast toward their rendezvous with fate: three hundred warriors under Chiefs Long Bull, Red Wind, and Crane. They carried every weapon they possessed; they carried their shields and their medicine bundles for protection. And in their hearts they carried their hatred for the white trespassers—in particular for the monument to that presence: Fort Alfred Sully.

Jenny knew that she was to be a part of their plan to take the fort. What she didn't know was how her captors meant to use her. And Iron Tail refused to say. She didn't know how long it would take to get there. No one told her anything.

The warriors were relaxed, one and all in a buoyant mood. Why not? They were on their way to engage in their favorite pursuit. With her the pivotal factor in their strategy. Would she survive it? Could the defenders protect her? They'd see her red hair from two hundred yards away. Unfortunately, they might be too busy fighting for their lives to even think about heroics.

They stopped for the night by Rabbit Creek. Iron Tail left her to herself, preferring Long Bull's company and that of other warriors. He did leave her with a second blanket against the cold. After a meal of pemmican and creek water she wrapped up as close to the fire as she could and went to sleep.

They were mounted and on their way before sunup. And so it went for the next two days. They crossed Cherry Creek and forded the Cheyenne River, which ran low between its banks this time of year. Ahead lay the tiny settlement of Hayes. Hayes they would avoid. But, unbeknownst to any of them, and to Jenny as well, two white men were approaching it from the west.

"Holy Hannah!"

Reed Samuels pulled up sharply; Wilton Benyus did the same.

"Injuns," muttered Benyus and swallowed hard. "Hunnerts of 'em. What are they up to, do you think? Where they heading?"

"Looks to me like Fort Sully if they keep straight on the way they're going."

"Damn!" burst Benyus. "They sees us!"

"So what? We're no threat. What do they care? You don't see any slowing down, coming this way . . ."

Benyus continued to eye the Blackfoot horde, bunched like a herd of buffalo. "They're armed for trouble, all right. Look, some is carrying two quivers."

"They're fixing to attack Fort Sully for sure," said Samuels. "Let's just hang back here, let them pass. Not budge till they're out of sight.

Jumping Bear's conscience gnawed relentlessly as he headed south toward Wind Cave, the Black Hills beyond, and home. Try as he might, he could not dismiss Jenny from his thoughts. And the longer he dwelt on her, the more ashamed he grew.

He'd been so quick to dash every idea she came up with that might help free her. She'd accepted his reasons for refusing to get involved. Only his conscience was proving less accommodating than she'd been. Why shouldn't he help her? He loved her.

He thought back to Father Drummond, the orphanage, and his days under the Jesuit's tutelage: the long lectures on sin and redemption, on morality, on the importance of living in accord with Christ's teachings. He recalled the father's warning that when this life comes to an end, God calls everyone to His tribunal. There, one of three destinations for all eternity will be assigned: heaven, purgatory, or hell, depending on how one lives one's life.

Another of his warnings came to mind, that man could suffer no pain more excruciating than remorse of conscience. It allowed no peace day or night. He had no peace since leaving the Blackfoot camp, leaving her without any promise of help, because he feared for his own life. He could rationalize his reluctance until his brain cracked, but fear had made him hesitate.

Father Drummond also said that conscience tells us what is good, what is evil. It gives us joy when we do right, and remorse and sadness when we fail to do right. It speaks when we don't want it to and it cannot be stilled. It never wearies, it hammers away, like the tireless woodpecker hammers a tree.

Should he return? Should he not skirt Wind Cave but instead ride in and go straight to Hammer? The Indian agent would recognize him from the time he and Jenny's husband questioned him and Walks Alongside when they were cutting up the buffalo. Wind Cave, Hammer . . .

"Yes."

He heeled the horse, picking up the pace. Far ahead someone was coming, following as he was himself, this old trail north. The sky had broken, snow drifted lazily down: huge flakes and few. Just enough to announce winter's too early arrival.

They drew closer to each other. It was a white man. What was he doing up here? And by himself? Was he an Indian agent? Was it Hammer? Closer and closer they drew. Not Hammer, it was Pryor. Her husband!

"Man alive, do you see what I see?" burst Benyus.

Samuels gasped. "That's the reddest hair I've ever seen. It's her!"

"What are they taking her to Fort Sully for?"

"Who knows? But it's got to be her, Wilton. How many red-haired white woman captives can there be? Let's go . . ."

"Wait, wait, are you crazy? You're going to ride up to 'em bold as brass?"

"And deal. You bet. I'm sure not about to let them sashay right on by till they're out of sight. That red hair's a thousand bucks. Come on."

"I'm afraid, Reed, I purely hate and fear redskins."

"I don't particularly fancy getting close enough to them to smell 'em either, only this is a chance we can't miss. This is big money, man. Let me do the talking. Come on."

"I hate this," muttered Benyus.

Jenny had seen the two white men sitting their horses about a hundred yards off the trail to the right. She watched as they bolted forward. She held her breath; they wanted to talk to the chiefs! They'd seen her! Were they going to bargain for her release? She watched them ride boldly up to Long Bull, who was in full regalia, war bonnet and all, with fifty eagle feathers trailing down his back. No one stopped, no one even slowed as the two ambled along keeping pace, talking to the chief, gesturing. Then one pointed straight at her.

They *were* trying to bargain for her! And Long Bull seemed to be listening. Then he pulled out of the pack and held up his arm. He was shouting something. From where she and Iron Tail watched, their line of sight was partially obscured by a hundred or more warriors.

Now down came Long Bull's arm. Arrows flew from the tightly bunched warriors, thudding into the two white men's chests, toppling them both from their saddles. They lay in the dust. Long Bull got back into the pack, the Blackfeet moved on. Two warriors rode out, dismounted, speedily and skillfully scalped the two, collected their weapons, took their horses, and got back into the pack.

Just as Jenny and Iron Tail passed. She could not bring herself to look down at the corpses.

FORTY-TWO

The light snow persisted. John gasped, recognizing Jumping Bear immediately.

"I must talk to you, Pryor. I have seen your wife."

John's eyes saucered. "Where? Exactly!"

"A good way up. They took her up to the Blackfeet." John heeled his horse and started away. "Wait, wait . . ." Jumping Bear wheeled about and caught up with him. Great clouds of vapor issued from the nostrils of both horses. John's pinto pranced, eager to move on. "Do not go up there. They will kill you before you get within a hundred yards. Where are your troopers?"

"Gone back to Fort Randall. Hammer's back down in Wind Cave. You *know* Jenny?"

"We became friends when she was with us in the Black Hills."

"The Oglalas . . ."

"You can not go up alone. You must have help. Get twice as many troopers. The Blackfeet are much more numerous, more powerful than the Oglalas."

"You saw Jenny."

"And talked to her. Do not worry, she's well."

"Mary's dead."

"Mary? Your daughter. I'm afraid so."

"Ottowa again . . ."

"Yes. He ordered her . . . killed. And the other woman and her son. They tried to get away."

"Woman and son? The Larimers?"

"I do not remember their name."

"Good God, we all thought the bodies in one of the burned wagons were theirs. Nobody knew they took them along with Jenny and Mary."

"Let us talk as we ride. Back down to Wind Cave, to Hammer. You and he can handle it."

John eyed him questioningly. "Why are you helping us?"

"I told you, Jenny is my friend. I helped her all I could when she was with us in the Black Hills. I . . . just could not help her get away."

"Too dangerous."

"For me. I did not have the guts."

"She's alive, that's all that matters. Only it'll take days and days to get help up from Fort Randall again. Hammer and I'll have to ride back down."

"What about Fort Sully? It is closer. No, wait, they do not have any more men than at Fort Laramie. Not until reinforcements arrive."

"This is fantastic! Oh, what a relief to finally know. At least where she is and that she's safe and sound. She is safe and sound?"

"Yes. I think life is even better, easier for her with the Blackfeet than with Ottowa. It seemed so when I saw her."

"I'd love to keep on, get up there, see her, talk to her . . ."

"You would be foolish to try."

"I know, you're right. Let's go back."

FORTY-THREE

Colonel Nelson Galsworthy was by nature extremely high-strung. Anything that made him nervous set his hands shaking slightly. And many, many things made him nervous. He had commanded Fort Sully for nearly two years and in that time had weathered attacks by hostile Indians no fewer than seven times. But his success failed to ease his anxiety over his position: sitting short-manned, surrounded by enemies. Occasionally in his sleep, bad dreams assaulted him—dreams that saw a thousand howling savages armed with Spencers charging Fort Sully on all sides, torching the walls, breaching the gate, sending the defenders scurrying for cover from withering fire.

His nickname, Nervous Nellie, his reliance on Dr. Wilden's Quick Cure for Dyspepsia to calm his rebellious stomach, his penchant for pacing his office by the hour, could not, however, obscure the man's character. He was conscientious, he was able, he was courageous, although as a company commander in the War of Secession, he had seen little action.

He paced now. Captain Oscar Schmidt sat shifting his glance back and forth following the colonel's movement.

"Pacing relaxes me, Captain. Let me see if I understand you correctly. The woman was kidnapped from a wagon train near Fort Laramie. Taken to an Oglala camp in the Black Hills and moved elsewhere shortly before you and your men arrived there."

"Correct, sir."

"Now Virgil wants us to pick up the traces."

"What Colonel Truscott said was that you, being closer to the Black Hills, might have heard of a white woman captive . . ."

"Not a whisper. And we're not that close. I wish I could help."

"Maybe you can, sir."

"I don't see how. If it's men you want I simply don't have them to spare. You saw that when you rode in."

"Colonel Truscott's aware of that, sir."

"He has no such problem, I hear. He got a thousand reinforcements, was it?"

"Barely four hundred."

"Barely. I'd give my eyeteeth for half that."

"He, the colonel, is taking the situation very . . . personal," said Schmidt. "Which is why I'm here."

"Personal?"

"A white woman, sir, a wife and mother."

"Yes, yes, yes, yes, yes. Who wouldn't take such a sorry mess 'personal?' How many men did you bring with you?"

"Four."

"Judas Priest, you're a brave man to come all this way through Miniconjou country, just the four of you. Blue coats are like a red flag to a bull to the Sioux."

"Sir . . ."

A loud rapping rattled the door.

"In!" barked Galsworthy.

A sergeant burst in out of breath, disheveled-looking, the widened whites of his eyes filled with fear. "Colonel! Injuns! At the front gate! They want in!"

Captain Schmidt noticed Colonel Nelson Galsworthy's hands begin to tremble.

Long Bull and the other two chiefs had seen to it that Jenny was tightly surrounded by warriors long before the war party came within sight of the fort's lookouts; that her hair was completely covered; that the main body of their warriors, roughly four fifths of them, were dispersed to either side and commanded to wide-circle Fort Sully. The fort itself was a 270-foot square stockade, the palisade rising well over twenty feet, with blockhouse tow-

ers at the corners. The entrance gate looked about twenty feet
wide. Armed soldiers appeared high up along the interior walkway running the full width of the fort between towers.

The gate stood slightly open, sufficient to permit an officer—a colonel—to emerge with other officers and twelve men
with rifles. All stared stonily as Long Bull, affecting his most im-
perious manner, swaggered forward, with Iron Tail trailing to
act as his interpreter. Jenny could hear much better than she
could see.

The warriors tightly bunched around her edged even closer.
Now she could see nothing but their backs. For a time all was
silent. Then the wind rose and began to flap the flag atop its
pole on the parade ground inside. Long Bull spoke. Iron Tail
interpreted.

"This is Chief Long Bull, chief of the great Blackfoot nation."

"Tell your chief I am Colonel Nelson Galsworthy, commander of Fort Sully. Kindly have him state his business."

"Chief Long Bull's business is a woman. A white woman
brought to us by another tribe. We have come to return her, so
that she may rejoin her people."

"Tell your chief his gracious gesture is appreciated. Where
is this woman?"

"Here with us. Safe and unharmed."

"Tell your chief I would like to see her."

Iron Tail addressed Long Bull. The chief barked an order.
The warriors bunched directly in front of Jenny separated just
enough so that she could see the colonel and his men. Then,
just as quickly, they closed ranks. Long Bull resumed speaking.

"Chief Long Bull will exchange her for eight Spencer rifles
and five hundred loads of ammunition."

"Tell your chief that army regulations forbid trading
firearms for hostages. We will give him four fine horses. Or
food. Or one hundred new, sharp knives. His choice."

"Chief Long Bull wishes rifles in exchange for her. Right now. After which we leave. Six Spencer rifles and three hundred loads of ammunition."

"Tell your chief no rifles, no ammunition."

"Chief Long Bull wishes to enter Fort Sully and discuss this further. Until we can agree."

"Tell your chief no rifles," Galsworthy repeated.

"May we enter?" Iron Tail asked.

Overhead on the walkway at least forty men now looked down. How many men did the colonel have? How much ammunition? And did he know what he was doing? Jenny's heart raced. Galsworthy responded.

"Tell your chief that he and the other two chiefs are welcome to enter. And you, his interpreter, and the woman. No one else."

"Chief Long Bull wishes to remind the colonel that we have come in peace. Voluntarily. To turn over this woman. In a fair trade."

"Tell your chief we'll trade fairly but only the five of you can come in. We will talk, come to an agreement, you'll leave the woman and withdraw."

Long Bull, Red Wind, and Crane fell into spirited discussion. Jenny could hear them jabbering. Then Long Bull spoke to Iron Tail.

"Chief Long Bull will do as you desire. He, Chief Red Wind, Chief Crane, myself, and the woman will enter."

"Tell your chief it is agreed. Tell him that his warriors must stay where they are. Approach no closer."

"Chief Long Bull agrees."

Jenny watched the gate open slightly wider as the warriors around her again separated, permitting her to move forward. She whipped the piece of cloth from her head, threw it away, shook her hair and ran her fingers through it. Iron Tail came up to her.

"Do not speak. Not a word. This is between Long Bull and him."

"All right, all right."

He held her arm lightly as they entered following the three chiefs. Inside were nine buildings of various sizes stretching in a line laterally, all but concealing the rear palisade. The chiefs, Iron Tail, she, the colonel and his men, assembled about twenty feet inside the gate which, as everyone entered, was closed.

"Are you all right, my dear?" Galsworthy asked her.

"Yes."

"What's your name?"

"Jenny Pryor."

"You're sure you're not injured in any way?"

"No."

"Where did they get you? Who from?"

Long Bear interrupted. Iron Tail spoke.

"Chief Long Bear says we must come to an agreement."

"Yes, yes," said Galsworthy. "Only tell him to stop asking for rifles. It's out of the question. I repeat, we will trade for horses, food, or knives."

"Colonel," Jenny interrupted. "I must warn you. The warriors who came with us are not all out front. Most of them cut away . . ."

Gunfire and loud whooping stopped her. Bedlam erupted. In seconds the fort was overrun with howling savages. Caught by surprise, the soldiers manning the overhead walkway suddenly found themselves easy targets for the attackers. One by one they were picked off, dropping like grain sacks to the ground. Smoke and the stink of cordite filled the air as the firing increased all around Jenny. She cast about helplessly, deserted by Blackfeet and soldiers alike as everyone leaped into action.

She ran for the nearest building some thirty yards distant.

Arrows flew all around her. Fire arrows thumped into building after building. Bullets whizzed perilously close. Fear clutched her heart, setting it pounding. Reaching the door, she pushed inside. Then paused to look back. The parade ground was a battleground. The howling Blackfeet outnumbered the defenders five and six to one. The savages were already torching buildings and the palisade itself. The warriors left out front had broken in.

But how had the main body broken in at the rear? Was there a rear gate? Or had they hacked their way in with tomahawks? The fort was ancient, in need of complete rebuilding, the palisade looked rotted with age. She slammed the door just in time, an arrow thudding into it and rattling to rest.

She looked about. A single small window at the rear admitted enough light so that she could see. Running to it, she looked out. And saw where the attackers had broken through: a hole a good six feet in diameter.

She was in a storehouse: crates of rifles and boxes of ammunition were piled high. The magazine!

"Good God!"

Even as the dread possibility flashed through her mind, more arrows struck the building. Smoke came curling through a slit in the wall not far from the door. How much time would she have before fire blazed and began to consume the place? Back to the door she ran, wrenching it wide. The fighting was now at its peak. Fires blazed everywhere. An arrow whizzed over her head, shattering the window behind her. She slammed the door. Then noticed the ring in the middle of the plain board floor, in among rat droppings and dried gobs of mud left by boots.

She ran to it, threw herself to her knees, and grasped the ring with both hands, pulling with all her strength. Up came the trapdoor, releasing a rotten odor. Steps led down. She looked about for a candle. There was none.

The fire was now eating through the wall at the spot where she'd seen smoke curling in. Within seconds the place would be ablaze. She threw a last look at the stacks of ammunition boxes then began her descent into the dank and fetid blackness.

FORTY-FOUR

Jumping Bear was ill at ease standing by the hitching rail with John in front of Lincoln Hammer's office. It had finally stopped snowing, leaving less than three inches in Wind Cave. Further up the line, up to where the Oglala and John had met on the trail, as much as eight inches blanketed the desolate land. Hammer had come out.

"So they took her to the Blackfeet," he murmured. "Come inside, I've got a fire going and you two look stiff with the cold."

Down the street John saw that the tent bar had been taken down. Wind Cave looked even sleepier under snow than it had earlier, the few residents staying indoors close to their fires.

Jumping Bear and John stood warming their hands over the squat Oakdale Sunshine stove. Heat filled the little office to the four corners. John yawned.

"There's more snow coming," said Hammer, sitting and pouring three tumblers of whiskey from his jug. "Could be a blizzard."

John eyed him. "Would that be code for 'I'd rather not traipse all the way up there'?"

"I'd rather not. Does that make you feel better?"

Jumping Bear shifted his glance between them. Were they going to fight? John planted his reddened palms on the side of the desk and leaned close to the Indian agent. His tone was absent of any threat when he spoke but his expression was deadly serious.

"I don't care if there's six feet of snow on the ground. She's up there, I'm down here, the army's back at Fort Randall. Somehow we've all got to get together. Got to."

"There's one way," said Hammer, and drank.

Jumping Bear and John did likewise and both took chairs. Jumping Bear removed his moccasins and set his feet close to the stove, talking back over his shoulder when he spoke.

"You shouldn't have to go all the way back down to Fort Randall," he said to John.

"That's what I was getting to," said Hammer. "I can write a letter to Colonel Truscott, explain the situation, appeal to his sense of duty, ask for twenty men."

"Thirty," said John. "At least. Better yet, the sixty-five that came up last time."

"Maybe it's better I don't specify; leave it up to him."

"I'll go down to Randall."

"I'd think twice if I were you before committing to that. Look at you, you're so tired you can scarcely keep your eyes open. You've been practically living in the saddle for weeks. Four hundred-odd miles more could conceivably cripple you for life, if it doesn't kill you outright. Remember your remark about me getting drunk and the danger of falling off my horse? You could fall asleep and do the same. And here come the buzzards."

"I said I'm going."

This Hammer dismissed with both hands. "There's got to be a better way. Put Randall to one side for a minute. I know Chief Long Bull up there . . ."

"What sort is he?"

"Actually, he shares leadership with two other chiefs. What sort? He's devious, slick, he can lie with a straight face, I don't turn my back on him. But bad as he is he's a distinct cut above your friend Bloody Sky."

"At least he does not rape and murder his own people," said Jumping Bear. Both looked at him sharply. "Ottowa had one of his wives murdered. The two who did it were the ones who took Jenny up to the Blackfeet for him. I know them well."

Hammer studied Jumping Bear. "Would you consider accompanying us up there?" Jumping Bear sighed. "On second thought, it might be embarrassing for you. You marching in with two white men. Long Bull might wonder whose side you're on."

"No side. I would just like to see Jenny and you back together," he murmured, looking John's way.

John stopped a yawn, then laid a grateful hand on his shoulder.

"I'm willing to take a crack at it," said Hammer.

"Good. Great! When do we leave?"

"Day after tomorrow."

"Why not first thing tomorrow?"

Hammer grinned. "If I had a mirror here you'd see for yourself why. You need fifteen hours sleep and at least two one-pound steaks behind your buckle. And it makes sense to hold off for another reason: the weather. Cold we can take but another heavy snowfall added to what's already down could turn two days into a week."

"I hate putting it off even a day. I . . . I . . ."

It was as far as he got. His face tilted down, his eyes shuttered, he was snoring lightly. Hammer smirked.

"It's the heat, the booze, the exhaustion. There's a cot in the back. Help me with him."

FORTY-FIVE

Rats. As yet none had touched her, even crossed her foot, but she could hear them scurrying about and squeaking softly. It was very dark; she could hold her hand within an inch of her eyes and was still unable to see it.

She had no idea of the size of her hideout, nor what was stored there. More ammunition? Had she dropped down into a potential bomb? Fearful of the rats, she hesitated to explore, instead keeping to the relative safety of the steps.

It was damp as a tomb and the stink of feces and decaying bodies was overpowering. But the cellar did seem large enough to provide her with sufficient air, in spite of its foulness.

A rat brushed her left ankle. She squealed and kicked at it, heard it scamper clear. She despised rats as much as she did snakes; they were so filthy, flea-infested, diseased. She had descended all the way to the floor. Now she started to back up the steps, ascending until the top of her head touched the trapdoor. Turning and reached upward she raised it slightly. Smoke came pouring in and the sound of crackling flames was all around.

Then she remembered where she was! Down came the trapdoor. Just in time. The ammunition in the stacked boxes began detonating; it sounded like muffled firecrackers. Then quickly it became deafening even through the trapdoor, a single extended explosion that rocked the burning magazine and sent shock waves shooting down the steps, shaking them under her. Overhead, the din culminated in an ear-splitting explosion, so powerful it knocked her off the steps. She landed, picked herself up quickly, and started back up. On the third step her moccasin came down on something soft. The rat squealed and jumped off. Up the steps she rushed.

Lying with her back against them she waited for what seemed hours, listening to the faint sounds of the fighting all around her gradually diminish until all was silent. The air was beginning to stale when she started upward. Using both hands, she pushed open the trapdoor.

Night. Stars and moon. The explosion had leveled the magazine. Ashes no more than six inches in depth surrounded her. Wisps of smoke rose here and there. She ascended to the top step and looked about the fort. Every timber of the palisade on all four sides had been reduced to ashes; every building was leveled; even the flagpole had been consumed by fire. Not a soul was in sight, but bodies lay about. Some were completely blackened, others only partially. There were also a number of corpses strewn about in the open, untouched by the flames. Moonlight bathed the grisly scene. So eerie did it appear she could not suppress a shudder. Death hung in the air like morning mist and the only sound was the low moaning of the wind, until far away there came the deep, penetrating hoot—five, six, seven times—of a great horned owl.

The eulogy?

The attackers' fire arrows had leveled Fort Sully. She footed the charred remains of the flagpole; a piece a foot long crumbled and disintegrated. Curiously, every corpse she came upon was white. She spied a captain, scalped and with five arrows in his chest. One arrow had found the medals neatly rowed above the flap of his breast pocket. In one gloved hand he still held his blackened saber. Lying partially hidden under his hip was his opened wallet. The money had been taken. According to his I.D. card he was Captain Oscar Schmidt, permanently assigned to Fort Randall. What was he doing at Fort Sully?

Wandering about, she came upon a slightly singed knapsack shoved under a blackened beam. The beam was too heavy to move; freeing the knapsack took a great deal of tugging but she finally managed to extricate it. In it she found a quantity of hardtack wrapped in butcher's paper. It was light brown with tiny holes like the ones in soda crackers. It was also brittle. It tasted extremely dry but was edible and filling. There was also beef jerky, a slightly different shade of brown from the buffalo jerky the Blackfeet and Oglalas favored. She found coffee and even a quantity of brown sugar. Searching further, she found a pasteboard box of Sears Roebuck Parlor Matches. Most welcome of all was a brown paper sack containing a brand new set of long underwear. There were also three freshly laundered pairs of socks, as well as other useful items, all necessities in the field. She decided that she wouldn't need a canteen. What she desperately needed was a horse, but none was about. She continued to search until the sun came up, white and wan looking, sending no warmth down on the desolation.

She tried to ascertain the location of headquarters and the colonel's office, but so complete was the destruction it was impossible. She needed one other item for her knapsack before leaving. She searched and searched. It wasn't until the sun nearly reached the top of the bleak sky that she found what she was looking for in the belly drawer of a desk that had somehow escaped total immolation—about the only piece of furniture in the entire fort that had.

She found a map. It included both the Department of the Dakota and Department of the Platte. She easily found Fort Sully and to the southwest was the North Platte River. Across from it was Fort Laramie.

Without a ruler it was difficult matching the distance against the scale. She settled for a rough estimate of 500 miles. Probably further than that; since she was not a crow, she would not be flying.

FORTY-SIX

Jumping Bear returned to the camp, his conscience unburdened at last, his spirits raised. He would never have Jenny other than as a friend—and he would never see her again. But she'd finally be reunited with John.

Dismounting, he looked around for Walks Alongside, needing someone to tell. And Walks Alongside would be pleased to know that Real Woman's days with the tribes were coming to an end. Walks Alongside, however, was nowhere about, and no one seemed to know where he'd gotten to. Jumping Bear noticed also that neither Pawnee Killer nor Four Hawks was in camp. Could the three of them be together?

Inside his tepee he knelt by the dead embers of the fire, piled sticks and, using a bow drill, ignited a handful of dry grass which in turn set fire to the wood. The small flame immediately began chasing the bitter cold from his bones. Let an early blizzard strike, he wasn't going anywhere.

He thought about Pawnee Killer and Four Hawks: the inseparables. Chief Ottowa's hands and his knife. Jumping Bear did not doubt for a moment that the old man had assigned them to do away with Flower Woman. Didn't Walks Alongside realize it? Did he actually think that one day she'd return? If that were so, why didn't he go out looking for her? Now was he off in the hills with her two assassins? How had they talked him into going with them?

Pawnee Killer led the way, Four Hawks followed, Walks Alongside brought up the rear.

"It was by pure chance that we found your sister Wacawin's grave," said Pawnee Killer. "We had no idea she was buried up here."

"Like you, we both thought that she just went away, Icamanu," said Four Hawks.

Walks Alongside grunted. It was much colder out in the hills than in camp. It had snowed lightly earlier, little more than a dusting, but the sky held more snow.

Walks Alongside's impatience began to show itself. "Where is her grave?"

"Just a little further now," said Pawnee Killer. "If you want, we will help you get her body out and bring it back, so she can be buried properly."

"Her husband would want that," said Four Hawks. "She was always his favorite wife. It is around this hill and up the slope."

"How did you find her?" Walks Alongside asked.

"By all the small rocks piled up in the crevice," said Pawnee Killer. "We spotted it passing through here on the way back to camp. It stuck out like a smoke signal in a clear blue sky."

"Just like that," added Four Hawks. "It looked strange."

"Strange, yes," said Pawnee Killer. "Suspicious."

"And who do you think did it?" Walks Alongside asked.

Four Hawks considered the question. "Maybe a Cheyenne? Caught her, raped her, and killed her to quiet her screaming?"

"That is possible," said Pawnee Killer. He stopped, dismounted, and pointed ahead and to the left. "That crevice there."

The other two got down. Walks Alongside brushed by Pawnee Killer to look. "Let me see."

"Move the rocks," urged Four Hawks.

"I will. But first . . ." Walks Alongside turned, levered a cartridge into the chamber of his rifle, and fired, killing Four Hawks instantly. Fired again, killing Pawnee Killer before he could ready his own weapon.

"Maybe a Cheyenne?"

He looked around. About fifteen yards away to the east was a crevice resembling Flower Woman's grave, only larger. Big enough to hold two bodies. Covering them would be hard work and would probably take him until darkness fell. It would also be enjoyable and immensely satisfying.

Shortly before sundown the sky broke and snow fell. It was wet and began to make quickly. Jumping Bear was outside his tepee talking to two other warriors when a hunting party came riding in. They had been out after buffalo in the Belle Fourche River country. They had killed only two. They brought interesting news. All nine looked exhausted.

"We ran into Siksikas," announced one as the Oglalas gathered around them.

"What were they doing so far out of their territory?" Ottowa asked.

Jumping Bear thought of Jenny with Iron Tail. He called over one of the hunters, Hoka—Badger—whom he had known since boyhood. He was short—he only came up to Jumping Bear's shoulder—but was solidly built, very muscular. Jumping Bear once saw him break the handle of a tomahawk with his bare hands.

He yawned wearily as he came up.

"That is the last time I go out until spring," he muttered. "You were smart not to go. All we did was wander around and freeze our arses. And found only two old cows."

"I was away," said Jumping Bear. "I did not even know you went out. What is all this about Siksikas?"

"A war party. They attacked Fort Sully, destroyed it. Three hundred of them. They lost twenty-eight. We met them coming back, bringing back their dead."

"How did they get past the cannon?"

Hoka smirked and winked. "They tricked them. They had a white woman with them. They used her for a decoy." Jumping Bear held his breath. Hoka nodded. "You remember Real Woman. Ottowa sent her up to the Siksikas. They brought her to turn over to the army. And while they were bargaining for her with the colonel, the main body of warriors broke in the rear and overran the place."

"No!"

"Yes. Do not look so glum, my friend. What, are you wor-

ried about her? She is all right. No wounds, no pain." He chuckled. "She died with the rest."

"Who says?"

"She is dead, I tell you."

"They saw her body?"

"They massacred every blueback. And she was killed. She
was in the middle of the fighting. They left no one alive."

"They said . . ."

"You do not believe it?"

Jumping Bear's mind was suddenly whirling like a dust devil.

"She cannot have been killed . . ."

Hoka's little eyes brightened with understanding. "That is
right, you knew her. Well. You used to talk to her."

Jumping Bear didn't hear him. Her husband and Hammer
were planning to ride up to Bull Creek and the Blackfoot camp
to deal for her release. They'd be wasting their time, risking
their lives for nothing.

"They were sure she was killed?"

"How many times do I have to tell you? It was a massacre.
Not a single survivor. Any whites who were not shot, burned to
death. The Siksikas left nothing but rubble. I have to sleep. I
will see you tomorrow. Maybe not till the day after." He
laughed. "I am so tired I may not wake up until next week."

Far to the east of the Oglala camp and the Black Hills, it was
snowing lightly as Jenny started out. She had taken the time to
dress warmly, using Schmidt's gloves and his boots—the latter
fit perfectly over her moccasins. She found an undamaged pair
of wool trousers and a winter coat to put over her Blackfoot
buckskins. All she lacked was earmuffs, but in their place she
found a knitted muffler which she put on over her head and tied
under her chin.

The knapsack was heavy; when she tired it would become a

boulder on her back. But she hesitated to dispose of anything. For weapons she settled on two knives and a pistol, in preference to a much heavier rifle. The map she'd found showed a number of streams on her route to Fort Laramie, but only two rivers: the Little Missouri close by Fort Sully and, at the far end of her trek, the North Platte, running northeast of Fort Laramie. It could well be frozen solid by the time she reached it. Three hundred miles plus. Would she make it? She would, but she must spare her energy, and resist the temptation to press on so hard and so long only collapse would force her to quit. That was risky; she might find herself too weak to make a fire, and there was no way she could pass a whole night without warmth.

The sun had long since vanished; it was getting on to late afternoon. She estimated that she'd cover no more than seven or eight miles at most before dark. The sky had turned an odd gray color: darker than slate and with a hint of green. It looked ominous. To the north and west heavy black clouds tumbled and rolled, propelled by high winds.

Despite resolving to spare her energy she would love to keep going all night, just this first night. But that was out of the question. She'd stayed awake throughout the previous night. She hadn't even realized how long she picked through the rubble until the sun appeared on the horizon. Curiously, though, she didn't *feel* at all tired. She was going on nervous energy, of course.

She wished she had a compass, wished she'd had the presence of mind to look for one. As long as the terrain was fairly level she foresaw no problem. When it became hilly, which was much further on, she could easily lose her way, particularly without the sun's position to confirm her direction.

She shivered. Winter never came this abruptly to southern Ohio. Here there'd been no fall. Hot one day, cold the next—then freezing. And already snow. Soon, no doubt, the sun would give up altogether and go into hiding. She thought about John. To come face to face at last, embracing, tears of joy . . . then the pain erasing his smile when she told him about Mary, confessed her part in her death. Every word out of her mouth would wrench her heart like a fist pulling at it.

Would John be at Fort Laramie? If not, he had to be in the area—whoever was in command would know. They could send out a detachment to bring him in. He had to be out looking. He'd never give up. As long as there was the slightest hope, as long as no one could offer concrete proof that she'd been killed, he'd keep searching. He'd never give up.

A dangerous business, though, and he'd need help, preferably 200 troopers. If only he'd gotten after the Oglalas sooner, he'd have caught up with her long before Milk Eye sent her away. But the raiders were very fast, riding in, overwhelming the wagon train, fleeing with her, Mary, and the Larimers all in a few minutes. And taking all the horses. No wonder he didn't get after them. She could think of a round dozen reasons why he and the army had failed to locate her since.

But now the worst was over . . . at least, was on the way to being over.

The snow came down all the way to Wind Cave. By the time Jumping Bear rode into town nearly five inches had accumulated on top of the earlier fall. He made straight for the brick building, hitching his horse and rushing toward the door. Someone must be around who'd seen them leave. He had to find out approximately when.

Inside, he hurried down the narrow hall to Hammer's door. Nobody was about. Could someone be in the office? He knocked.

"Who is it?" Hammer called.

Jumping Bear's heart leaped. Why should he be surprised

that they hadn't left in this weather? He quickly sobered. He'd have to tell John earlier than he'd anticipated. The door opened. It was Hammer. John sat in a chair behind him, holding onto the arms. He looked fidgety, about to jump up, anxious to get moving.

"Jumping Bear!" he exclaimed.

"What brings you back?" Hammer asked.

"I am glad I caught you . . ."

Jumping Bear entered, pulled off his gloves, held his hands at the stove.

Hammer grinned. "You didn't think we'd leave in this? They say it's coming down in barrels up the way."

"It'll stop soon," said John. "It better . . ."

"There is no sense going, John," said Jumping Bear.

He explained, relaying what Hoka had told him, his detailed description of what Fort Sully looked like when the war party left there. As he went on he watched the color gradually drain from John's face. Hammer, too, appeared shaken by the news. Jumping Bear finished. There was a trenchant pause; he looked from one to the other.

"I don't believe it," murmured John. "I have to see her body."

"They said she was . . . burned."

"*They* said. That's not good enough!" He was up and pacing. "It can't end like this!"

"John . . ." began Hammer.

"It can't! She survived so much." He sank back into the chair and buried his face in his hands. "Mary murdered. Now this. It's not true, it's not . . ." He raised his eyes, fastening them on Jumping Bear. His suffering dulled them.

"I am . . . sorry," said Jumping Bear.

John shook his head, lowering it, propping his forehead with one hand.

"I appreciate your riding all the way up here."

"She was my friend."

"*Was* . . . Bloody Sky." He hammered the arm of the chair. "He's to blame for everything!"

Night. Still snowing in the Black Hills. Ottowa slept, snoring lustily. Around him his wives slept. The entrance flap lifted. A face peered in. A warrior came stealthily in, padding up to the chief. He raised his rifle, holding it stock high, inching the muzzle down to the chief's mouth . . . the cold metal touched his lips . . . Ottowa could not even get his eyes fully open before the intruder fired.

FORTY-SEVEN

Chief Ottowa's wives screamed in chorus; within seconds, the entire camp was roused. But not until Walks Alongside was up on his waiting horse and galloping into the hills, heading for the Wyoming border.

Jenny fed the fire, wrapped herself up in her overcoat and two blankets, and lay down. She had come upon a lonely grove of boxelder interspersed with a few willows near a stream. It looked to be the best concealment available on the barren prairie, where different species of grass dominated and trees were notably few. The canopies of the trees trapped much of the persisting snowfall, permitting her to get a fire going without too much difficulty. Lying close to it, warming her back while her face absorbed the chill air, she pictured herself awakening in the morning to find two feet of snow blanketing the land. Realistically, she held out little hope that anyone would find her before she found Fort Laramie.

To the northwest the Black Hills rose, some to 3,000 feet, in the shadow of Harney's Peak, which was more than double that height. She avoided looking at them. She didn't know if Indians hunted during snow season but common sense cautioned that some might. She decided that before she stopped for the night she would take time to locate the best hiding place she could. There was simply no avoiding many of the risks that went along with traveling so great a distance through hostile country.

Her hand felt the pistol under the blankets and coat. Its presence was reassuring, although she'd never even picked up any firearm before this one—unlike Sarah Larimer, whose husband had taught her how to use both pistols and rifles.

Poor Sarah, poor Willis, poor Mary . . . poor her, if she didn't make it.

Over the next two days, she got her legs, her stamina increased and so did her optimism. The snow had stopped shortly after she fell asleep in the grove, depositing only about three inches to add to what had fallen previously. The skies continued bleak, the wind blew tirelessly, drying the snow and flinging it about. Time after time, she had to raise both arms to ward it off. On she plodded until early afternoon of the fourth day. Then, within minutes, the temperature began noticeably rising. It went up sharply—at least twenty degrees within the hour. The sun emerged and, for the first time since leaving the Blackfoot camp, she could feel its warmth against her cheeks. The snow began melting. It became slushy underfoot. She thanked the Lord for Schmidt's boots as she sloshed along.

Then thunderheads as black as a starless night appeared ahead. They were rimmed with white and changed shape swiftly, as if invisible giant hands were molding them. It began to rain.

For less than ten minutes it poured. It was ice cold but not frozen, and fell straight down. Again and again she wrung out her muffler.

She could see no cover for miles in any direction. Everything got soaked through. Her overcoat felt as if fifteen pounds had been added to its weight. It hung dripping, pulling at her shoulders. She began shivering. Removing the coat, she wrung it out as well as she could before slipping it back on. It still hung heavily and the dampness made its way through her buckskins, through the long underwear, into her body.

Still she sloshed along, her pace measurably slowed by the deep slush. She had rolled up both blankets upon arising that morning and tied them over the top and down the sides of her knapsack. With no protection from the downpour, they, too, had become sodden and heavy.

Still, she had no choice but to keep on. She crossed her fingers that the freezing cold would not return, but shortly before sundown back it came. The temperature plunged, the trail became slippery, and her coat became as stiff as planking. So stiff that she worried she might fall and crack it.

She felt utterly miserable, her spirits dashed, her optimism sent packing. She sighed. What she'd give to strip naked in front of a roaring fire, wrap up in a cozy comforter and sleep till the chill wracking her from her shoulders to her feet left her. She was slipping and sliding more often now, battling to keep her balance. It was exhausting and ahead she could see no place where she might pass the night in at least partial protection. Not a tree was in sight, no houses, no barns, no structures of any type. Not even rocks where she could possibly find a fissure large enough to crawl into to get out of the wind.

And the wind was up. It turned bitter cold and blew almost continuously. There'd be no fire tonight; it would be impossible to build one out in the open. She was mulling this over when she slipped and fell. She turned her ankle but only slightly, there was no pain. She sat looking about. A membrane of ice enveloped the world, a crystalline skin that slowed her hourly progress. Distance, the barren landscape, and the weather had joined to conspire against her. To reach Fort Laramie, to be reunited with John, she would have to endure. Whatever happened she'd have to keep going till dark. Stop, eat, lay out her stiffened blankets one atop the other on the ice, bundle up in her frozen coat, and try to sleep. . . .

And before sleep came, pray that no Indians would pass her way during the night . . . pray that she'd awaken in the morning . . . pray that she would not freeze to death.

FORTY-EIGHT

John had long since departed Wind Cave to head south. He vowed—"as God is my witness"—to find the Oglala camp and kill Bloody Sky, unaware that Walks Alongside had already done it for him. But time in the saddle and the gradual easing of his anger combined to change his thinking. He ended up following Hammer's advice: heading west, avoiding the Black Hills entirely, eventually to cut south. He followed the crude map the Indian agent had drawn for him.

Riding down the plain he pictured himself finding the camp, asking for Jumping Bear. They would talk privately. But for all the Oglala's sympathy for Jenny, for all his willingness to help in rescuing her, John could scarcely expect him to join in executing the chief. And he wouldn't be able to bring it off alone, not in their very midst. Thinking about it as objectively as he could, it amounted to risking his life for vengeance. Forget Bloody Sky, forget all Indians, Indian agents, colonels, and troopers, get back down to Fort Laramie and hole up for the winter. When the ice broke in the North Platte and the first wagon train came along, he would join it and get back on the Oregon Trail.

Both Jenny and Mary dead. . . . Instead of continuing on, should he go back to Cincinnati? He couldn't. It offered only the past; the years to come had to be in Oregon. Why *not* keep on alone? Jenny would have approved, and there was something cowardly about giving up on it because there was no one left to share his dream. All that had happened, bad as it was, really had no effect on the dream.

The next morning he came upon the vast open area where he, Hammer, and Schmidt and his men had questioned the buffalo hunters—where he'd first met Jumping Bear. A thin covering of snow stretched as far as he could see. The snow's arrival provided one service to anyone traveling the plains—it kept the dust down. And the sun wasn't burning him to a crisp while he lived skinned in sweat day in and day out.

From Wind Cave to Fort Laramie was roughly 225 miles, according to Hammer. Having crossed over into Wyoming, he'd be coming upon any number of settlements along the way; places where he could hang his hat for the night and buy a drink and a bed.

Snow fell intermittantly but there was no real threat of a blizzard. Hammer had warned him when they said good-bye to avoid getting caught between towns when a blizzard threatened, for if his horse gave out, he'd be doomed. He missed Hammer. They'd had heated arguments. Thinking back on their relationship, they'd seen eye to eye on very little. And the man's weakness for alcohol bordered on disgusting. But, like Jumping Bear, he had a good heart. He was conscientious, he was helpful, he was honest; he didn't paint rosy pictures in order to ease John's pain. And he was there when John most needed him. Their failure to rescue Jenny wasn't his fault.

He patted the horse affectionately. He dreaded to think of

trying to cover such a distance on foot out in the open like this at this time of year.

He missed Jenny. Now, knowing she was dead at last, his view of the situation changed drastically. Up until Jumping Bear's disclosure of what had happened at Fort Sully there had been hope; there was the possibility, however slender, that their luck would change for the better; there was even the chance of a miracle. And there were the periodic reports of her whereabouts that confirmed she was still alive.

Now there was nothing. What hurt as much as her death was the fact that she'd survived so long, survived so much so bravely, only to have it end like this. In a way she'd have been better off, as would Mary, if they'd been killed in the attack, along with the Foleys and the others. It would at least have saved her from suffering, from false hope, from unanswered prayers.

So many wagon trains had passed through since 1841, the first year of emigrations—nearly 300,000 souls. Casualties were many, more than a few trains had been massacred by hostiles—but accident and disease, not Indians, were the worst killers. And comparatively few women and children were kidnapped.

"Why Jenny? Why Mary?" he shouted. "Why?"

The wind howled answer.

No more snow, no rain, the temperature locked below freezing. Midday and Jenny kept on, hoping and praying that she might soon see a house with smoke issuing from the chimney. Just one night under a roof in the warmth of a fire would restore her.

Before nightfall she came upon an abandoned ranch. The corral fence was kindling, the house had been burned to the ground, but for some unknown reason, the Indians had left the barn standing, although so many planks were missing from the sides, so many shingles from the roof, that the wind poured through it. Inside it smelled musty but there were no rats, no evidence of any varmints. Scattered about the floor were rusty tools, among them a spade which she used as a crowbar. She removed planks from the rear wall and used them to patch up one corner at the front. She broke up additional planks to make a fire on the dirt floor. She painstakingly warmed one article of clothing at a time, melting the ice in the fibers and drying her trousers, coat, buckskins and everything else. The overcoat actually felt cozy when she put it back on. She also restored both blankets so that she could wrap herself in them over the coat when she slept. And the pemmican took on a pleasing flavor when warmed.

She fed the fire before turning in. She had broken up one last board removed from the back wall and was laying a piece of it in the flames when it began to snow. It came drifting slowly down through the holes in the roof, a few flakes hissing as they landed in the fire. Looking upward, watching the snow descend, she wished she could repair the roof directly above her corner but there were only two holes, and they were small.

One other hole did worry her. Nearly the entire lower panel of one of the two doors had rotted away, leaving only the framing to support the upper portion. In rushed the wind, passing her and the fire in the corner on its way to the rear of the barn. The wind didn't worry her—she was more concerned about possible two- and four-legged intruders.

The warmth of the fire, combined with her exhaustion, brought sleep within seconds after she lay down. She didn't even have two minutes to think about John, as she usually did. She slept soundly and without dreaming.

It was still dark out when something woke her . . . not a sound—a presence. Someone or something was standing close. She raised to a sitting position, and gasped. In front of her stood three staring wolves, eyes gleaming evilly, tongues lolling. One bared his teeth and a low growl issued from his throat. They stood so still they looked carved. Her heart tightened with fear as she swallowed. She could see that they sensed her fear. In the next instant they would leap and begin tearing at her face.

She had removed her pistol before lying down, setting it on top of the knapsack a few feet to her right. She berated herself silently; *if you're fortunate enough to have a pistol, you keep it close at hand when you lie down.* She measured the distance. It would take her at least three, possibly four steps to get to it. She could dive for it, but any sudden movement and they would surely attack. To her left the fire glowed. Four pieces of the last board she'd broken up lay beside it. Slowly filling her lungs, her gaze shifting from one wolf to the next, she held her breath and sent her left hand inching toward the wood. Seizing the nearest piece, with a slight movement of her wrist she set the end of it in the embers. It flared up almost immediately, causing the wolves to raise their muzzles and back off a step.

She began waving the torch, simultaneously rising to her knees. She got to her feet, the blankets slipping from her and heaping around her ankles.

"Hi-eeeeee!"

The wolves started, retreating, racing out the hole in the door. She dove for the pistol, righted herself, and, cocking it, followed slowly, warily.

Outside only their tracks heading off into the darkness could be seen. Would they be back?

Food was hard to come by in this weather. Did wolves eat humans? Doubtless they ate anything if they were starving. She had no way of knowing the time, but she'd had all the sleep she was going to get this night. She turned to refueling the fire, to keep warm until sunup. It wasn't until then that she realized it had stopped snowing.

For how long?

FORTY-NINE

It had snowed heavily around Fort Laramie, and as John approached the front gate, slowing to talk to the guards, the skies threatened an additional fall. As expected, Colonel Thomas Moonlight was gone. Neither man knew where. His replacement, according to the older of the two guards, was a Major Orson Roebling: "a underfed pipsqueak with peach fuzz on his cheeks, a voice like a whistle and a Adam's apple that he can't hold still nohow."

John glanced at his wagon, the bonnet capped with snow. He hoped his oxen were under cover and healthy, being fed regularly, as Moonlight had promised. He stood staring at the wagon. It looked old beyond its years, worn out getting them this far. Would it make the more than 900 miles still to go? Not in this weather. In the spring, hopefully. Of course, he could always swap it with a few dollars for one in better condition at Fort Hall, up the line in Idaho.

He walked over to the front, eyeing the seat, far enough under the bonnet so that no snow landed on it. He envisioned Jenny, Mary, and himself sharing it—singing or just talking, covered up against the burning sun, against torrential rains, the wind and the dust assaulting them. Braving it all to send the miles out from under the wheels, climb the mountains, ford the streams and rivers, and eventually make it to Oregon.

Traveling alone would be lonesome, even hooking on with another wagon train. With no one to share the seat, no one to talk to, he'd get to thinking too much—about the two of them. About what might have been.

"Can I help you?"

Major Roebling waved and beckoned him over. John introduced himself. The major's smile darkened. He knew. Everyone must know. The major took him into Moonlight's office. It was unchanged from the last time he saw it, a hundred years ago. Roebling was young and looked as if he wasn't old enough to shave but he was no "underfed pipsqueak," although his voice was unusually high-pitched and his Adam's apple had yet to stop moving.

"Thomas Moonlight told me all about your situation. I'm sorry you weren't able to find your wife and daughter."

"They're both dead."

Roebling gasped. "How dreadful for you. I'm so sorry. I wish there were something . . . Ahem, may I offer you a cigar? How about a drink?" John declined both. "What are your plans now? Will you be going back to . . ."

"Cincinnati? No. There's nothing to go back to. When the first wagon train comes through in June I'll join it, although hanging around until that late in the season seems a waste of time."

"You'd be wise to wait, however. Safety in numbers and all that. I hear the country gets rougher and rougher the further you get up the Oregon Trail."

"Mmmmm."

"You're welcome to stay here the rest of the winter, of course. It's the least we can do."

"Thank you. Are my oxen being cared for?"

"Oh, yes. They're in with the horses. We'll fatten them up till you leave."

Abruptly, John's grief rose in his throat, momentarily blocking it. He felt suddenly devastated. It was, he told himself, a delayed reaction. He'd had so much to occupy him since Wind Cave and Jumping Bear's disclosure of Jenny's death in the fire. He'd been on the move almost continuously since then. The enormity of the tragedy had not hit him, not fully. Now it did.

Concern seized Roebling's boyish features. "You're white as a sheet. Are you ill?"

"Can I have that drink now?"

"Of course."

The whiskey was bitter and too fiery going down. It reminded him of Lincoln Hammer's Buffalo Gap jug whiskey.

"Feeling better?" Roebling asked.

"I'm fine," he lied. "Just run down, I guess, from so little sleep."

"What you need is a hot meal and twelve hours. Let's get you over to the mess hall. We had turkey last night, I'm sure there's some left." He refilled John's glass. "One more, to hold you till you tuck in your napkin."

"You're very kind. May I ask where Colonel Moonlight was transferred to?"

"Oh, he retired. Two weeks ago. Gone back to Minnesota."

"Did he get his promotion?"

Roebling shook his head. "Unfortunately, no. Shall we go?"

For seven more days Jenny walked southwest through freezing rain, bitter cold, and no fewer than four snowstorms, all of which were of mercifully short duration. By the third day of traveling after leaving Fort Sully, she felt as if she were gaining strength and stamina. At the time she attributed it to nervous energy. Now, approaching the end of her second week, she was beginning to feel a weariness that even a decent night's sleep failed to dispel entirely. It invaded her whole being. She struggled to keep going. The knapsack grew heavier daily. Her posture suffered. Time and again, she had to catch herself and straighten. She pictured herself looking like an old man slogging along minus his cane: head well forward of his body, shoulders forward, his back with a pronounced curve, his gait discouragingly slow.

She reckoned, estimating conservatively, that she had yet to pass the hundred-mile mark—she blamed the weather. At this rate, she could be ten weeks or more getting to Fort Laramie. Her body simply couldn't stand such prolonged abuse.

She had to find a horse!

The day dawned clearly and cooperatively mild; the wind rested, at least for the present. The sun rose, if not warm, at least the color the sun ought to be—not as white as it had been the past few days. She set forth and walked until the sun was halfway up its morning path. Then some helpful instinct alerted her, suggesting she turn and look back. Far down the road a black shape smudged the lower edge of the sky. As she stood watching it out from under one gloved hand, it began shifting slightly. Gradually, it grew larger and assumed shape.

A farm wagon! Closer and closer it drew, pulled by two draft horses, one black, one bay, vapor issuing from their nostrils. They tossed their heads, the breeze tossed their manes. Their step was high, they pulled effortlessly. Up on the spring seat bouncing lightly, dressed entirely in black, the floppy brim of his hat bending up and down, sat a big, raw-boned, middle-aged man. His face was red, his long brown beard trailed off behind him, the ends of his mustache flattened against his cheeks. Jenny stood aside as he drove up.

"Whoa, whoa, whoa, whoa, whoa . . ."

"Good morning."

"Good morning yourself, Missy. What in thunderation are you doing out here in the middle of the back of beyond walking by your lonesome?"

"I'm on my way to Fort Laramie."

"Fort Laramie! You got some way to go . . ."

"Could I ride with you as far as you're going?"

"You're more'n welcome to. I'd enjoy the company. I'm on my way home to Cottonwood." He sent down a hand the size of a small shovel, helping her up. The seat was unpadded, and as hard as plate steel, but once they got going the two-leaf springs under each end would absorb the bumps and she'd get quickly used to it.

Much more importantly, she was off her feet!

"You're an answered prayer, Mr. . . ."

"Woods. Elmer." He tipped his hat.

"Jenny Pryor."

"Heyyyyy-yup!"

Reins slapped flanks and away they went. She looked around. The wagon bed was filled with loose hay, a single bale, and three sacks of what she took to be oats.

The team pulled with little exertion, as if the wagon were as light as a fly. Elmer besieged her with questions. Where had she come from? How long had she been on the road? Questions, questions. She told him briefly what had happened and described her travels since her capture, detailing only her experiences at Fort Sully, the attack, the fire, and her departure. Then changed the subject.

"And you're going home."

"Can't wait to get there. Been away a month. Up to Manila. At my brother's. Our daddy died and we had to settle the will. There was lots to do. But I never meant to stay away that long. I sure do miss my Elsie and our three boys: Cleland, Wesley, and Donald. My boys are the biggest, strongest youngsters you ever saw—like young bulls. Wesley's got arms like tree trunks. Donald can lift two ninety-pound cast iron anvils over his head, one in each hand, like you'd lift your bonnet to put on. Strapping, handsome fellows. And their mother's a beauty. She's twelve years younger than me. I'm fifty-two, I don't look it, do I? How old are you?"

"I'll be twenty next week."

"Oh my, just a child. But you're married and you're going back to your husband. Isn't that nice? And the two of you'll go on to Oregon."

"I think. Elmer, how far from Cottonwood to Fort Laramie?"

"A long way—almost four hundred miles."

"Oh dear . . ."

She got out the map, spreading it on her lap. "Here's Fort Sully. And down here's Fort Laramie. I measured it, it's over five hundred. I've been on the road nearly two weeks and haven't even reached the hundred-mile mark. It's so discouraging."

"Well, now you're able to leave off shanks' mare for a while you'll make lots better time. At least Cottonwood will get you over the first hump, your first hundred miles. That's one thing we've got no shortage of out here: distance. Let's see your map." He indicated. "You see here? You'll be crossing the border, cutting off the corner of Nebraska, skirting hills right here, just above Harrison. Then you cross over into Wyoming and make a beeline on down."

Discouragement had taken firm hold. "You make it sound like a Sunday stroll."

"Oh, I'm sure we can find you a horse in Cottonwood."

"Really?"

"Depend on it. And you'd make it even without one—you come this far and you're still going strong. You got gumption, Jenny Pryor, you're like my Elsie. She's got gumption to burn. And blessed the boys with it, too."

On and on he went about his family, raving about each member individually. He was beginning to bore her, he repeated himself so often. And despite his warmth and friendliness there was something strange about him. She couldn't put her finger on it, but it made her uneasy.

"Cleland's the reader in the family. Always got his nose in a book. My brother's got a wooden leg. Lost his leg in an accident mishandling his shotgun. Fool."

Jenny's glance strayed to Elmer's own weapon in its leather boot attached to the seat on his side.

"Have you seen any Indians?" she asked.

"Not one—wouldn't expect to. This time of year they stick close to their fires, except the ones out chasing buffalo. Donald's been sick. We thought it was the pneumonia but it turned out just a bad cold. I had a sister but she died. She was only nine, can you imagine?"

And Mary was seven. . . . As the afternoon wore on, his talk became more and more disjointed. He jumped from one subject to another like a frog; his eyes were strange, too. Oh well, it would only be for the one night. She'd sleep with pistol in hand under her coat. And they'd get to Cottonwood sometime tomorrow and part company.

The horizon was slicing the sun perfectly in half when he pulled to the side of the road. "You can sleep in the wagon tonight if you like. The hay'll be warm. It makes *me* sneeze. I'll just curl up on the seat, like I usually do." He looked overhead, staring for what seemed at least two full minutes before lowering his eyes and smiling. Quite strange . . . eerie. Her hand slid slowly across her middle until it came in contact with the pistol underneath. If he noticed he gave no sign.

"Sky's clear," he said. "No more snow, not tonight. But it's on the way, I can feel it. You live out here long as I have, you get a sense of snow, you know? Tomorrow late, maybe. Would you mind fetching some of those oats back there for the horses? I'll start a fire, melt some snow for water for them."

She got down and made her way down the side of the wagon to the tailgate. The sides were almost twice the height of emigrants' wagons. She had to climb over the tailgate into the bed to get to the nearest bag of oats. There was only a water bucket up front under the seat. Elmer was busy making a fire. She felt around in the hay for a bucket for the oats. And touched something . . . not a bucket. She knelt and cleared away the hay. It was large, wrapped in a piece of dirty canvas and with a rope tied tightly around it. She cleared more hay from the end of the thing . . . and gasped. A face. The flesh had a distinct bluish cast. The eyes gaped, the tongue protruded.

She looked forward. She'd have to get to her feet to see

Elmer. Instead, she undid the middle button of her coat. He had climbed back up onto the seat and stood facing her—staring, grinning maniacally, his eyes wild.

He threw back his head and roared with laughter. It was so loud it startled the horses. They jerked, nearly upsetting him. Holding onto the back of the seat with one hand, he reached for his rifle in the boot. Out came her pistol. Two-handing it, she aimed, fired. He gawked. His hand stopped. He pulled his hand slowly back and set it against his chest. Blood seeped through his fingers. He stared questioningly down at it, then back up at her.

And down he fell.

FIFTY

The fall had broken Elmer's neck. His head lay to one side awkwardly. But it was the shot that had killed him. The first shot Jenny had ever fired, and it had killed a human being. The fact that it did so before he killed her somehow didn't seem important. She'd taken a life.

Standing staring down at him, her pounding heart gradually slowing, her trembling finally ceasing, she could see more madness in his eyes dead than when he was alive. Taking hold of his ankles, she pulled him out from under the wagon and to the side of the road, leaving him temporarily to return to the tailgate. She climbed into the bed. She finished uncovering the corpse. And, as she expected, found three other corpses. The woman was about forty, the three men in their late teens, early twenties. All were wrapped in canvas and bound around their chests and legs. All had been strangled or hanged. All still had the ropes around their necks. Uncovering the woman she took one look, her stomach rebelled loudly and she vomited over the side. When she was done searching she covered up all four corpses again.

She had a hard time dragging Elmer's body down to the rear of the wagon. It was even harder standing him up, leaning him against the back. She'd never be able to lift him, dead weight, over the tailgate. She lowered it, set his shoulderblades against the edge of the bed and tried lifting both legs. But he had to weigh close to 200 pounds, and she couldn't get his feet more than a few inches off the ground before his body buckled and down he fell. Night was coming on when she gave it up, dragged him to the side of the road, and left him face down.

As she did so, panting with exertion, leaning against the wagon to catch her breath, it occurred to her that somebody might come along, find him, continue on, and catch up with her. His death she could explain, but what about his family? The whole situation was suddenly getting too sticky too fast. Somehow, she had to get him into the wagon and under the hay with the others.

She made a fire and ate, hoping to reinvigorate herself. She analyzed the problem. If she only had a board to lay him on, lift the end, and slide him into the bed the way corpses were slid off planks and buried at sea. It wasn't just his weight that prevented her from lifting him, it was her inability to keep him from doubling in the middle.

Inspiration! The plank she so desperately needed was right in front of her! She searched the tool box under the seat and found a screwdriver and small wrench. The tailgate hung from the rear by two plates, each boasting four small bolts. At the top of each plate a rod ran through the width of the bed. It permitted the gate to be freely raised and lowered. The bolts were rusty but she finally managed to remove all eight, taking off the nuts and poking the bolts out with the screwdriver.

It was dark by the time she was done. She lay the gate vertically at an angle against the edge of the bed, lay Elmer's corpse against it and lifting the foot, slid him into the bed. She then covered him with hay and placed the tailgate in alongside him. Before setting out in the morning she'd restore it to the plates. Her hand went to her chest as she caught her breath. Something was missing. What?

Her locket with Mary's silhouette! When had she lost it? She recalled having it coming down from the Blackfoot camp. Running toward the door to the magazine she'd covered it with her hand to keep it from flying about.

She must have lost it in the cellar. Running up and down the steps, kicking away rats, holding her breath during the explosions overhead—the final one knocking her off the steps. The chain had broken and the locket had slipped off; she'd never even felt it. She'd preserved it throughout her ordeal, right up to the attack . . . only to lose it. How very sad.

FIFTY-ONE

John awoke from a dream. He saw Jenny, whip in hand, driving a surrey. She had on a polka-dot summer dress and matching bonnet. She flicked the whip over the horse and it sprinted ahead. He saw himself standing on the sidewalk watching her pass. She waved and batted her eyes coquettishly, laughing gaily. He waved back. Up the street she flew, coming to a stop at the corner. Traffic was light, she had no difficulty turning around and coming back. She pulled up in front of him and gestured for him to take the seat beside her. He climbed up. She flicked the whip . . . the horse started off. Faster and faster it ran until he felt it leave the ground, flying. He looked down. The wheels were slowing . . . stopping . . . the street dropped and dropped. They were thirty feet in the air. Into the sunset they flew, Jenny laughing spiritedly, he hanging onto the grab rail with one hand and his hat with the other.

What did it mean? Jenny insisted that every dream had a meaning. What did riding in a surrey together, leaving the ground, leaving earth and flying off signify? Freedom? Like the freedom to drop Cincinnati and run off to Oregon?

A knock sounded.

"Yes?"

"Mr. Pryor, Major Roebling would like you to join him for breakfast in the officers' mess."

"Thanks. Tell him five minutes."

He hurriedly washed and dressed. At the mirror he ran a hand down his cheek. Shaving would take five minutes and his five were already almost up. He settled for scrubbing his face and neck a second time and running a comb through his hair.

Roebling looked as if he'd been up all night. He confessed to having been up and working almost two hours. John got the impression that the major averaged about five hours sleep a night. He was at least bringing conscientiousness to his new command. He was eating oatmeal. John requested the same and poured coffee from the tin pitcher.

"I had an interesting conversation with two Sioux about half an hour ago. As I'm sure you've noticed, the ones who live around here pitch their tepees near the outbuildings and we let them in the gate to trade with the enlisted men. Helps to smooth the waters. I was on my way out with Lieutenant Frasier when I overheard them telling some of the enlisted men about the Blackfoot attack on Fort Sully."

"Where my wife was killed."

"I know. I mean, *if* she actually was."

"What are you saying?"

"Now don't get excited. This may be the wildest hearsay

imaginable, but the two I talked to claim to have heard that a bunch of Miniconjous camped not far from Sully picked through the rubble a couple days after."

"And?"

"One Miniconjou found something interesting. It seems that in the attack the magazine blew up. All that was left was the floor. But there was a trapdoor. It was still in one piece, undisturbed by the blast. I imagine the Miniconjous descended the steps looking for guns and ammunition. Who knows? Guess what this particular one found?"

"Major, stop it! Spit it out!"

"I apologize, you're absolutely right. Brace yourself, John: The fellow found a heart-shaped locket with a silhouette of a little girl inside." John gasped. "He was wearing it, so those two say. Showing the silhouette to everybody."

"It's Mary! Jenny never took that locket off . . ."

"I figure that in all the uproar, running around as she must have, the chain broke. John, your wife was in that cellar under the magazine."

"They found her body . . ."

"No, no, no. That's the whole point. There was no body. Don't worry, I asked. Only the locket—evidence that she'd hidden there during the fighting. Don't you see what this means?"

"She could have survived down there!"

"I think she did. She must have. Obviously, no one would bother to take her body out of there. I think she climbed out under her own power. Probably the next morning. I bet she wandered about, put together a winter outfit, and left. The question is, where?"

"For here! Where else?"

"But it's over five hundred miles from Fort Sully . . ."

"I don't care if it's five thousand. She's on her way here, I tell you! She is! God in heaven, she is!"

*   *   *

Jenny had a decision to make. Would she be better off dispens-
ing with the wagon, riding one of the horses while pulling the
other along behind her? The first day or two would be torture
riding without a saddle of some type—even a high-pommel,
high-back Indian woman's saddle. But there was another reason to keep the wagon: The bodies should be brought in so that
they could be properly buried. It seemed the least she could do
for the poor souls. Even mad Elmer deserved a Christian bur-
ial. This in turn brought another concern: Would they keep?
Was it cold enough to prevent their rotting?

She shuddered . . . then smiled. What a sight she'd
be, entering the gates of Fort Laramie dressed half-army,
half-Indian, and driving a wagonload of corpses! At that, her
whole experience would have been hilarious, had it not been
so nerve-wracking. The myriad dangerous situations aside,
the travel alone had taken its toll—two hundred-odd miles
up to the Oglala camp, another hundred up to the Blackfeet,
two hundred plus down to Fort Sully, five hundred to Fort
Laramie.

Over a thousand miles. Almost as far as from Fort Laramie
to the Willamette Valley in Oregon! Which prompted a firm
decision. Once she and John got to Oregon and built their
home, she wouldn't travel more than two miles in any direction
for the next ten years at least!

Would John be at Fort Laramie? He'd realize that if she did
escape, she'd head straight there. Again she pictured his expression when they came face to face. The first few seconds
would be priceless: the staring, the hearts hammering, relief and
joy pouring over them both. Indescribable. Heavenly!

Only then he would ask about Mary and she'd have to tell
him what she'd done.

"Oh, John . . ."

* * *

Major Orson Roebling insisted that John borrow his personal buggy to go out and meet Jenny. As if she were four miles up the way.

"She'll be exhausted, in no condition to ride a horse. She can't have gotten more than a hundred miles from Fort Sully."

"On foot, I'm sure."

"Please take the buggy. It's upholstered, the top's leather, it has roll-down side curtains if you run into a blizzard. Think of her, John."

"I'll take it. Thank you."

"You'll also need an escort. I'd like to give you a whole troop but I'm afraid . . ."

"I know, you can't spare a man."

They stood outside Roebling's office at eight in the morning. Overhead, the flag flapped loudly. Immense black clouds sped eastward. The heaviest snows of the young season threatened. The snow that had blanketed the bonnet of John's wagon had melted. By spring, the canvas would be rotted from the cycle of freezing and melting.

"I can give you a couple of men, John, volunteers. Most likely you won't run into any hostiles this time of year, but just in case . . ."

Two guns added to his own would hardly intimidate a horde of well-armed buffalo hunters, but John discreetly hesitated to mention this. The major was trying to help. He'd already done a better job of it than Thomas Moonlight.

"You've saved her life, Orson."

Roebling blushed furiously. "Not really. She's in no great danger on the way here."

"Maybe not from savages, but she could be from the weather. If the snow holds off we should be able to cover sixty to seventy miles a day, catch up with her in a week, possibly less. She *is* shortening the distance herself."

"I'm sure."

"Walking. Good God . . ."

"She's a trooper, your wife. You've every reason to be pleased and proud." He clapped a friendly hand to John's upper arm. "Before I forget it, don't stint on blankets when you pack. Take more than enough, and a couple of buffalo robes to boot. Firewood'll be scarce out there."

"We can bring some."

"Keep in mind you'll be at least a week getting to her and another getting back here. That's not taking blizzards into consideration . . ."

John smiled grimly. "Plural?"

Roebling was studying the sky. "We'll get the one up there before sun-down. I'm from Maine, I know winter."

"We'll see . . ."

Jenny couldn't get the Woods family out of her mind. Why had Elmer killed them? Of course he was mad as a March hare, but what actually had driven him over the edge? Why kill so brutally? And how had he worked it? Had he brained all four in their sleep, then strangled them? Hanged them? In the few hours they'd been together he hadn't quoted the Bible; he was no religious fanatic, prepared to justify the most heinous crime with scriptural example. He rambled but he wasn't incoherent. Just too many blue devils resident in his troubled mind, too many and too powerful to control.

Where was he heading with their bodies? And had he planned to add her to their number the moment he laid eyes on her? He'd sent her back to get a bucketful of oats. He knew the buckets weren't under the seat as he claimed, that she'd have to search through the hay. He had known she couldn't help but make her grisly discovery. Then, too, he was reaching for his rifle when she shot him.

"Self-defense."

It sounded more an excuse than justification. Her first shot ever, and one dead. She thought back. She could have killed Milk Eye, even Iron Tail . . . possibly Flower Woman, if she'd pushed her much further.

She glanced back. No part of any one of the bodies could be seen. It was getting late, getting to time to pull off the road, build a fire, tend to the horses, eat, bed down for the night. Where? Not in the wagon bed! Maybe under it, in the event the skies broke during the night.

Even as she decided, it started to snow.

FIFTY-TWO

The wind blew furiously, driving fine particles of choking, blinding snow in icy clouds. It had shifted over the past hour and was now coming from the northwest, the source of all blizzards in the central plains. Before the wind roused itself, an enormous coal-black cloud had lowered. The land beneath lay silent, expectant, bracing for the onslaught. John drove the buggy following the two troopers assigned by Major Roebling. Both had wrapped their faces in mufflers. John felt sorry for the horses. How much of this cold could they take before giving up? They lacked his incentive: his fierce determination to keep on however bad it got, knowing that Jenny was doing the same coming the other way.

The biggest problem was the distance separating them. And in conditions like this, they or she could too easily wander off the road. The wind grew stronger, raging, forcing the blizzard sideways. It came from the left and at a sharp angle.

In minutes, John's horse became covered with snow. As the

snow blew off, more replaced it. The horse slowed to half its gait. Drifts materialized on both sides of the way, then in the road itself. The troopers had little difficulty getting around the obstructions, but the buggy was light—less than 500 pounds, counting John's 175—and the wind toyed roughly with it. While getting off the road and back on, it nearly toppled. From the way the horse was beginning to behave it was clear that it wanted out of the shafts, wanted to run, get away from the monster.

They couldn't see ten yards ahead. The snow billowed down. The wind howled continuously and so loudly his mittened hand found his left ear to block out the sound. He hesitated to roll down the side curtains for fear of increasing the possibility of the wind bowling the buggy over, and likely shattering one or more wheels. He carried no spares. He'd have to mount the horse and ride bareback. The pile of blankets and the buffalo robes covered by a tarpaulin in the rear bed, along with all their food, would have to be abandoned.

Scouring his memory for comparisons, John thought that this had to be the worst blizzard he had ever experienced. And it had to be here and now, and up ahead Jenny was surely caught in it. It appeared to test the limits of the sky. It was as if the snows of the next ten winters had all gathered over the plains and were now descending.

The wind struck again, tilting the buggy. For an instant it balanced on its two right-side wheels, teetering, deciding whether to fall over or settle back on all four wheels. John held his breath and stiffened, debating whether he should jump out or not. The horse, sensing impending trouble behind it, had stopped. Back settled the buggy. The horse went on, catching up to the troopers who hadn't even noticed what happened. One turned in his saddle and shouted back to John, but the wind caught his words and carried them away. Again he shouted, but it was useless. He came back.

"This is really rough on the horses, Mr. Pryor . . ."

"What do you suggest we do?"

The other man came back and joined them. Their horses looked frozen. Standing, hoofing the ground, tossing their heads in resentment, sending up clouds of vapor which the wind dissipated immediately, they shivered with the cold.

"We could stop at the next big drift and pull off behind it," said the first trooper. "At least get out of this fucking wind."

"This fucking wind don't respect drifts, George," said the second man. "Look up there."

He indicated a drift only a few yards away. They could barely distinguish it. It was less than five feet tall, but even as they watched, the wind attacked its summit and in seconds reduced it to half its size.

"I say we keep going," said John.

"We're not making headway worth a shit," said George.

"Maybe we'll spot a house or barn, even just a shed," Louis replied. He was older than George, longer in service, and seemed to take his partner's impatience in stride. Looking for any type building, however, was absurd. If anything, visibility was shrinking. They decided to keep going. John cracked his whip over the horse. It refused to budge. He struck its flank; it whinnied and sprang forward, breaking into a trot. But almost immediately it slowed to an amble, then a walk. So they went on for the next few minutes. And the howling wind became more furious and it snowed and snowed and snowed. . . .

FIFTY-THREE

The wind sang and danced with the snow in celebration, and a biting and invasive cold found the marrow in Jenny's bones. She got under the wagon to sleep, but the bully wind came after her, flinging snow at her face.

She dreaded morning. She worried so, sleep refused to come. The horses stood unprotected, shifting position occasionally to keep their tails to the wind, and neighing plaintive objection to the onslaught. Would they freeze to death?

She arose to find them lying on their sides, their legs rigidly protruding from under nearly a foot of new snow. During the night, the wind had filled the wagon and raked the top perfectly level. Snow continued falling, although not as heavily as when she had crawled under the wagon. Now, at least, she could see nearly two hundred yards in every direction.

See the white-hidden land as flat as a board. It looked so beautiful and so treacherous, and the riveting silence was eerie. She could not see a single tree, no buildings of any type, nothing but glaring, pristine whiteness supporting the horizon and here and there snow devils whirling briefly like maddened dervishes.

She tried to kindle a small fire using wood from the box Elmer had packed with fuel. A small fire so as not burn the bottom of the bed. But she could not light a fire, the wind was too strong.

She crouched, the top of her head nudging the wagon bottom, staring at the wood which she'd stacked like a tepee. Then a powerful gust scattered it. It was symbolic: her hopes raised, only to be knocked down. She duck-waddled out from under the wagon.

Horses, corpses, Elmer's rifle, the wagon—everything save her knapsack would have to be abandoned. Shielding her eyes from the descending snow, she squinted skyward. Was it brighter than the day before, or did she imagine it? The wind amplified the cold, jarring her teeth, shrinking her extremities in their sleeves of flesh, stealing her breath when it struck her face, freezing her tears, bringing a numbness to her ears.

She couldn't squat like a toad under the wagon all morning: Without moving, she'd freeze to death. She had to keep her blood circulating, keep up her body temperature. Adjusting her knapsack, checking to make sure she hadn't dropped her pistol, she eyed the wagon bed.

"Good-bye Elmer, Elsie, Cleland, Wesley, Donald. I'm sorry to shirk my responsibility but, under the circumstances, I'm sure you understand."

One hand against the side of the wagon, she deliberated. Should she get back under, put her back to the wind and pray that it would all end before she froze to death . . . or strike out, search for some kind of cover, something better than under the wagon? If she stayed, it could be all over before noon. If she left, she at least had a chance.

She started out, sinking up over her knees with every labored step, shading her eyes from the rapidly increasing glare, looking for shallow spots between drifts. Fear set adrenaline churning, lending her energy, but it would not last. She felt as if she were dragging a sled piled with anvils. The lack of hot food the past two weeks began to tell. On and on she plodded, turning now and then to look back at the wagon and the horses' legs still visible, to see how far she'd come.

She struggled forward, her upper eyelids pushed downward. She tried to raise them. Give this up, she warned herself, turn around, go back. Smash the wagon to pieces with the rifle. The wind was letting up; she could try to start a fire again.

"Yes!"

A big fire. Huge! Somebody would see the smoke. The snow was letting up as well; fewer and fewer flakes lazed down, spared the wind's pummeling. She turned around.

But as she started back her legs became heavy. She stopped to catch her breath. Dizziness struck, setting her mind spinning; she fought it off. Stand, rest a bit, then try.

She was so tired, sleepy. The sensation came in a warm wave, dispelling the cold, enveloping her. Her exposed flesh came alive, myriad tiny needles poking, pricking. The wind gusted and pushed her over. She lay on her side in fetal position. Snow flew against her face; the muffler slipped away, exposing her cheeks.

Summoning her will, fighting off the mounting yearning to sleep, she sucked in a freezing breath that stabbed her throat, and tried to get up. She could not. The mental effort by itself was exhausting. Drowsiness came swirling in, knitting a thick drape, spreading over her, tucking in around her whirling mind. It felt as if her body were emptying, hollowing, changing into a vessel. Warm slush poured in. It filled her limbs and her torso, and ascended her throat.

She wanted to yawn but could not find the strength to open her mouth even a crack. She wanted to sleep . . . sleep . . .

It came. Sweet, welcome, warm sleep.

═══════════ FIFTY-FOUR ═══════════

Within less than an hour the wind died, the skies cleared, the sun emerged, and the temperature began to rise. John could never remember seeing such an abrupt change in the weather. The gray overhead fled and the sun began melting the snow.

The thaw persisted and three days later, bare brown spots began showing. John, George, and Louis had stopped for the night and were sitting around the fire.

"How far do you think we've come?" John asked.

Louis consulted the map. "We're out of Nebraska. Kyle, right there, is no more than ten or fifteen miles ahead."

"We made some goddamned great time before the storm hit and since," said George, biting a chaw off his plug and grinding away at it. "We got to be pushing three hundred miles."

"I'd say so," said Louis to John.

"A day, two at the most, and we'll meet her," said John.

He managed a tight smile. The troopers exchanged looks. He noticed. Louis cleared his throat embarrassedly.

"It was pretty rough, sir."

"So? Jenny's intelligent, she can see a storm coming. Certainly in time to get under cover."

Sitting with his knees drawn up, Louis studied the toes of his boots.

"If she could find any. Coming down from Fort Sully there's no more than a handful of houses until you get to Cottonwood. It's all the savages' hunting grounds. Few folks dare to build."

"Oh shit, Louis," rasped George. "You heard the man, his wife's not stupid."

"Let's turn in," said John.

"It's not even eight o'clock yet," protested George.

"Turn in early, get up early," said John. "Bear with me, boys, indulge me." He scanned the heavens. No sign of another storm. The stars looked frozen, brittle. "Two days. Less . . ."

"Jesus saves all." The sampler was done in red on a white background. One corner of its wooden frame was becoming unglued. It hung against the log wall. Jenny blinked. Sampler and wall vanished, then came back.

"Awake at last?"

She lay on a heap of goose down, so it felt, a comforter snugged under her chin, her head against a small cloud of a pillow. She had on a nightgown too large for her. The face before her wore mail-order spectacles above fat cheeks and over eyes glowing with warmth and kindliness.

"Where . . . ?"

"I'm Elizabeth Hornbecker, my dear. This is my home. I live here with my son, when he's not gallivanting about the territories, hobnobbing with Indians. Don't speak, it can wait. Here . . ."

She brought up a steaming bowl of soup and began spoon-

ing it into Jenny. It was chicken. It was delicious, if a trifle hot.
Elizabeth blew on each spoonful. Jenny ate her fill.

"Let it settle. You'll start getting your strength back. It's a
miracle you didn't catch double pneumonia."

"How did I get here?"

"My son found you. Zebediah!"

"Coming," said a voice from the other room.

"I'm Jenny Pryor."

"Pleased to meet you, Jenny."

Jenny looked around. The bedroom was tiny, the furniture
crammed into it, but like the bed it was cozy. Snow layered the
outside windowsill like a white rabbit stretched across it sleeping. Outside it was clear, the sun was out. A man came in. Jenny
gasped.

"You . . ."

"Zebediah W. Hornbecker at your service. You remember . . ."

"From the Oglalas' camp."

"The same. Before anything else I do owe you an apology
for that. For looking right through you. I . . . sort of had to."

"I know."

"I wanted to finish doing business and get out of there with
my scalp intact."

"Of course. But how . . . ?"

"Do you come to be here, in Maw's bed? I found you. That
simple. Sheer luck. One of my burros got out of the barn. Pure
carelessness on my part. I came away from feeding the three of
them and failed to latch the door properly. The burro broke its
tether and came wandering out. I went to bring them water later
on and imagine my surprise.

"I went out looking. It was still snowing. Blinding . . ."

"It came down like I've never seen it," said Elizabeth. "And
we've been here going on thirteen years."

"How did your horse get through the drifts?"

Elizabeth beamed. "Oh, he didn't take Emmaline."

"I did like the Indians do," said Zebediah. He held up a finger, excused himself, left, and returned with snowshoes: rawhide webbing attached to a round frame with straps at the toes and insteps. "The deeper the snow, the easier getting around."

"Did you find your burro?"

"Dead and buried under a drift. Then I found you. I thought *you* were dead."

"I feel asleep . . ."

"You did. You looked frozen stiff. Like the two horses near that farm wagon."

She told them what had happened, beginning with Fort Sully, to her meeting Elmer Woods on the road, to his death, and the blizzard. Recounting it tired her. She covered a yawn.

"That'll do for now," said Elizabeth. "I'll warm up what's left of the soup, get it down you, and then you go back to sleep."

"I'm fine, really."

"Doctor's orders," said Zebediah. "So you were heading for Fort Laramie. That's a long, long way."

"I know."

"Let her sleep," said Elizabeth. "You go on back to your catalogs."

He withdrew.

"When winter gets real bad he comes home and does his homework. Gets all his spring ordering ready. He's a trader, mostly with the tribes. Of course you know, you met before." She smoothed the hair away from Jenny's forehead. "You're sweating, that's a good sign. Such lovely red hair. However did you keep it living among the Indians? You'd rather not talk about it. Relax, rest, we'll save the soup for when you wake up."

"I don't remember a thing."

"You were unconscious when he found you."

"Wait. One thing. I must have opened my eyes for a split second just as he was bringing me into the house. I saw the front, the stone chimney, the roof, the white frame around the door."

"Please. Back to sleep."

She fell asleep before Elizabeth reached the door.

John's buggy threw a wheel, but he managed to stop before tilting downward and possibly damaging the axle. The troopers collected the wheel, also undamaged, and restored it. All three searched for ten minutes before locating the decorative knob that had fallen off when the cotter pin snapped. George broke a tine off his mess kit fork, replaced the cotter pin, and affixed the knob. It was about one in the afternoon, the weather continuing fair, the sky cloudless, when John pulled up.

"What's that up ahead?"

The troopers in front of him, conversing animatedly, paused and looked forward. Then sprinted away. John followed.

"It's a box brake farm wagon," exclaimed George.

They got down to inspect it.

"Their horses gave out," said Louis indicating.

"That isn't all that gave out," said John, leaning over the tailgate.

"Jesus, Mary, and Joseph," murmured George and crossed himself. "All wrapped up for Christmas, it looks like."

"This one isn't," said John.

George furrowed his brow and spat. "Somebody had to have been driving. They must have left."

"There's no footprints leading away," said Louis.

"Because the snow's so melted," said John. He pulled the rifle from its boot. "And nobody's been along since or they surely would have taken this, if nothing else."

"Do you suppose whoever was driving made it to that grove of trees we passed?" George asked.

John didn't answer. When the trooper began repeating what he'd said, John silenced him with his upraised hand.

"Let's think a minute. Whoever was driving was heading toward Fort Laramie."

"There's a lot of settlements between here and there," said George. He gawked. "You think your wife was driving? This thing all the way from Fort Sully? What would they be doing with a farm wagon at Fort Sully?"

"I don't think it came from there. This one with the beard; he's the only one not wrapped in canvas. He's been shot."

"You think your wife shot him?"

"It could be. She wouldn't have left Fort Sully without arming herself. There had to be some weapons the Blackfeet overlooked. She started out on foot and somewhere up the line this one picked her up. All this hay was dry back then and covered these bodies. Snow fell into the bed, matted the hay, exposing them . . ."

"So what happened to her?" asked George. John shook his head. "You think she wandered off in the storm and died, froze to death?"

"Shut up, George," growled Louis.

"If she headed down the road in the blizzard there's no way she would have made it to that house. It's much too far." John shook his head.

"Shall we have a look around, sir?" asked Louis.

"Definitely. She wouldn't go back the way she came, wouldn't go to either side, she had to go forward. We would have passed her. Damn, I wish there were footprints . . ."

"If we got here yesterday," said George, "there woulda' been a few left. On second thought, maybe she wasn't ever here. Didn't get this far."

"That's possible," said John.

Louis nodded. "He could be right."

"I said it's possible! I'm sorry. Maybe you *are* right, George. Maybe we should just keep on. Leave this mess."

"Let me get my glasses," said Louis.

He got a pair of issue field glasses out of one saddlebag, adjusted the focus, and scanned the area ahead.

"Let me see," said George.

"There's nothing *to* see. Not a house for miles. That one we passed with the stone chimney, the barn in back, is the only one in the last twenty miles. Are you thinking what I'm thinking, sir?"

"It wouldn't hurt to go back and check."

"Waste of time," said George. "I'm right, I feel it. She just plain didn't get this far. We're a hundred miles from Fort Sully. That's a long walk."

"But in over two weeks?" asked Louis.

"It's hard to believe anybody would pass somebody walking. Before we start searching let's go over the wagon. If she was here maybe she left something. Like she left the locket in the magazine cellar," said John.

Louis shook his head. "She didn't leave it, sir, she lost it. That Miniconjou found it."

They searched every inch of the wagon. Discouragement was rapidly dispelling John's meager optimism.

"I don't know, boys. George, you may be right; we could be wasting valuable time. Here and going all the way back to that house. Maybe we're complicating it. Maybe she set out, the storm drove her off the road, and she wandered around."

"Until she froze to death," added George. Louis glared at him. "No. I'm sticking to what I said before. She's back up the road. She never got this far."

"Possibly," said John. "The question is, what happened to whoever was driving this thing? They couldn't just vanish into thin air . . ."

FIFTY-FIVE

Jenny was completely restored . . . and becoming increasingly impatient at the delay in leaving—a delay due mainly to Elizabeth's reluctance to let her leave.

"I really have to get back on the road," Jenny said to her.

Zebediah was in his room, poring over his catalogs. Elizabeth's benevolent expression gave way to skepticism.

"I say it again, you'd be foolish to leave this soon. As far as that goes, you're welcome to stay till spring."

"I'm very grateful, Elizabeth. I owe you two my life, but I simply have to get to Fort Laramie. I've already lost so much time . . ."

"You can't walk it and the only horse we've got is Emmaline."

"I know."

"There's the burros. They're sturdy; one could carry you all the way."

"No, thank you."

"We won't let you leave unless you take one. Please, Jenny . . ."

Zebediah came in hat and sheepskin jacket. "I'm going out to the barn, ladies. I have to take inventory."

He went out the kitchen door.

"He and I've discussed it," Elizabeth went on. "The least we can do is loan you a burro."

Jenny shook her head. "I wouldn't know how to ride one."

Outside, Zebediah was heading for the barn when up the road he spied two cavalry men and a man in civilian clothes driving a buggy. They waved him over.

*   *   *

Jenny paced the parlor, listening politely to Elizabeth's arguments. She got the feeling that eventually she'd give in. It seemed ungrateful to refuse. Did Zebediah have any kind of saddle for the burro? She'd never even ridden a horse. Easterners called burros donkeys. Her grandfather favored jackass— although he didn't restrict the term to the animal. They were reputedly patient creatures: obedient, but much slower than horses, though capable of bearing a heavier burden. She knew she'd end up accepting the offer; it made more sense than for her to resume walking. She shouldn't be so quick to turn down such a generous offer.

The door opened.

"Someone here to see a Mrs. Pryor," said Zebediah.

Jenny stiffened. She stared, her mouth slowly opening. The troopers stood aside. He came in slowly, swallowing, his expression grave, his eyes large, filled with amazement. She felt the Hornbeckers staring. The troopers remained outside.

Their eyes fixed on each other, neither made a sound.

"Say something," murmured Zebediah good-naturedly.

"Hush," said his mother. "Are you blind? They're talking volumes. Come . . ."

They withdrew to the other room. He came forward. He took her in his arms, held her tightly. More tightly. She closed her eyes and yielded to his embrace, sighing softly.

The Pryors waited at Fort Laramie until the first wagon train of the following year passed through in early June. Completion of the journey to Oregon was without incident, apart from shattering a rear wheel in the Blue Mountains. Fortunately, at the time they were within sight of Fort Walla Walla, where a replacement was available.

Reaching Oregon, they settled in the Willamette Valley south of Portland. The city, founded twelve years earlier, was growing rapidly. Under the Homestead Act of 1862, the Pryors took title to 160 acres of prime land and, with the help of neighbors, were able to build their house before the winter rains.

Over the course of the next ten years, Jenny kept her promise to herself never to venture more than two miles from her home. In that time she gave birth to four sons and two daughters, all of whom inherited her red hair.

She studied nursing, became a midwife, and cared for neighboring settlers. John Pryor died of cancer in 1895, two days before his sixty-fifth birthday. At the age of fifty-one, her family grown, her sons and one of her daughters married with families of their own, Jenny took up the study of medicine and surgery. Eventually she passed her state examination, was awarded her certificate authorizing her to practice medicine and surgery, and undertook private practice in Portland.

Her first surgical patient was a Kalapuya Indian chief whose appendix she removed. For years afterward she recalled the chief's uncanny resemblance to Chief Ottowa of the Oglalas.

At least 20,000 emigrants—about one in every seventeen who started the 2,000-mile trek to Oregon Territory—were buried beside the Oregon Trail.

"audaces fortuna juvat"

AFTERWORD

Jenny Pryor's experience with the Oglalas and later the Blackfeet was atypical of white captives. The majority of abducted white women were not sexually abused by their captors. But at the time of Jenny's capture (1865), hatred ran particularly strong between the Army and the Sioux Nations. It reached its climax in June of 1876 at the Little Big Horn, where General George Armstrong Custer and his men were annihilated. The Army's campaign against the tribes came in December of 1890 when two hundred Sioux men, women, and children were massacred by U.S. troops at Wounded Knee, in southwestern South Dakota.

The history of white captivity begins with the first settlers in New England in the seventeenth century. In the West, perhaps the most widely documented experience was that of Olive Oatman, who was only thirteen in 1851 when the Oatman family, on the way to California, separated from the train and was attacked by Yavapai Indians in a desolate part of the Gila River Valley. The family was massacred except for Olive and her seven-year-old sister Mary Ann, who were carried off to be slave laborers. A year later their captors sold them to some Mojaves, who walked both girls north to near the Colorado River. Two years later drought struck the area and many of the Mojaves starved to death. Mary Ann Oatman died.

Fortunately for Olive, her older brother Lorenzo had survived the massacre, and started on a five-year search for his sis-
ters. Olive was barely recognizable when he found her and she
was many months recovering. As was their custom, the Mojaves
had tattooed her arms, chin, and along her jawline.

Fanny Wiggins Kelly, captured by the Oglala Sioux, escaped tattooing by pretending to faint every time her captors
brought out their instruments. She was nineteen and only nine
months married, when she was captured. She became the property of a chief who was over seventy-five and partially blind.
After five harrowing months in captivity, Fanny was finally ransomed at Fort Sully, exchanged for three horses and a quantity
of food. Neither Fanny Kelly or Olive Oatman were violated
by their captors. Said Fanny, "The Oglalas treated me at times
with great harshness and cruelty, yet I never suffered from any
of them the slightest personal or unchaste insult."

But accounts of white women's experiences as captives of the
Indians, particularly those that cited sexual mistreatment, ap-
pealed to newspaper readers in the East, who preferred to think
that Indian captives were systematically raped and forced into
unwanted marriages.

Like today's tabloids, yesterday's similar publications pan-
dered to the lowest taste and carried bizarre and heartrending
wildly exaggerated accounts of captivity, citing every conceivable atrocity. But sexual abuse, although *believed* to be wide-
spread among women captives, was actually quite rare. Even
during the 1860s and 1870s, when resistance to white invasion
of their lands peaked and native American hostility was at its
highest—a period when the number of white captives sharply
increased—the relatively small percentage of women who were
sexually abused by their captors, did not increase.

Many women captives elected to remain with their captors,
when families, friends, or the Army sought to effect their release. Some had taken Indian husbands. Of, for example, 569

Indian captives of both sexes (but predominately female) recorded in a New England study cited in "Crossing the Cultural Divide," by Vaughan and Richter, 228 chose to remain with their captors, roughly one half. No such records are available for Western Indian captives, but interestingly, after Olive Oatman was ransomed, she spent the next few years grieving and unsatisfied, longing for her native husband and children.

Some authorities maintained that redeemed captives who failed to fit back into white society reacted so because they were too brutalized by the Indians to be able to recover their civilized ways, or too ashamed to face families and friends. There is some evidence for this assumption, but many such captives were treated with great kindness by their abductors, and long after they were ransomed, retained benevolent, even affectionate feelings toward them.

A few even went so far as to renounce their "white life" insisting that they had become Miniconjou, Hunkpapa, or Arapaho, whatever their captors' tribe.

In the West Army, wives were considered special targets of hostile Indians. But the government's fears for their safety turned out to be groundless. According to Army records, after 1861, not a single woman was killed by Indians at any Army post.

And yet at Fort Phil Kearney, in Wyoming Territory, where Indians attacked often and in force, the post commander issued a standing order that if the post were overrun, the women and children were to be herded into the powder magazine and blown up.

Emigrants traveling one of the five main trails West (the Oregon Trail and its offshoot, the California Trail; the Sante Fe Trail and its offshoots, the Gila River Trail and the Old Spanish Trail), were confronted with probably their most difficult decisions at the jump-off place, towns like Westport, Independence, and St.

Joseph, on the eastern bank of the Missouri. Generally, wagons
were ten feet by four feet, and everything they owned had to be
packed into them. Treasured possessions and heirlooms had to
be kept to an absolute minimum in favor of necessities. Unfortunately, among the first things discarded as wagon trains struggled through hills and over mountains were treasures retained:
china, books, furniture, etc. And many a dining-room table was
cut up for the wood to build a wheel to replace one damaged
beyond repair en route.

Wagons could carry 2,500 pounds. No more. Getting down
to that weight limitation at the jump-off place was trying for
every emigrant wife. A cast-iron stove selling for $25 in the East
cost $200 in the West. But, depending on its size, such a stove
could weigh up to 300 pounds, making it dispensable. Luxuries
included stoves, furniture, canned foods, plant cuttings, school-
books, fine linens and china, silverware, and musical instruments.

Some bulky, if not heavy possessions, proved expendable because they could be easily built once arrived. Churns, for example. Filling a bucket with fresh milk starting out in the
morning, hanging it from the tailgate, subjecting it to the jolt-
ing of the wagon throughout the day, resulted in butter, by sundown. One way of insulating bacon against the heat of the plains
was to pack it in a barrel of bran. Eggs were packed in barrels
of corn meal; as the eggs were consumed, the meal was used to
make bread.

To their ultimate chagrin, many emigrants refused to pack
sensibly. They would lay in an oversupply of flour, beans, bacon,
and other foodstuffs, some of which proved perishable. They
packed frivolously, everything from brooms and brushes to
boiled shirts. What they failed to pack: lanterns, candle molds,
tallow, liniments, bandages and surgical instruments, for example, often made a harsh and hard crossing more difficult than it
should have been.

But Yankee common sense and ingenuity prevailed in most instances. And sharing necessities was common practice. Wagons were tightly pitched to make them waterproof, enabling emigrants to float them across streams and rivers. Wagons were circled to form a corral for livestock and protection for their owners at night. Heavy chains linked wagons securely.

Accident and disease, not Indians, were the emigrants' worst enemies. Extreme heat, cold, violent wind, dust, rain- and hailstorms, tornadoes, buffalo stampedes, and prairie fires where constant threats. And the mountains destroyed many a wagon after they had survived the rigors of the plains.

Despite difficulties and life-threatening situations, which turned many trains and more individual wagons back, by 1869, the year the first transcontinental railroad was completed, approximately 350,000 Americans had crossed to the West to stretch the nation coast to coast.